I0598247

**He'd been sent here to do *what*?**

"Mykhael," Kendra warned, sitting up completely. The sheet fell away from her, and she felt the early morning chill of the cabin against her bare skin. Now was not the time to worry about such things. "You're making even less sense than before."

"I was called to take care of the situation."

"Why you?"

"A heritage. Some are watchers, some are guardians, some are...enforcers. Alastor, my clan name, was misinterpreted with all the different translations throughout history."

"Alastor..." she mused, searching for an elusive nugget of information. Then the book opened in her mind's eye, and the answer appeared. "It was the duty of Alastor to ensure that the sins of the father were visited upon the son."

"Not precisely. It is the duty of the clan of Alastor to ensure that the sanctity of the places and balance of power is maintained at all times. When violations occur, a member of my clan is called, and we are given an image of the person responsible for the violation."

His eyes were even more remote, with

that far away, almost sad, look she'd seen so many times before. A chilling premonition came to her and she lifted her chin, seeking the strength to ask the next question.

"Quit the games, Mykhael. Why exactly are you here now, in this place, at this time?"

He looked at her directly, and she saw the agony he had to be feeling.

"Darling, I've been sent here to kill you."

**She came to the woods to heal and found evil lurking among the trees...**

Upon her grandmother's death, Kendra inherits a cottage deep within a sequoia forest, along with the powers given only to certain women in her family—powers she doesn't know she has. Recovering from a vicious attack in Phoenix, Kendra returns home to the remote cabin determined to heal both her body and her spirit. But the forest is ailing, too. Evil stalks its dark places, turning its quiet glades into a battlefield. When a strangely beautiful man appears at her cabin intent on punishing her for a crime she didn't commit, Kendra needs all her strength to protect her forest, her life... and her heart. Can she learn to use her powers and to trust Mykhael in time to save the ancient forest?

**He came to the woods to redeem himself and found an innocence that would be his undoing...**

Throughout his long life, Mykhael has struggled, often in vain, to please the Atrahasis, immortal overlords of the sacred places in the universe. Now they have given him one last chance to redeem himself. He must punish the person they think desecrated an ancient forest in Northern California. But when he meets Kendra, he realizes he's doomed to disappoint them once more. Not only is she innocent of the crime the Atrahasis have accused her of, Kendra is the missing part of the soul Mykhael didn't know he still possessed. Can he defy the Atrahasis yet again and live long enough to save the only thing in his life that matters?

## KUDOS for *My Killer, My Love*

Mona Karel writes about love with a deft hand, a deep heart, a sexy eye and an intelligence that has been all too rare these days. In her romantic fantasy, *My Killer/My Love*, Karel leads us on a journey that is both magical and grounded in all too familiar earthly realities of fear, selfishness, arrogance, pride and caution. – *Rebecca Forster, USA Today, Best Selling Author*

Karel has given her characters strong traits like courage, determination, and a firm sense of justice. She's tempered these traits with emotional baggage, physical disabilities, and a charming innocence. The female lead, Kendra, is especially interesting. With her strong heart, shy courage, and broken body, she's not the usual type of heroine we see in modern paranormal romances. Mykhael's innocence comes not from his lack of sexual experience, but from his inexperience with modern-day humans, particularly innocent, unassuming humans like Kendra. Of course, being in solitary confinement for the past two-hundred years didn't help. – *Taylor, Reviewer*

*My Killer, My Love* by Mona Karel is an outstanding achievement for a debut author. I can't find enough good things to say about this book. Why do I like it? The title for one thing. How could you not read the book with a title like that? For another thing, the characters are different. Take the heroine, Kendra Weiss. Kendra is not beautiful. Not only is she not beautiful, she's handicapped. She walks with a cane, and she wears glasses. Not contacts, glasses. How many heroines have you seen recently in romances that wear glasses? It's delightfully refreshing to find a new author with the guts to deviate from the norm and give us a heroine who actually feels like a real person. I'm impressed. – *Regan, Reviewer*

# MY KILLER MY LOVE

By

**MONA KAREL**

*A Black Opal Books Publication*

GENRE: Paranormal/Fantasy/Romantic Suspense

This is a work of fiction. Names, places, characters and incidents are either the product of the author's imagination or are used fictitiously, and any resemblance to any actual persons, living or dead, businesses, organizations, events or locales is entirely coincidental.

Published by Black Opal Books

# DEDICATION

*To Tom, the true love of my life, who supports me even when he doesn't understand me.*

# CHAPTER 1

Kendra Weiss braced herself on her walking stick, contemplating the place she'd always thought of as her talisman against the cruel realities of the modern world. Whatever life had thrown at her, she'd always had Gran, her dancing, and their home deep in the sequoia forest. Now Gran was gone, the doctors marveled Kendra could even walk, and the forest held no refuge.

Once she could take care of herself again, she'd headed here, deep within the ancient forest. Television, automobiles, and the frenzied pace of progress were far away.

The evil she'd tried to leave behind seemed closer than ever.

She remembered a cheerful harmony of songbirds, chattering squirrels, and rustling leaves. A mélange of growing scents had once tickled her nose in giddy promise. Now a watchful stillness lay over the ancient forest.

She moved painfully along the overgrown path. Even the ground cover seemed out of control, snaking across the pathways, threatening an already perilous journey. At least no one saw her halting, ungraceful progress.

Or did they?

"Right." She hobbled forward as she muttered, keeping a close eye on errant vines and loose stepping stones. "Next thing you know, I'll be blaming my problems on alien invaders."

Generations of harmony with the creatures of the forest seemed to be at an end. What hadn't been chewed by deer or mutilated by snails had become hors d'oeuvres for bunnies. The bunnies and deer she could handle later. For now, she had to deal with the snails or face starvation the next winter.

"I'm sorry to do this," she murmured, her spirit as dark as the woods had become. Her innate reluctance to harm another warred with the need for survival. "But times have gotten tough, and there won't be enough in the garden for me at this rate."

She navigated the three stone steps with a fraction of her former agility and set down the wooden cane. Someone, most likely her cousin Clarissa, had stocked up on all the deadly chemicals never allowed at the cottage in Gran's day. A box of them sat on the porch. Donning plastic gloves, she reached for the slender bottle guaranteed to deliver a quick if not merciful death to snails.

"Are you absolutely sure you want to do that?"

The voice came from everywhere at once—and nowhere in particular. Deep, commanding, it filled the garden, echoed in the trees, rumbled across the sky. Kendra wheeled around, steadying herself on the rough-hewn porch timbers.

Now the clouds moved, driven by a high wind to mass even more densely above her. Crows took flight, calling to each other as they fled to the safety of the deep forest. Tree branches rustled at the other end of the clearing, though no breeze touched her cheek.

A shape formed, deep within the shadow at the edge of the forest, just beyond her perception. A man stepped forward.

The sun's last rays eased through the

clouds, gracing the high cheekbones of an aesthetically carved face and limning his dark hair in a halo of gold. The tanned beauty of his skin and the luxuriant mass of his dark red hair drew her eye. Classic would be the only way to describe this man. His image had been carved from marble in Greece and preserved on canvas by the Italian masters. No doubt there were still small wooden statues with his likeness deep within the druid forests. She knew she'd seen those same high cheekbones, flaring nostrils and bow-shaped upper lip a thousand times in her study of ancient concepts of beauty.

This modern version decorated a tall, lean, and very much human, male body. On the whole, she preferred this interpretation. A heated flush washed through her as the subtle differences between man and woman became very clear to her.

Green fire flashed from his narrowed eyes as he strode forward, a warrior spirit bent upon vengeance. She had only a moment to be aware of him, to acknowledge his unearthly beauty and innate grace before her common sense asserted itself. Bracing herself against the porch railing she stepped back, seeking to maintain as much distance as possible between herself and this stranger. Her foot brushed against the walking stick, knocking it off the porch before she could reach for it as support or protection.

"Who—who are you?" she demanded, hating the quaver in her voice. She knew she should move back, run, get inside where there was at least a pretense of safety. But like a deer caught in the headlights of an oncoming truck, she was mesmerized. She tried to move but her feet grew leaden as an unnatural calm permeated the resistant part of her mind.

The man continued forward without speaking. Sounds ceased in the forest around the little cottage. The few remaining birds fell silent, waiting in breathless anticipation.

"Whoever you are, please stop now." She tried to project firmness in her voice.

Still he came forward, growing larger by the second. At another time she could have appreciated the grace of his walk. Now she only feared and resented the speed with which he covered the area between them, and the fact that she would not have been able to avoid him even if she could make herself move.

She squinted as the fading sun glinted off her glasses. Surely the sunset was the reason she could almost see a glow, bright orange and red, outlining his body. It deepened in hue, and heat seemed to wash off him, warming her uncomfortably.

With one stride he ascended the low retaining wall. This final reminder of her inadequacy was too much. Pointing the bottle of snail killer in his direction, she thumbed back the spout.

"This is your last warning, mister."

He stopped at the edge of the porch steps, one hand on the pillar. Peridot green eyes looked from the bottle to the carefully cultivated angry look on her face, back to the bottle.

"What, precisely, do you intend to do with that?"

"The label says it's 'guaranteed to rid my garden of slugs and unwanted pests.' Whoever you are, you seem to qualify." Her voice still quavered, but since he no longer approached, she could at least pretend courage.

Both brows rose, just before the finely sculptured mouth twitched at both corners. His eyes continued to study her in an intense, feral way before they, too, crinkled at the corners. At last, he threw back his perfect head and laughed.

The forest resounded with mirth that echoed in the hills, reminiscent of summer storms and winter thunder. This was no polite chuckle, no quiet appreciation of her once common, madcap humor. Laughter overcame the stranger, and the world laughed with him.

She lowered her hand. It had been a silly idea, just the kind of thing she used to do. The last of her strength drained away as his laughter washed over her. She leaned against the closest support, the aged wooden porch rail. Eventually, he would get over his amusement and tell her who he was. She wondered why she wasn't screaming down the forest but was distracted as the bright orange glow seemed to fade around him. Had she really seen it?

As his laughter quieted, his perfect mouth quivered at one edge then stilled as he looked at her more closely. In baggy linen drawstring pants and a wrapped top, he certainly dressed like one of Clarissa's many friends. But not even her gorgeous cousin would be enough woman for this man. There wouldn't have been a chance for Kendra even in the past. Now...

Kendra closed her eyes, wishing for the oblivion of sleep, or at least a reasonable facsimile thereof. The tiny scuffling sounds of animals setting out on or returning from food-gathering chores resumed as though there had never been an interruption. Kendra wearily opened her eyes. The Adonis in front of her stood very still, intently studying her face, her hair. A frown marred his perfect brow, making him appear gorgeous and serious at the same time. He nodded toward the bottle in her hand.

"The contents of that are poison."

"I believe that's why it was developed. If I don't do something about the snails in my garden, I won't have anything to eat this year."

"There are better ways," he said in the condescending tone she'd heard from males so many times.

"Unfortunately, 'better ways' aren't getting the job done at the moment." Pretending courage, she dared to step toward him, off the porch.

She'd made the move hundreds, thousands of times when she lived here as a child. She stepped out as though she had two whole legs under her and pitched forward. Then she remembered she didn't have the equivalent of one.

She fell down the steps, toward granite stepping stones. It would be an ugly fall, with no way to soften the drop, and Adonis too far away to help. Resigning herself to more pain, she relaxed as much as possible.

There was no fall. As her knee buckled, a warm wind blew against her side, and she was held, supported, and lowered to the porch step. Large, gentle hands straightened her trembling legs. Seeing the masculine hands against her jeans-clad leg broke through her curious sense of detachment. Could this be a dream, induced by the drugs forced upon her in the hospital? Would she soon wake sweating, trembling, rigid from the effort not to scream, not to strike out? She tried to pull her leg away, to stand and hobble out of his reach, away from this fantasy.

From his hands radiated a sensation of limitless power. She felt a shift, as though the fabric of the universe had been strained then rewoven in another pattern. Her pain diminished, replaced by tingling warmth and a singular sense of familiarity.

The large hands stilled, not quite touching where her knee was ugliest under the denim. Time hesitated, drawing a deep breath, while Kendra tried to bring herself back to a semblance of reality. The warning voices in her head quieted as she again felt the touch deep in her mind and realized there was nothing to worry about.

His head raised, the mane of dark auburn curls falling back from his brow as he looked at her. It was as though he saw her for the first time.

His intense hunter's eyes looked from her casually held back hair to her aged, comfortable T-shirt and jeans. Again, he looked at her glasses, and again, his perfect brows drew together.

Kendra was prepared to hear herself inanely ask if they had met before when he spoke again, softly this time.

"Do I know you?" His deep voice soothed, like the rumble of distant thunder on a summer afternoon.

"I think that's supposed to be my line, isn't it?" She managed the whole sentence without stuttering and imagined herself almost sophisticated in the process.

"Line?" He frowned as though the concept were totally foreign to him. Was he intelligent in inverse proportion to his appearance? No. No one could be that stupid and remember to pick his feet up to walk.

"Never mind. Look, if you're not going to go away and not going to tell me who you are, could you make yourself useful and take this so I can stand up?" She held the bottle of snail bait out to him.

Maybe she'd blinked without realizing it. She didn't see him move, yet he now stood well away from the porch. Hands raised as though in a defensive measure, he crouched slightly, like a big cat preparing to lunge. In which direction? Then he straightened and shook his head, as if to rid himself of unwanted instincts, and Kendra wondered where in the world these ideas came from.

"If you will put that to one side, I will be happy to assist you in rising."

Had his voice been that formal before? Shrugging, Kendra carefully fastened down the spout of the bottle, making sure it locked shut before she looked around for a place

11

near her to set it. Against the railing would have to do for now.

"It would be better to put it further away." There was a new note of tension in his voice. Could he dislike the stuff as much as she did?

"That's as far as I can reach without getting up." Still holding the bottle, she peeled the disposable glove off her left hand, covering the top of the bottle. The other glove covered the bottom, so she could handle the bottle without actually touching it. She wrinkled her nose in disgust as she set the bottle out of her way.

"If you dislike the poison so much, why is it here?"

"I'm not sure. I think my cousin brought it while I was in the hospital."

"Your cousin?"

"Clarissa. She came by to take care of things while I was hurt. Gran and I never had a problem with the snails. They had their part of the garden and stayed out of ours. The same with the deer and rabbits." She heard the words babbling out of her mouth but couldn't stop herself. "It seemed as though we had a bargain."

"One which worked very well," he said,

as if it were perfectly natural to think you could reason with slugs.

She leaned back, looking at him again, trying to understand him. "Who are you, one of the Forest Guardians?" Again with the jokes. She seemed to be a regular comedian around this stranger.

Another of those heavy silences fell over the woods as he tensed, staring at her. Then the corners of his mouth curved. He gave her a smile to make the masters weep. They'd tried, all of them, many times, to preserve this upturning of lips, this all-knowing expression. None of them had come within a prayer of portraying it. Youth, wisdom, mischief, knowledge were all exposed in the movement of a pair of lips.

"Not hardly," the lips said, parting enough to give a glimpse of strong, depressingly white teeth.

Then he looked away, studying the neglected garden.

He seemed to have forgotten her, his face lifted to the sun, as if he sought what little remained of the heat and light. Under the loose linen shirt, his chest rose, drawing in great gulps of the rich air, and his hands lifted away from his sides. As though he tried to feel the forest with every pore of his body.

Kendra looked away, once more thanking whatever powers Gran had believed in that mind reading was not a common talent. Her words had sounded silly enough, without her thoughts. She stared at her serviceable sandals, not wanting to intrude on his absorption in the forest. Once, she'd felt that same connection to her surroundings. After a moment, he collected himself, pushing his hair back with both hands, and looked down at her.

"Do you tend this land?"

"This was my grandmother's cottage. I grew up here and came up whenever I got the chance. Were you interested in the area?"

"I was told of the gardens and the wise woman who tended them."

It seemed reasonable, if archaically put, but Kendra's days of trust were long past. "Did they also tell you she's gone?" She tried to say it with a firm voice. The best she could manage was not to break down completely.

"I knew that." He spoke more gently than before. "It seems she turned care of her land over to someone she loved and trusted."

Kendra stared unseeing at the ruin of the garden. "It appears I haven't done all that well at caring for her legacy."

"I am learning appearances are not always what they seem at first."

She looked back at him, wondering, almost as an afterthought, who in the world he was. But she lost the thought before it had time to develop, almost before she had time to wonder how he got there. "Since you seem to have come a distance to see the gardens, I can show you around while there's still a little bit of light, before you have to leave."

He didn't react to her hint about leaving. After a moment she shrugged, leaned down to reach for her stick, and levered herself to an upright position.

"You have been hurt," he said, watching her struggles, "and you need to rest. We can inspect the gardens later."

Before she could speak, before she could tell him she didn't like to be touched, that she had learned to be particularly wary of a man's touch, his warm hand braced under her elbow. Energy she'd forgotten she possessed flowed through her limbs. She rose, yielding to his guidance to turn away from the garden.

Instead of staggering, she managed a near normal walk into the cottage.

Any unease she'd experienced before was gone. In its place was a peace she hadn't known since her childhood. Later, after she rested, she would think about that.

"Would you care for a snack before you leave?" she asked, no longer worried about subtlety. "I have a few things made up. I'm afraid there's no meat."

His shudder nearly shook her body, and the force of his hand on her arm was almost painful.

"I do not eat meat." His calm tone belied the tension in his fingers. He looked around the cottage as though this, too, was a strange and wonderful place to be studied with an unsettling intensity. Every hand-thrown bowl, every rough-carved piece of furniture, every patiently woven or crocheted blanket was examined and categorized.

"You need to rest," he informed her. "I could prepare a meal, if you tell me what you want."

"You cook?" She leaned away, wanting to get a clearer look at this true paragon among men. Not only beautiful, but useful as well?

16

"I have not done so before, but it cannot be too difficult. Women have been doing it for years."

He was absolutely, totally, no-grin serious. Gorgeous or not, this was too much. Kendra stopped dead, wrenching her elbow away from his grip.

"I have offended you?"

Kendra knew she should protest what was, after all, a sexist remark, but it would require too much energy. Sighing, she shook her head. Maybe the sexism was a natural by-product of the looks. She yawned deeply, more weary than she realized.

"You rest." He urged her toward the narrow cot where she'd slept since her first visit to the cottage so many years ago. Gran's small bed, built into the wall, had been piled high with boxes. Somehow, not keeping it as a sleeping place made the cottage seem less lonely.

She would rest, for a minute. Only because she suddenly felt so very tired, not because he told her to. Setting aside her glasses, she collapsed more than sat on the cot, letting herself sag back amongst the brightly covered pillows.

Serenity swept over her in smothering waves as a voice which seemed to be inside her head urged her to lie down, to lift her legs, to sleep. The soft, familiar warmth of a woven throw settled over her. As she hovered between sleeping and waking, a nearly forgotten longing came to her. She remembered an old desire to find the missing part of herself, someone to share her life with. It seemed such an old dream, and so foolish. It had been years since she'd given in to that particular whimsy.

Before her eyes slid shut she watched him drift around the cabin. Some items he just looked at. Others he touched, stroking his lean hand along the wood of the spinning wheel, caressing the stone of the fireplace with his fingertips. The mantelpiece was a solid slab of mahogany, tended lovingly for many years until the wood grain gleamed like a precious gem. Under his hand it seemed to reflect an even deeper light.

Gran had kept a collection of photographs on the mantel. Mostly group family shots, there were a few individuals whose pictures sat in a place of honor. Kendra waited for the inevitable question.

"Who is this?"

She inched one eyelid open, identified the photo by his general location, and let her eye rest again. The image leapt up at her from memory. Two young women with light blond hair, standing with their arms linked, showing loving faces to the outside world.

"My cousin, Clarissa, and myself, outside this cabin a couple of years ago."

"You look very much like your cousin." He made it a statement of fact, not opinion. There was another note in his voice as well, as though he had solved a great riddle.

"No I don't. Clarissa is beautiful." She heard him take a breath, as though to protest, and forced both eyes open again. At least he played the part better than most. He deserved a modicum of her attention. "I'm attractive. I was athletic. Clarissa is beautiful."

"Who are you, precisely?" He asked the question as though the answer mattered greatly to him.

"I am, precisely, Kendra Weiss."

"Kendra?" His eyes widened, pinning her with the relentless stare of a cougar. "Do you know what that means?"

"Of course I do. It means my father was

so disappointed he didn't have a son, he named his daughter after himself, instead." There was no bitterness in her voice. Her naming had long been one of the family's favorite jokes.

Again that smile decorated his face, this time tinged with an exasperation she could see without her glasses. He shook his head, and the auburn curls fell around his shoulders with more grace than her own silvery-blond hair ever managed.

"It means much more than that, but you do not seem prepared to listen at this time."

He fell silent, standing very still by the fireplace. It was as though he sought to become one with the ancient stone and wood. Telling herself she was definitely hallucinating, she faded into sleep.

გთავ

Once the woman slept, he moved more freely. With the stealthy tread of a stalking wolf, he searched the darkening rooms, letting his senses hunt for a specific location. He settled in a corner window seat, bathed by the moonlight inching its way toward her bed.

Many puzzles existed here, and he knew he was not yet prepared to face them.

He breathed deeply, then more slowly, his body becoming motionless. The atmosphere around him thickened, a silent wind lifting his hair away from his face then dying abruptly. After a long moment of hushed tension, he emitted a sound of exasperation. The answers had never come to him easily before, why should now be any different?

He studied the woman. Even in her sleep, her thoughts spoke to him in unclear muttering, a not unpleasant sensation. He wondered about the part he had been sent to play and knew the ending would not be as originally planned. He could no longer think of her as he had been instructed.

This small, fearful female had given him something he had forgotten existed. She had given him back his laughter. For that alone he would protect her beyond life.

# CHAPTER 2

Kendra's eyes opened as dawn began to coax the world into existence. In spite of an even worse than normal sleep, she woke with the glimmerings of life coursing through her veins.

For the first time in so long, she looked forward to the morning, and she hovered between sleep and waking, enjoying herself. She stretched, feeling the texture of her shirt against her skin as her thoughts wandered, searching for the source of this sense of well-being.

A shadow drifted at the edge of her vision, a faint impression of movement. Wrenched fully awake, she sat up.

He hadn't been a dream, or the result of too many days with too little food. Outlined by the early sun, he sat in the window seat, far larger and more imposing than she remembered or could ever have imagined. As though realizing any movement on his part might throw her into a panic, he sat very still, until she could wake all of her mind.

Finally, sleep stopped clouding her inner and outer vision. She let out the breath she'd drawn to speak. There was nothing to say. Never had she stayed in this cottage with anyone but Gran. Never had she stayed anywhere with a male. Yet nothing seemed more right than waking like this. Worried at this last impression, she asked the first question that came to mind.

"Was there a storm last night?" No, that wasn't the first question she had in mind.

"Why do you ask?" He seemed genuinely interested, as though no question of hers could ever be inane.

"Perhaps I just dreamed it." Drawing a deep breath, she prepared to move her legs off the bed and ask them to support her body.

He appeared in front of her his large hand reaching for her arm.

"Please, don't touch me." She spoke with the candor of the barely awake. Realizing her rudeness, she ducked her head, trying to hide her blush.

He stilled, again reminding her of a cougar she'd seen atop a rock, pretending to rest, planning that night's hunting. His hand slowly drew back.

"Why not?"

Kendra delayed answering while she went through her morning routine. First lift the legs off the side of the bed and bend them slowly. If only she could tolerate drugs. During the inevitable dispute with her body over the necessity of movement, she hesitated on the edge of the bed.

"When I was in the hospital, they tried different ways to make my legs heal faster. One of them consisted of attaching electrodes along my nerve endings and running a low level current. I get the same kind of feeling when you touch me." To forestall any further idiocy on her part, she reached for the glasses she barely remembered laying to one side the night before.

His brows drew together, in no way marring the beauty of his face. "It was most likely an atmospheric oddity," he said, staring at her. "What do you have on your face?"

From long habit, she checked for crumbs, bits of food, perhaps a piece of hair.

"No, covering your eyes." His voice was

as intent as his gaze. "You have no need to hide your eyes."

"I have a need to see," she said. "Where have you been the last two hundred years?"

His head jerked sideways then he tilted his head, studying her.

"Why do you ask?"

Briefly, she wondered at his reaction then decided he had said nothing unusual.

"These ugly things are on my face because I can't tolerate contacts, and I've become addicted to seeing clearly."

She used the glasses now to look at him more closely. In the ever-growing light, his physical attraction did not fade. But who in the world was he?

"Who in the world are you?" she asked without thinking about it first.

He seemed stunned, as if she should not have asked. "I am..." He hesitated, a frown shadowing his face." I am called Michael Alster," he said then nodded as if agreeing with himself.

"Michael Alster?" She repeated the name as it sounded to her: "Me-khal Al-a-stor," yet there was something different about the way he said it. Almost as though she heard it on two different levels at once. To herself, she preferred the softer sound she had heard. Mykhael.

"Michael," he corrected. "Michael Alster." Now the name came easily. "At your service, Kendra Weiss. Would you care to break your fast with me?"

Her stomach reminded her she had neglected dinner in favor of a night's sleep. Strange. Mealtimes were one of her few indulgences. She reached for the stick that had once been Gran's and levered herself upright.

"Give me a moment, Michael Alster, and I'll put something together."

A small, hot fire burned in the old wood stove though she didn't remember banking the coals. It would require just a few minutes to heat water for tea and toast thick slices of bread. Trips to town were rare. Lacking ordinary fare, Kendra reached for a large jar in one of the open fronted cupboards. She hesitated. Not everyone shared her diet preferences.

"PB and toast all right with you?"

"Whatever you eat will be suitable for me."

Michael had apparently gone outside, leaving the cooking to the female of the species. He followed his voice into the cottage, arriving at her side in time to relieve her of the large teapot. She set plates of lightly browned bread, decorated with a stream of honey atop thick peanut butter, in front of each chair. Two slices for him, one slice for her. She hoped she could finish the whole slice.

"You do not eat enough." He slid his chair up to the table without scraping on the floor, a trick she'd always wanted to learn.

"This is plenty for me. I haven't had much of an appetite since I was in the hospital. Besides, I'm moving around less now, so I can't eat as much." She sliced strips off her toast then lifted the first piece, almost salivating in anticipation. The first bite was always so good.

"What is this?"

"Homemade bread." She didn't bother to hide the smug note in her voice. "I used one of Gran's recipes." Anticipating his positive reaction, she took a small taste of her meal.

"Yes, of course, but what sort of cheese have you put on your bread?"

Kendra held the bite in her mouth, un-chewed. She would not allow herself to become upset by his calm acceptance of what was, to everyone she'd ever met, a lost art. Then his question filtered through her irritation. She swallowed abruptly.

"It's peanut butter, not cheese. Good grief, what did your mother feed you? Peanut butter is a staple of childhood."

From polite interest, his face went to stony solemnity. "Not where I come from, I'm afraid."

"Would you like me to get you something clsc?" She forced herself to remember the manners Gran had believed in.

"If this is your morning meal, I would not ask for special foods." Following her example, he cut into his toast with the smooth edged table knife.

"Peanut butter is my main source of protein. I think I would have starved more than once if not for nut butters." Before he could say anything else, she took another bite of the still warm treat. Memories came along with the taste, and she was once again a child who didn't quite fit in.

"Gran always had lots of PB around when

I came to visit. She knew my parents preferred more—you would probably say 'civilized' foods."

"Such as?" He gingerly picked up one of his own strips.

"Dad's in upper level business management. They ate out a lot, so at home we had nutritious foods. Low-fat, that kind of thing."

"No peanut butter." Drawing a deep breath, he bit off a small piece of toast and chewed carefully. After a swallow that worked the muscles of his throat, he dared a larger bite.

"Why not?" he asked, his voice thicker when he tried to talk through the mouthful. He hesitated, apparently realizing how much of his meal stuck to the roof of his mouth.

Kendra held back her laughter, making inroads into her own breakfast while he dealt with the new sensations. Another swallow traveled into his throat and she watched, fascinated, while the morsel began its journey down his gullet. A sip of tea seemed to clear his mouth, and he regarded her over the rim of his cup.

"This is your favorite food?" he asked, his voice like his expression, neutral and polite.

She nodded, picking up another piece and chewing on it without savoring the taste as much as she had at first. It was only food, for pity's sake. Nothing to make such a big deal about.

"I believe my gastronomic experiences have been lacking." He applied himself more eagerly to the meal.

Finally allowing herself to relax, Kendra reached for her tea cup. Whoever this stranger was, he was at least an entertaining guest. Too bad she would have to ask him to leave. Too bad he wouldn't want to stay anyway.

&#9756;&#9758;&#9756;

Herbal hedges awakened by the sun's kiss scented the morning air. Heady fragrances waxed and waned, wafting across their path. Bees droned happily, collecting and distributing pollen on their way to creating rich honey.

Motes of dust outlined the sun's rays. How had she ever thought the cottage had lost its magic?

Reveling in the rediscovered charm of her

garden, Kendra took Michael on a delayed tour. Her injuries slowed their progress but he made no comment. Instead, he matched his pace to hers, stepping aside to look more closely at something when she had to rest a moment.

"Whenever Gran planted, she made herself a garden here." Kendra indicated the once orderly rows with protective herbs and bright flowers interspersed among the vegetables. "Then over there." She pointed to a shadowed area on the other side of a hedge comprised of rosemary, comfrey, bryony and other herbs. "She planted a garden for the forest creatures. She explained to me, since we existed in the same area, we had to get along. There's even a bed of ivy for the snails."

"She controlled snails by planting ivy over there?"

"The ivy gave the snails a place to go. She used more aggressive methods to encourage them away from this garden." She shrugged, managing a laugh at herself. "I guess the snails voided her agreement once she left."

"Perhaps you need to renegotiate."

"Perhaps. For right now, I need to renegotiate this pathway, so I can walk without tripping."

"That would be no problem, as long as we have some way to tie back the vines until they agree to grow elsewhere."

Kendra glanced at him. Did he mock her? His face seemed utterly serious as he knelt in the pathway. If he mocked, he was too subtle for her to notice. She did notice his assumption he would be helping in the garden. For some reason, this seemed perfectly normal.

For the better part of the morning they worked on coaxing the vegetation into more civilized growth. Toward noon, as the increasing temperature intensified the herbal scents, Michael looked up, staring toward the road. His brow furrowed and he seemed to listen intently. He bent again to the task at hand, encouraging vegetation away from the walkway. As he pushed back the stubborn growth, Kendra handed him covered wire ties to restrain the vines.

She'd spent twenty more-or-less-comfortable hours in the company of a large, powerful male. She'd been cautious around men even before the attack, particularly men like Mykhael, no, Michael. Not that she'd been around men like him or, for that matter, many men at all, except on a casual basis. That was more Clarissa's style.

As her thoughts babbled, Kendra gave thanks Clarissa was not there. Whoever this man was, he obviously didn't care for the chemicals her cousin purchased and used so liberally.

She wondered if the strange substances had something to do with her feeling as though the woods and garden were preparing to rise up and take back control of their destiny.

Such foolishness. Maybe her cousin had been right when she said Kendra had become too goofy for words. Like Gran.

A rumble from the direction of the county road drew her attention. She heard a vehicle turn up the steep driveway. No one had been invited, and if Clarissa or her friends thought they could camp back here again...She moved purposefully toward the front of the house.

It was a police cruiser. Probably Deputy Matt Hawkins, coming around to check on her. She could interpret a visit from any other member of the small local law force as professional concern. Hawkins would be here to spy on her, and maybe try to wangle information about Clarissa.

The cruiser, actually a Jeep, complete with light bars and a heavy duty winch, nearly disappeared in the cloud of dust preceding it up the hill. Kendra waited while the dust settled on her and the garden as much as on the vehicle, finding in herself a confidence she'd never achieved before.

"How-do, little lady." The large, solid man unfolded from behind the steering wheel. Mirrored sunglasses in place under a felt cowboy hat, revolver strapped to his hip, Hawkins looked like a stereotypical bad-county lawman.

"Deputy Hawkins."

"Shoot, name's Matt. Not like we haven't known each other for a long time, sweetie."

"We've known each other long enough for you to realize the 'No Trespassing' signs apply to everyone. Unless you have a specific reason for being here?"

Hawkins hesitated, pushing up the brim of his hat with one finger. Then, swaggering even more, he continued his approach. "Just bein' neighborly. You out here alone and all. Hurt too, accordin' to what I hear." He stopped a few feet away, bracing his hands on his hips and looking around. Finally, his attention settled on her. In his expressionless silvered glasses, he looked like some bloated poisonous bug.

"You heard from that cousin of yours?"

"Not since I got out of the hospital, Deputy. If I do hear from her, I'll be sure to pass along your interest."

"No reason to get uppity. Some reports came in about some of the fellows were up here with her. You know any of them?" He barely allowed her to shake her head in the negative before continuing. "Seems some of them were suspected of a robbery up Sacramento way. Just thought I'd pass along the warning, you bein' up here alone and all. It's not safe for a woman alone these days."

"I'm not—" she began. The words she wanted to use, that she was not alone, wouldn't emerge the way she intended. Frustrated, she shook her head, trying again. "I've been here alone, and Gran before me. I doubt any harm will come to me."

Kendra knew some women found Hawkins' tall, solid build and rough-hewn face handsome. She'd never given it much thought, since she knew from earlier experiences how he enjoyed being casually cruel. She suppressed a shudder as he took a step closer. Then the courage came back. Not quite as strong as before, but enough.

"As you can see, Deputy, I have no need of your company."

Though she strove to remain outwardly composed, Kendra's stomach clenched in the old way, and she drew a sharp breath.

Hawkins continued to stare around the clearing, peering into the thick darkness under the trees. "You could grow all sorts of things around here, and no one would ever know."

"I do grow all sorts of things around here, including vegetables and herbs. If you refer to illegal plants, none have ever been grown here, as we discussed before."

He grunted in response, heaved a deep sigh, and turned away. "Seein' as you don't have a telephone, I'll be stopping by from time to time to check on you, you bein' hurt and all."

"That really won't be necessary."

"No problem, Kendra. No problem at all." He turned his head in her direction, and his sunglasses made a slow survey of her. His thick lips curled in what had always passed for a smile for him. Finally, he shrugged, stepped up into his Jeep, and left with no further delay.

"That is not a friend of yours, is it?"

Kendra wheeled, barely catching her balance with the walking stick. "No. That's Deputy Sheriff Matt Hawkins, just coming around to check up on me, ask if I'm growing strange things in the woods." Only then did she realize Michael had not been around while she spoke with the visitor. Nor had she thought about him.

"He cannot check for himself?"

"Every time he goes in the woods around here, something goes wrong: sprained ankle, poison ivy—something. The forest doesn't seem to like him." Kendra didn't feel odd about saying such things around Michael.

"He is an evil man, with a mean nature."

"You won't get any argument from me there. Hawkins was a bully in school. He's the last person who should be in law enforcement."

She turned back to the garden then hesitated, frowning. "He said something about the people here with Clarissa, that they were more than just careless."

"Would that be unusual?" He tilted his head in question.

"Now that I think of it, I guess not. Clarissa never chooses to be by herself, and she's not always particular about the company she keeps. Gran didn't like her bringing that kind of person here."

Michael looked around at the sun-graced clearing and snug cottage. As she'd noticed the evening before, he seemed very aware of everything that went into the makeup of the area. Kendra watched him looking at the only place she'd been able to call home and realized peace was still here for her.

She made no sound, but he turned his head, his piercing eyes studying her as he'd studied the cottage. Something, perhaps her rediscovered happiness, must have shown. His lips lifted, gentling the lines of his face. Then he took a deep breath and looked away as though disturbed.

"That deputy who came by. Would he be one of your cousin's friends?"

The day grew suddenly grayer. What had she done, that he spoke with such abrupt coldness? Kendra shrugged mentally. This was a male reaction she knew.

What had happened before, the interest, the kind smile, must have been her imagination.

"Wanna be." At his questioning frown, she went on. "Matt Hawkins has wanted to be Clarissa's friend for years. Unfortunately, she only visited. I was the one who lived here."

"Your parents stayed here?"

"Dad's job took him all over the world, and sometimes it was more convenient for me to stay with Gran." More pleasant, also, to be away from the rush and glitter of her family. "I went to high school in the next town."

"Hawkins went to the same school?"

"Yes." She turned away. Time to get back to the garden. Maybe she could salvage enough vegetables to make it through this year without spending too much of her savings. Next year would have to take care of itself.

"You did not enjoy going to school with this deputy?"

"You seem awfully interested in my formative years." She turned her head just far enough to look at him. Maybe it would be safer if she could only see part of him at once.

"The deputy upset you. I wanted to understand why in the event he returns."

Now she stopped, bracing herself against a tree, and dared look at him directly.

"Michael, you never told me why you're here. I know it's not just to see the gardens. So, why?"

"I needed to rest. I decided to find out about the woman who had the beautiful garden."

Of course she could trust him, her mind told her. And she believed.

"You have a stressful job?"

He shrugged. "When I arrived, you needed help, and I had free time." He wouldn't quite meet her eyes, but his voice held the ring of sincerity.

"You're a good man, Michael Alster." She softened his name so it sounded the way she liked to hear it. "That's so rare."

"You see the world the way you want to. It is not a bad habit, but it could bring you trouble." His expression appeared more remote than ever.

Kendra chose to smile instead of frown at

his dire words. She'd heard many variations of this same warning in her lifetime. Only one person had read her a different way. "Gran used to say, if you wished and dreamed for something hard enough, you could make it happen. She believed people were as good or bad as you wanted them to be."

"What did other people believe?"

"My father loved his mother, though they were very different. Once he had grown up, she moved up here to stay with her aunt. And probably so she didn't interfere with his business. The townspeople thought she was strange, but kind."

"What about your visiting deputy? Did your grandmother see him as bad or good?"

"She saw him as barely human and not really worth bothering to classify." She grinned. "Gran could always manipulate things to suit her."

"A worthwhile habit, to be sure." He matched her smile then indicated the garden they'd worked in all morning. "We could continue here or we could find something in these woods to help your leg."

A brief flare of hope rose in her, to be

tamped down at once. "Some of the finest doctors in the field studied my knee and pronounced it unusable. At one time, most of them doubted I would ever walk again."

"Since they were wrong in that respect, why would you believe them in other things?" he asked mildly as he led the way toward a path she didn't remember being there the day before.

Dark coolness surrounded them, in sharp contrast to what had become a bright, warm day. Michael's path seemed far easier to walk on than any she'd encountered recently. Kendra found little trouble following, though she could never move as he did in the woods. It was as though tree branches leaned out of his way as he approached, and there was always a level place, without leaves, for him to set his foot.

Kendra felt like a three-legged goat in a crystal showroom. After all her years of dancing she knew how to move well. But even when both of her legs had worked to perfection she'd never walked through the woods as he did.

She accepted her limitations with a shrug and struggled on as best she could, appreciating his silence and his tactful lack of assistance.

"Did your grandmother ever tend to your knee?" he asked as they stepped into a small clearing, and he began to search along a stream bank for something that seemed to be very tiny.

"It—she died the day after I was hurt," she managed to say before her throat clogged with the tears she had yet to shed. Attempting to distract herself, she looked around the clearing.

No birds fluttered in the trees, matching their songs to the murmuring brook. No squirrels peered from between leaves, terminally curious about everything around them. Her breath hesitated before leaving her body, as though unsure of its welcome. Since her guide seemed disposed to stop for a while, she sank to the ground, stretching her leg in an attempt to ease some of the stiff soreness.

A large tree served as her backrest. Michael crouched near her.

When his shadow blocked the sun wending through the branches, seeking to touch her face, she pried one eye open, attempting a baleful glare. From the smile on his face, he remained remarkably unimpressed. "You seem content."

She shrugged, her eye drifting shut once more. Relaxing the muscles in her neck, she leaned back against the tree.

"I think I actually am. My leg feels good as long as I don't move, and I managed to stand up to Matt Hawkins for the first time in my life."

An increase of warmth along one side indicated he'd settled next to her. For a moment, he let her enjoy her tiny triumphs without question.

"You feared him before?" His low-pitched voice eased between the layers of her consciousness.

"Him and just about everything else to do with being around people. I always thought I wasn't meant to lead a regular life. Then today." She paused, relishing the memory. "Today, I felt stronger, braver than I ever have before. Maybe because I realized fear is relative. Matt Hawkins' casual meanness is nothing compared to what happened to me."

"You mean to your leg?" He went on once she nodded. "What did happen?"

Kendra drew in a deep breath, intending

to tell him it was none of his concern. But she'd brought this onto herself and somehow, she wanted to share it with him.

"I danced. Not ballet or chorus line, but folk dancing and some interpretive pieces. It wasn't a high dollar career, but it paid the bills."

"And you liked it." His voice slid under the tension of hers, supporting her words while she regained some control.

"I loved it. I could get away often enough to help Gran keep this place going. It was the next best thing to being here all the time." She stopped again, shifting her seat then squeezed her eyes against the pain and against the pictures that wouldn't go away. Michael sat silent.

"We were working at a small theater in Phoenix, with some local dancers, men and women. Some of the men in the other group were larger and more aggressive than I was accustomed to. When I backed away from them during the dances, they thought I was snobbish. They wouldn't believe I wasn't interested.

"The last evening, I had to go back to the theater for some of my things. The rest of my troupe was at dinner, so I went alone. The men had been striking sets or just hanging around. I never did get the whole story."

Her calm disappeared from one moment to the next as she remembered that night. The shock, the fear, the confusion of trying to explain to the men she hadn't come back to keep them company. She saw no need to bore Michael with petty details when he was kind enough to let her talk this out.

"I guess they thought I was there for some other reason. When I tried to leave, one of them grabbed at me. I fell." The largest of the men had lunged at her, tackling her around the waist and landing on her legs. They'd rolled into one of the partially dismantled sets. "One of the sets fell over on me, pinning me down. Then—they left. I couldn't move the set off my legs. One of our group found me later." The next morning, after a night spent in the dark theater, her legs pinned by the massive wooden set.

Kendra forced her eyes open, refusing to remember the rest, refusing to attach any more importance to the incident. The sun no longer peered through the trees. Instead, ominous clouds filled the open area above her head. Waves of cold, then heat, then cold, drifted across the clearing. From deep within the earth, or beyond, something stirred.

"Did you feel that?" She dared a look at him. He sat a foot or so away from her, calmly sorting through a collection of small plants and leaves he must have picked up while she rested.

"Feel what?" He looked up, one eyebrow raised. A spark burned deep within his eyes, but his face appeared calm.

"Almost like a tremor?"

"You must be hungry, or perhaps more tired than you realize. I have what I need for now." He rose gracefully and extended a hand to her. "After such an experience, you will need to take extra care with your legs."

His hand was cool against her fingers, but she could feel the hot beat of his pulse when their palms met. An impression of blazing fires, quickly banked, came into her head then vanished. Maybe she was as tired as he told her, for her imagination was working overtime.

When they emerged from the forest into her garden, evening shadows were beginning to march out of the trees and attach themselves to her cottage. Kendra frowned. "I didn't realize we were gone that long. Did I fall asleep in there?"

"Time does not always move the same way, everywhere you go." Michael offered his hand to help her up the porch steps.

"Are you a philosopher in your real life, Michael?"

"Not precisely." He smiled enigmatically. "If you must have an occupation for me, I am part of a group responsible for discipline in an uncivilized area."

"You're a soldier, or a policeman?" Kendra pictured him standing strong against evil. Her heart melted for this man who loved things of the light and happy, positive forces.

"After a fashion, one could say that."

"Oh, one of those jobs you can't talk about. I see." A part of her questioned why she accepted his story so readily. It was only a very small part, easily silenced.

Dinner was soup and more of the bread she'd made a few days before, which they devoured. While they ate, Michael kept pots bubbling on the old wood stove. After he picked up the dirty dishes, refusing her help, he brought sweet, spiced tea in heavy mugs.

Kendra sipped slowly, letting the tea warm her. Propping her chin in her hand, her elbow on the table, she watched him from under increasingly heavy eyelids. Her exhaustion was odd, but they had spent a lot of the day outdoors, and she'd been in the hospital not all that long ago. Still, a tiny voice, deep inside, tried to insist. Still.

"Are you ready?" Michael turned as he asked. He smiled at the sight of her almost falling into her mug.

"If you are," she said, trying to be gracious. She seemed to be a source of constant amusement for him. This almost unpleasant thought followed her as she hobbled through her evening routine, emerging from the simple old bathroom in a nightshirt and heavy robe. Setting the walking stick to one side, she lowered herself onto her cot.

As he approached, a towel over his arm and a steaming bowl held between strong hands, she saw him backlit by the lantern's light. He looked even larger, with a vivid golden glow outlining his powerful body. Within this she saw other, less happy colors. Then she felt again the cotton gauze sensation of something slowing her thoughts, overlaying her natural caution. The glow disappeared as if it had never been.

Tomorrow she would have to ask him to leave. After she found out why he was here. After his clever, deft fingers had prodded at her knee, exposed her pain, soothed her hurts. It felt good. So good. Too good. He'd have to leave. Tomorrow. After she slept.

⌘

Dreams, nightmares, waking fantasies of storms and earth tremors chased Kendra from sleep hours later. Sensing a difference in the cottage, she lay very still in her bed, seeing through barely opened eyes.

Michael sat in the deep window seat as he had the night before. The confusion of warm and cold washed across her skin, clearly coming from him, with flashes now of extreme heat. Thickened air coursed through the cottage, along with the feeling, almost, of the earth moving. Or was it the universe?

Daring more than ever before in her life, she edged open her eyes. Whatever else she didn't understand, she knew this was not for her to see. Her deep, slow breaths mirrored sleep, and she concentrated on not allowing her heart to race in her chest.

Michael sat curled in on himself, his head on his knees, sinewy legs hugged against his naked body. Long, dark hair fell along his legs and rose around his head as if lifted by a silent wind. Light and dark swirled around him, exposing, then hiding, the tension in his body. He seemed to concentrate on deep, rumbling thunder, far in the distance.

There were almost voices in the restless air, words nearly discernible. If she could only concentrate enough, she could understand what they argued about. The more she strained, the harder she listened, the less distinct became the words. Was that her name Michael used?

Finally, shaking from the effort, she relaxed against the pillows. When she ceased straining to listen, impressions came to her rather than actual thoughts. Her name? Then, something about another person. From the unknown non-voices a feeling of total indifference then derision. Warmth and concern for her emanated from Michael as he argued with someone who belittled him.

So much warmth, so much caring from

someone who barely knew her. Maybe because he didn't really know her. Forgetting her role as silent observer, Kendra allowed herself a tiny gasp, not quite a sob.

Shocked attention shifted toward her. Anger flew at her on a shaft of dark red light. The red splintered off a golden cloak flung around her so hastily, slender dark red darts seeped through. Freezing pain slashed at her mind until the cloak thickened, warming her. Her dreams faded into numbness and the blanking out of every thought in her head.

# CHAPTER 3

Kendra hesitated at the bottom of the drive, clutching the steering wheel of her aged green hatchback. She debated going on against staying on her mountain as she balanced clutch and accelerator. A twinge in her knee made the decision for her.

It was not a fast drive. The hatchback was ancient and tended to guzzle gas and belch smoke when pushed too hard. She was in no rush, one of the advantages of no longer working. The trip was for foodstuffs not produced in her garden, and she needed to check her mail. Besides, she wanted to speak with the sheriff. Matt Hawkins was not a welcome visitor at the cottage. Secure in her new-found courage, she hummed a little as she headed for town.

Michael had taken one look at the faded green car and declined to accompany her.

Even after she teased him about being afraid of her driving or of a silly little old car. Things she would never have said a few days before. He just gave her that unearthly sweet smile and shook his head.

∽∾∽

The session with Sheriff Danvers was brief but satisfactory. Without patronizing, he reassured her he would take care of the situation. He would speak with Hawkins, who had not been authorized to visit Kendra on official business. If she had any further problems, Hawkins would be disciplined.

Digging her short nails into her old leather purse to brace up her courage, Kendra ventured a request that the sheriff not discipline Hawkins solely on her behalf. She was assured hers was not the only complaint, and the situation would now be handled officially.

Mollified, Kendra continued with her errands. She was familiar to the residents of the town, and they greeted her impaired movement with polite concern. Even this was tiring after a while, and she was very glad to head for her car.

"Miss Weiss! Miss Weiss!"

The unfamiliar voice hailed her from across the street. Not wanting to face further conversations, Kendra decided to pretend she hadn't heard. It couldn't be anyone she actually knew.

"Miss Weiss—Kendra."

Heavy, hurrying footsteps approached along the sidewalk. Kendra eyed the distance between herself and her car. Too far to make it, burdened as she was with groceries. She turned.

The man approaching was unfamiliar of face or dress, his three-piece suit entirely too formal for the small town. The stranger's manner she'd seen many times—unctuous, self-absorbed. He continued to talk as he slowed, speaking between panting breaths.

"Miss Weiss, I heard you were in town. You should have stopped by my office. Have you made a decision yet about the property?"

As he drew closer, Kendra turned to fully face him. When she lifted her face, he stopped and frowned, taking in her thick-lensed glasses and unstylish clothing.

"Excuse me," she said, reminding herself that she was no longer afraid of strange men.

"But I believe you have me confused with someone else."

"No, I don't think so. You're Kendra Weiss. I spoke with you last week at your cottage. You expressed an interest in selling as soon as possible." His breath was coming back to him, very slowly. The confusion grew on his florid face. "Wait a minute," he said, really looking at her for the first time. "You're not Kendra Weiss."

"Yes, I am, but I never spoke to you last week. You must have spoken to my cousin, Clarissa."

"No, I don't confuse names. I distinctly remember the name Kendra. Besides, Kendra Weiss is listed in the county records as owner of the property."

"The records are correct. The property is mine. Last week I was at my parent's home in California."

"How confusing," he said, his mild words not masking the race of thoughts and plans she could almost see going on in his devious mind. "Well, whatever. If you are Kendra Weiss, then I will buy the property from you."

"I am Kendra Weiss," she said as patiently as she could manage, while the straps of the canvas bag began to cut into her arm. "But I have no intention of selling my property."

"You haven't heard my offer yet."

"I don't care. The property was left to me, alone. I cannot, I will not sell."

"You're being ridiculous. Last week, you, or whoever I spoke with, said the property held no value beyond whatever it could bring on the open market. I already have an interested buyer."

"Then sell him or her some other property. Whatever my cousin told you was her idea, not mine." Shifting the bag, she turned away. "Now, if you don't mind, I have to get back."

He must have believed her. At least, he went away, which was all she could ask for at the moment. If he was trying to mask his anger, he wasn't doing too good a job of it.

Setting the tote bag on a bench near her car as she searched the large purse for her keys, Kendra wondered what in the world Clarissa was up to now.

They were similar enough in appearance to fool a casual observer, at least for a few minutes. But even at her most irresponsible, Clarissa had never lied about being Kendra. Why would she bother? The problem would have to wait for now.

Her knee was beginning to protest the concrete sidewalks, and the night's bad sleep had caught up to her.

"Well, lookie here. If it isn't little miss tattletale."

This voice was familiar, as was the cold wave of nauseous fear that came over her when she heard it. Hawkins. Reminding herself she was not afraid, she turned, leaning against the back of the bench to take some weight off her leg.

The reminder didn't work. Seeing Hawkins standing only a few feet away, his thumbs tucked into his belt loops, a look of craft on his face, she backed away as much as she could. No words came to mind, but none were needed.

"You had to come running into town and try to get me in trouble, didn't you? Just like a baby. You can't solve your own problems, so you tell lies about people."

"I—I didn't lie about you, and you know it." She said it in a small voice, holding onto the courage she thought she had finally found.

"You're so jealous of your cousin, you can't even think straight anymore," he sneered, rocking back and forth on his booted heels. Still, he stayed far enough away to not pose an immediate threat.

Kendra wondered about that then realized they were in full sight of most of the town. Anyone watching would only see a conversation between two people, not an attempted intimidation.

Taking some courage from this, she let herself settle against the bench.

"I talked to the sheriff because I want you to leave me alone. Since you won't listen to me, I hope you listen to him."

There, it was said, with little tremor and no stammering, though her stomach churned. While she continued to meet Hawkins' mirrored gaze, not wanting to show any more weakness than she had to, Kendra wondered at the development, then loss, of her courage. She had a suspicion, but it seemed too outlandish.

"You win this one," Hawkins growled, stepping away. "But Danvers can't be everywhere." With this final threat, he turned away.

Kendra took little notice of his departure. From a lifetime of always being the dutiful daughter, the submissive female, the lady who never raised her voice, for once, for the first time, Kendra allowed herself to be angry. She let the blazing heat grow in her from somewhere deep within, building and expanding until she felt ready to burst.

At first, the anger was too great to even allow her to move, to see. Then vision returned to her. And mobility. Slowly, then with ever-increasing purpose, she headed for her little car. If her leg held her back, she didn't notice.

Closing the car door behind her with a satisfactory slam, she started the engine and headed home. For once she was not aware of how much gas or tire tread she used. The little hatchback shuddered then went to work, buzzing down the paved road like an arrow of vengeance.

The turn onto the dirt road was made with little slowing, and soon vision was almost impossible because of the cloud of dust and exhaust enveloping the car. Still, she did not waver. She was going to rid herself of her unwanted houseguest. Now.

❧❧❧

He was in front of the cottage, heading for the road, when she arrived. Unaccustomed to driving at this kind of speed, she dropped both feet onto the brake, barely stopping a few feet away from him as the engine stalled. She ignored the shooting pain in her knee.

Flinging open the car door, she stepped out, retaining just enough sense to reach for her walking stick. She used the stick and door to brace herself. Once firmly on her feet, all control fled.

He stepped forward, that kindly, attractive wrinkle in his perfect brow. "Kendra?" he asked, a note of strain in his voice.

"Just who the *hell* are you, and what have you been doing to me?" Casting aside all lessons in diplomacy, she yelled at his beautiful face.

He stopped, tilting his head as if listening to more than her words. Silence reigned for a moment, punctuated only by her ragged breaths and thunder in the distance. Then she felt herself calming. Why in the world had she been so upset? Michael was just here to help her.

"Stop it!" Stepping away from the car, she advanced on him. "My-khael Al-a-stor, stop that right *now*." The calming sensation disappeared as he took a half-step away from her.

"Where did you hear my name?" Thunder growled, closer, louder, as he spoke. For once, she heard no amused tolerance in his voice, saw no seductive smile on his lips.

"From you, before you started trying to tell me how to think." Kendra knew her words could be imprudent, but her anger had burned away all cautions.

"What else have you heard?"

Her inner voice tried to tell her to stop where she was. She ignored it. "Last night, I heard you arguing with–someone."

"That is a rather vague statement, Kendra."

She flinched at the inferred slight in his drawling voice. Still, she did not allow herself to back down. She'd backed down too many times in the past.

"No more vague than your 'need for a

holiday' and certainly far more honest." Turning her back on his chilling anger, she reached for the canvas grocery bag.

In one of his swift moves, Michael, no, Mykhael, was at her side, taking the bag away from her. Kendra leaned away before he could touch her, although she couldn't keep her hold on the tote. When one of his clever, long-fingered, dangerous hands reached for her arm, she stepped away, leaning on the stick and the side of the car.

"I asked you please not to touch me. Whatever it is you do to control my mind is worse when you touch me."

"You make no sense, Kendra. How do I control your mind?"

"Stop playing stupid games with me! I may be plain and dull and a coward, but I am not stupid. And don't bother trying to deny drugging me."

She pushed away from the car, heading up the now cleared path as best she could. Mykhael paced alongside her, keeping a careful distance. He also kept a close eye on her but said nothing until she had managed the steps onto the porch and was lowering herself onto one of the kitchen chairs.

"Thank you for bringing in the bags. If you'll set them on the counter, I'll put everything away in a moment." Now that the anger was seeping away, Kendra felt incredibly weary. Maybe, just maybe, if she lay her head down on the table, she would wake in the morning and it would all have been a very bad dream.

Mykhael was no better at taking orders than any other man she'd ever known. While she sat in numb exhaustion, he put away the powdered milk, honey, and other dried goods she needed to supplement her diet. Then he folded the canvas totes into a neat square and put them in the proper drawer. Taking a glass from the cabinet, he filled it with water from her tap and brought it to the table. At all times, he made sure she could see everything he did.

"Drink this. It contains nothing but the water from your own well. The trip, and your talking, would have dried your throat."

She drank automatically, watching him sit across from her. Gone was her anger and with it, the humor and the warmth she'd felt around him. Now Mykhael sounded like he looked, an ancient statue come to life. He watched while she drank most of the water without stopping then set down the glass. When she began to make patterns on the table with the wet glass base, he removed it from her slack hands.

"How did you mean it when you said I influenced your mind, Kendra?"

She hesitated, waiting for the suffocating control of calm. When it didn't come, she drew a deep breath and let it out before she tried to answer.

"You made me think I was brave." She remembered again the shock of realizing she still feared Matt Hawkins and her numbing sense of ineptitude with the unknown real estate agent.

"What happened in town?"

His voice demanded instant obedience. She'd heard the same voice all her life: '*Answer me now, young lady.*' The time for being a young lady was now very much past. Still, it was no great secret.

"Hawkins happened in town," she said with little inflection. "And someone else. I realized I hadn't changed. When I'm not around you, I'm as much of a damned coward as ever. And I hate it."

He reached to cover her clenched fists but pulled back his hands when she glared at him. Her breaths came close together while she pulled into herself, trying to protect herself from invasion.

"You can read my mind, can't you?" she said, suddenly understanding the monstrous extent of his crime.

"No more than you can read mine." His voice was still calm, but the air was beginning to sparkle like the beginning of a huge storm.

"That makes no sense. Whoever you are, you know more than you should." But it was said with little anger. She had no energy left for anger. "I really wish you would leave."

"I cannot," he said in the same toneless fashion.

"I suppose you have some sort of secret mission here?" she roused herself enough to sneer.

He hesitated, as though debating how much to tell her. "There were rumors of damage being done to this area. Damage that could have been irreparable. I was sent to assess the situation."

"Damage?" She struggled with her doubting mind to understand what he was, and was not, saying. "You mean, like the snail bait?"

He shuddered then nodded. "That, and other things. When your cousin and her friends were here, they had no respect for the woods or the clearing."

"Why you?"

"It is my..." He hesitated. "It is the duty of my family. We are sent when damage is done."

"What are you supposed to do after you assess the situation?"

Again, the hesitation. As though he didn't think she was ready to hear it all. Maybe she wasn't.

"You seem very calm about this," he said, apparently having decided to ignore her question.

"I've lived here off and on for the better part of my life. Gran taught me nothing can be ruled impossible as long as one person believes it can happen. You obviously believe you're telling the truth." She rose slowly and went to the sink for more water. "Besides, I'm too tired to be anything but calm. I haven't had a decent night's rest since I got here." She paused, realizing for the first time how unusual that was. This glass of water she sipped, more for something to do than from actual thirst. Leaning back against the counter, she crossed her free arm in front of her body and let herself look directly at the gorgeous stranger who'd invaded her life. It had been a lovely fantasy, for the little time she'd allowed herself to dream.

"If I were to leave here, would that appease your bosses?" she asked as though she were serious.

"Perhaps."

She drew a deep breath, cautioning herself against careless speech. What the hell, life was short.

"Tough. This is my home. If I won't let a slimy land shyster buy it, I certainly won't let you try to chase me out. For all I know, you could be in cahoots with him."

He straightened in the chair, his interest piqued. Kendra waved away any questions. Placing her glass in the sink, she turned to the cupboards.

"It's obvious I can't make you leave until you're ready to go. You seem capable of taking care of yourself, but you're welcome to share my meal. I intend to make myself a small dinner then turn in early. Something tells me tomorrow isn't going to be much better than today."

⟨⟩⟨⟩

The woman slept. After tending to their dinner and attempting to tend to her leg, she lay still, fighting the pain by herself. Eventually, the demands of her body overcame her uneasiness.

Even in her slumber, she managed to resist his gentle probing. A stronger effort would have broken through her novice guard, but it could also cause her harm. In spite of his background, in spite of his history, in spite of his duty, he did not want to cause her any harm.

Any more harm. She had been harmed physically by the men in this Phoenix place, and in other ways by many of the people in her life. Something in the village had scared her. This 'deputy,' with his ugly mind and debased spirit, took perverse delight in harming her psyche. Someone had done something to her today that she had not been able to deal with, and she again had the aura

69

of feeling worthless which Mykhael had first sensed in her.

There was something else, also. Something that had her thoughts flinching and darting, her mind refusing to face some fact. Kendra had received a shock so extreme, it did not seem she would recover quickly.

He probed again, his touch a shade stronger than gentle. Again, he heard music ranging from lilting to powerful, overlaid with children's songs and a sense of swirling colors. And pain. So much pain. He could sense betrayal, on more than one level. His own, of course, and that ate at him bitterly. Kendra Weiss had been well on her way to becoming dangerously attracted to him. Still, there was more.

Raising his head from his knees, he shook back the hair that was in his way as often as not and looked over at her still form. In the moonlight, she had even less color than when he had met her. She shifted, grimacing slightly, and her fine silvery hair fell loosely about her head.

There was no artifice in this woman, not a touch of the guile he had known in females for more years than he was allowed to remember. Her honesty, her lack of subtlety, was a dangerous lure to him. Kendra Weiss represented a potentially greater threat, or greater victory, than he had ever known. Her slender, weary body and melancholy eyes could very well be the end of him. Or the beginning.

Snorting in derision, chastising himself for such late moonlight foolishness, he put away the imprudent thoughts and set himself to rest. Humans were at their weakest just before dawn. He would try at that time to breach her defenses.

∾∾

Kendra woke in the darkest hour before dawn. Mykhael slept, or at least he gave every appearance of it, laying his head back against the wall of the window seat, his mouth drooping open. Even with his breath moving heavily in and out of his nose, he was devastating.

He dreamed, this man of no history, no place. She sensed his dreams held desolation and doubt, dark areas of his thoughts only lightened in a few places. Whoever Mykhael was, whatever the job he had to do, he was not a happy man. A small part of Kendra hurt for him, in spite of her better sense.

Although her knee ached, her clumsy efforts the night before, plus the sketchy sleep, had done some good. At least the pain no longer shadowed every move she made, and she was able to consider her options. She needed to act now, before dawn. It had always been her strongest time of day.

For one thing, she had to get away from Mykhael. The sadness in him reached out, even in his sleep, to threaten the limits she placed on relationships with other people. This would not do. Not until she could go somewhere, far away from here in thought if not in distance. She remembered a place, deep in the woods, where she'd often gone to be alone.

Once she knew where she wanted to go, she filled her thoughts with memories of a lifetime of dancing, to block Mykhael from learning her destination. At one time, thinking of the career wrenched away from her had been too painful. Now, she understood pain much better than before. The worst pains were never physical.

# CHAPTER 4

Dawn moved into the glade, touching leaf and bark with a hint of the new day. It had still been dark when Kendra slithered into the spot she thought of as her very own. No one had ever been here with her. When she'd first found the spot, the entry, which tunneled through stubborn vines, was too low for a woman the age of her grandmother.

She remembered little of the trip to the glade. Not wanting any encumbrances, she'd left her glasses behind and let her feet remember the way. As she walked, she concentrated on the clearing she'd visited with Mykhael a few days before.

Every branch and ripple was recalled, with utmost precision, along with the pathway they'd taken. Only when she bent to enter the vine tunnel did she abandon that image. Half-crouched to crawl through the dark opening, she couldn't allow any wasted energy.

In spite of the years, there seemed to be little change. Certainly, in that period of time, there must have been something. Perhaps the sheltering trees had grown larger. If so, other bushes had grown into trees, to provide the same shielding branches. They grew just a few feet or so above her head, completing the sanctuary.

The peace she'd sought was here, and she wondered why she hadn't thought to come here before. In fact, until that morning, she hadn't remembered this place at all. As she settled herself on the mossy roots of the benevolent old sequoia, she wondered about that.

Immediately, she felt the searching probe, and she re-directed her thoughts. In spite of his restless dreams, Mykhael was awake and again trying to reach her. Now, instead of confusing his search with inane detail, she let her mind go blank and opened herself to the rising sun. As the first rays stroked her face, she breathed in the serenity of the clearing and breathed out her confusion, anger, and fear. The familiar ritual worked as it once

74

had. Soon, she was immersed in tranquility, far away from any touch.

The thought of Mykhael she rejected as soon as his image appeared in her mind. He was too close, too clever, too attuned. Thinking of him would bring him here, before she was ready to deal with him. Instead, she allowed herself to think of her cousin.

Clarissa. Child of the light, with moonbeams threading through her hair and eyes the blue of the finest summer skies, though her inner person did not match her appearance. Clarissa, for whom beauty and success were a foregone conclusion. It was known in the family that Clarissa was beautiful and Kendra...well, Kendra was smart, which was quite good enough for her.

Her cousin had come to visit in the hospital, overcoming an aversion to things imperfect. When Kendra expressed worry about the garden, Clarissa had been happy to come up, to help out. Why hadn't Kendra seen the danger? In her whole life, her cousin had never done anything for anyone else without expecting something in return. Still, Kendra had wanted to believe Clarissa's stated desire to help.

Even knowing the truth, and knowing what kind of a person Clarissa had grown into, Kendra could not accept the duplicity. To even think of selling Gran's home was impossible. That Clarissa would intentionally pretend to be someone she'd always despised meant the purpose behind the act was darker than Kendra could conceive.

It had been too long since she opened her mind to contemplation. Thinking was as hard on her body as it was on her mind. She shifted, trying to find a more comfortable spot on the ground, and her heel caught on a root.

The pain came unannounced, ripping through her knee, rushing up and down her leg, piercing her heart. Kendra had not cried for her grandmother and could not cry for her cousin. Not yet. She could, and very nearly did, cry for the destruction of her knee, and of her life.

It was the warmth, first, that let her know she was no longer alone. Not only physical warmth, but something far more than that. A gentle, nurturing warmth, reaching through the ice that had formed in her thoughts, around her heart.

Reaching, searching for a way to help, to touch. To invade.

Mykhael was in the glade with her.

"No." Her eyes snapped open, but for a moment her mind refused their message.

He sat close enough to touch, far enough away not to frighten. His green eyes regarded her with the unblinking stare of a predator. His legs were folded into the complicated knot she could no longer achieve, and his expression was one of benevolence. Kendra doubted that expression, and when he reached a long-fingered hand in her direction, she recoiled before she could stop herself.

Mykhael paused, his hand in mid-air, reaching for her but not quite touching. Then he let his hand drop to rest on his thigh. From kindness, his expression froze into the remote aloofness she told herself was more in keeping with the person he really was. She would not allow his implied hurt to touch her. Not this time.

"I could never hurt you, Kendra. Not in the way you think."

In the hush of the glade, his voice filled an emptiness she'd never noticed here before, yet she knew it had always been there.

"You already have."

He tilted his head to one side, and the entirely-too-thick fall of dark auburn curls draped across his shoulder. "How have I hurt you?"

"By making me think I was better than I am, that I have courage and value. I've been a crawling coward all my life. I was perfectly content to remain that way. Now that you've made me experience valor, I know what I'm missing in my make-up."

He allowed himself a small smile, as though amused by her explanation. "Your courage was always there, Kendra. I did nothing to force it."

"Oh, like Oz and the lion?"

This time his puzzlement was absolute, but he didn't pursue what she said. Instead, he looked around the glade. "Is this a place you came when you were afraid or worried?"

"I found this place when I started high school," she answered obliquely. "Gran never wanted to come here. She said it should be my place alone."

"No one ever joined you?"

"No one ever knew anything about it. I'd forgotten about it myself until this morning."

She looked away from him, lifting her face to the sun's growing warmth. On the edges of her mind, she could feel his delicate touch.

"Go away, Mykhael. Get out of my mind and my life."

"What is it you fear?" he asked, his voice low.

"You," she answered without hesitation. "I fear you."

There was none of the condemnation or argument she expected, nor any derisive amusement. Instead, a void suddenly appeared where his thoughts had been. Puzzled, Kendra allowed herself to look, really look, at him, for the first time that day.

Backlit by the sun, he sat very still, his rising and falling chest the only sign that he was more than a statue. The belt of his shirt had come loose, exposing the knit silk undershirt. Mykhael had gone into himself, shutting her out as completely as she had tried to shut him out. Now she saw her own efforts as amateurish. Had he wanted in, he could have invaded her mind whenever he wanted.

"Touch me, Kendra," he said into the blank silence that had taken root between them.

There was no force in his voice, and he did not change his position. With his legs wrapped up within themselves, it would be difficult for him to leap toward her. Yet she felt trapped. She pulled away, readying herself to rise.

"You have no need to fear me. I think you realize that. It is yourself you fear."

"Why would I fear myself?"

Whatever her fears, or lack thereof, she knew she could not respect herself if she backed away now. Finally, her eyes on his face, she braved a touch on his forearm. Just a light brush of her fingertips, trailing through the short dark hairs.

She saw his pupils dilate, then his eyes narrowed and his nostrils flared, while his mouth opened slightly to grab a breath of air. She watched his chest rise as his breath caught. His small nipples hardened and rose against the silk undershirt. Fascinated, she continued to stroke as she recorded his reactions. A bulge began to show in his loose linen trousers, and she jerked her gaze away, to focus on his hands, forming into fists on his legs.

"It is not just you, touching me. It is us. It

is something concerning you and myself." He swallowed, and she tracked the movement of his throat then was distracted by the pulse beating at the base of his neck, the abrupt rise of his chest. "I was sent here to investigate rumors of people violating your grandmother's garden. I did not expect you. I am as shocked about it as you are."

He lifted his hands, opening them, looking at them then at her. "I have tried to only touch you to heal, to help. But I cannot control what happens when our skin connects. I find I do not want to control it. Kendra, may I touch you?"

Helpless against the honest longing in his voice, the torment in his face, she nodded. Her eyes squeezed shut as she braced herself for the now familiar shock.

A warm breeze skimmed across her cheek, brushed the edges of her hair, traced the outline of her jaw, then swept on. Intrigued, she leaned toward rather than away from the promise of his touch. A lightening came to the glade, as though the trees themselves breathed a sigh of happiness.

Finally, she felt the slight roughness of his fingers against her skin. Through some oddity of the communication they shared, she also felt the softness of her cheek under his fingers. He traced her eyebrow, the edge of her nose, the folds of her ear. Everywhere his fingers touched, sparks kindled. Soon she felt as though her entire body was on fire. The fire chose no one place, but she felt heat pooling in her thoughts, melting the lump in her chest until it ran into the center of the most feminine part of her being.

Gasping a near sob, her eyes squeezed shut, she edged closer to his touch. His arms reached out, circled her, lifted her, and she was settled on his lap. Shocked, at first she held herself aloof, stiffening her spine against the desire to give in, to melt against him. He only held her, raising his leg to support her hip so she didn't need to brace herself.

He continued to brush her face, her neck, her shoulder with the merest hint of his touch. Until, at last, she gave in and let herself settle against his shoulder, trusting her weight to the powerful arm behind her back.

Replete with sensations, she let her eyes edge open and her head loll back. Immediately, she felt his fingers encircle her neck, sliding around and tunneling into her hair to support her head. His face lowered to hers, the glitter in his eyes like the heart of the finest emerald. For the first time in her life, Kendra felt the brush of a man's warm breath against her skin. Where he had touched her with his fingers he now used his mouth, nibbling and tasting, as though savoring the feel of her against his lips.

Not so cautious now of the link between them, Kendra let herself feel just a bit more of what Mykhael felt. A flood of sensations overtook her mind, including a raging arousal that shocked her out of her complacent stupor. Before she could do more than think about pulling away, he'd dropped a screen over that sensation.

Resting his face against the base of her neck, he held her, sheltering her from the world and himself. After a moment of feeling the security of his arms around her, Kendra dared greatly and lifted her arms to slide them around his waist. The shudder that raced through his body shook her—and seemed to affect the clearing around them.

The branches of the trees swayed in a slight wind, always managing to shade them from the sun as it tracked across the sky.

Offering and receiving comfort, he held her close, and she felt the harmony grow between them.

Nestled against Mykhael, Kendra felt welcome, safe, for the first time in years. There were so many questions still needing answers, so many problems yet to be solved. Here, for now, she could rest her head and her heart. She didn't sleep. Sensations as beautiful as these were not to be wasted in slumber.

Mykhael seemed content to stay in the glade. From time to time, he would lift a hand to her head, touching her hair as though enjoying the fine texture. Then he would stroke his hand along her back, searching out the areas made tense by her limping. Warmth without heat slipped out of his fingers, tracing along nerve endings she hadn't known she possessed.

When the sun no longer shone into the side of the clearing but instead filtered in through overhead branches, Mykhael lifted his head. He urged her with a gentle hand to sit up. "We need to return. It will storm this afternoon, and you do not want to walk on wet ground."

"Can't you control the weather?" she asked, through a yawn that snuck up on her unannounced.

His laughter rumbled against her shoulder. Raising his hand, he pushed her hair back behind her ear.

"Sorry, no. That was one of the skills I never quite mastered."

Her question had been meant as a feeble joke, but his reply seemed serious. Wondering at the softening in his face, Kendra dared to lift a hand and trace the smile curving his lips. As her fingers touched his mouth, he took a gentle hold of her hand.

"If you start to touch me now, we will never return."

The statement was mysterious to her at first. A flaring of his nostrils as he caught at a lungful of air, and a sudden tension underneath her legs, explained without words. Feeling her face heat as it had not for years, Kendra scrambled off his lap.

It was not as graceful a movement as it once could have been. Mykhael supported her without comment until she could stand without swaying, but there was a rigidity to his mouth she hadn't noticed before. This time she kept her curious fingers to herself, accepted the walking stick in silence then led the way out.

The day seemed much cooler outside the glade. A weight began to press on her, reminding her of all her failures, all her fears, all her shortcomings. She remembered, also, what Clarissa had done to her, and how Mykhael...

"No," he said quietly

He stood very still, next to her. Behind them, the vines fell together, masking any hint of an entrance. In the cold gray of the coming storm, she felt very alone.

"In there..." she began and hesitated.

"In there you could think more clearly, without the world intruding. Do not let the world come between us, just because we are not in there now."

She wanted to believe him. With every lacerated fiber of her being, she wanted to believe peace was possible wherever she was. It was a lovely fantasy.

"I've always been happy in there," she said, deciding for now to avoid the issue.

"It is unique," he agreed, leading the way to the cabin. Then he stopped, looking back along their path. Although they had moved only a few feet, there was no indication anyone had touched the vines for years. He nodded, as though something were confirmed for him.

"Remember this place, Kendra. Do not let yourself forget again where it is, no matter what happens."

He watched her face intently, until she nodded. Seeming to be satisfied, he turned again. This time, instead of leading, he waited for her to join him. Together, they went back to the cottage.

# CHAPTER 5

By the time they returned to the cabin, the weather had shifted seasons into autumn. Kendra didn't argue when Mykhael insisted she eat some warm soup and drink her fill of hot, sweet tea. Today, she had no fear of what he prepared for her. It was as if the baring of emotions in the clearing had eradicated much of the mistrust between them.

There was something else between them, something growing, no matter how much they might try to ignore it. At first, Kendra tried to act as she had in the beginning. She avoided his touch, avoided meeting his eyes.

Then his hand closed over hers, resting on the table. Once again, the heat flared, this time even more quickly.

"It will not go away, Kendra."

"What—what can we do about it?"

The smile he gave her now was different,

softer, more beguiling, as he looked at her through lowered eyelids. He raised his free hand, touching her cheek with one long finger.

It was as though he had completed a circuit. Kendra felt the charge along every nerve ending in her body. Most strongly, she felt it in her suddenly tense stomach, her over-sensitive breasts.

His gaze dropped to her chest, and his smile broadened. Kendra looked down. The sensible button-down shirt she donned that morning had managed to lose a button some-time today. Instead of a conservative one button undone, it now gaped open to the top of her bra. On either side of the opening, rising nipples tented the material.

"I imagine we could find something to do about it," he said, not raising his voice above a husky whisper.

Tugging gently at her captive hands, he pulled her forward and onto her feet. In spite of her many misgivings, she relented, moving to stand between his legs. He shifted his hold on her, pinning her hands behind her back, using the pressure to move her closer.

With his free hand, he unbuttoned her

blouse the rest of the way, never lifting his gaze from what his fingers were doing. Each small button gave way before the deft movements of his fingers. She felt a draft of cool air against her stomach.

It was a brief moment of chill. Uttering an inarticulate murmur, Mykhael pulled her against him and rested the side of his face against her bare skin. The weight of him was foreign to her, as was the feel of his lush hair against her torso. She looked down at his supplicantly bent head, the dark red hair contrasting with her pale skin and sensible white bra. Behind her back, her fingers twitched, and she pulled against his gentle hold until he released her wrists. Lifting her hands, she touched just the ends of his hair. It was cool, springy, inviting her to explore just a bit further. Working her way slowly upward, she soon felt the heat of his scalp under her fingers.

Remembering earlier sensations, she slid her fingers through hair that seemed to have a life of its own. His sigh breathed against her skin, and he wrapped his arms around her, below her waist, as though he was reluctant to ever let her go.

He stood abruptly, scooping his arm beneath her thighs and lifting her as he rose. Kendra was too surprised to utter any sort of a protest beyond a tiny squeak. Her hands slipped from his hair and closed on his shoulders, bracing against the unaccustomed movement.

In the waning light of the stormy afternoon, he carried her to the narrow bed she'd slept in much of her life. Fully clothed, he set her on the bed and lay down next to her.

"Mykhael..." she croaked, unable to verbalize what was very wrong with a man in her bed. Partially because having Mykhael next to her on this bed was so very right.

"Hush, darling. I just want to hold you, to feel you." Pulling at her hip until she turned on the bed, he settled her body against his. As their bodies touched, he uttered a soft groan. "It is as I thought. So good. So very good."

It was good. After a lifetime of repression, Kendra's frenzied nerve endings clamored for more, ever more. In an unconscious move, she edged forward, tilting her hips just a bit, reaching, striving.

Mykhael shuddered and moved. Bearing her back on the bed, he lifted his body over hers. For the first time, she felt the differences of their bodies, male and female, the eternal meshing that was so alien, and so natural.

Even if she was ignorant, her body knew what it wanted. Drawing her hands away from the secure hold around his neck, she reached between them. Her trembling fingers fumbled at the button of her loose jeans, bumping against him, encountering strange and wonderful new shapes. Uttering a breathless laugh, Mykhael took possession of her hand.

"Slowly, my darling. There is no need to rush."

He encircled her hand with fingers that trembled only slightly less than hers. Bringing her hand to his mouth for a brief, hot kiss, he set her open hand against his chest until she could feel his nipple hard against her palm.

While she rubbed slowly, enjoying the catch of his breath, he reached around her.

A hook was loosened, cloth barriers were swept away, and before Kendra could be embarrassed about him seeing her small, bare breasts, his hands covered her.

"Lovely," he whispered, lowering his head.

She wanted to tell him how strange all this was, to ask that he go just a little more slowly. She wanted to explain that she was just the least bit scared—maybe even a lot scared. Before she could draw a breath, it was jerked out of her body by the fiery wind rushing through her.

His warm, moist mouth settled over her breast. Against her nipple was the stroke of what could only be his tongue. She arched, pushing against him, a high keening cry sliding from her tightened throat. Grabbing at whatever was closest, she took hold of his head, his shoulder, his back.

Low muttering, in a guttural language she'd never heard before, painted sultry words across her skin. She tried to concentrate on his voice, and at first missed the work of his hands. Bare skin touched, first their chests, hers soft, yielding to his hard. Both damp with a sensual heat.

While she tried to absorb the unfamiliar feeling, his hands swept down her back, along her thighs. His gentle touch eased her onto her back. A hesitation, a bitten off word, then soft kisses on her scarred knees, before he continued. When he came back to her, there was nothing between them but the truth.

"Mykhael..." she tried again. "I hav—"

Muttering what might have been an apology forced out between tight lips, he moved over her again. A touch along her thighs made a place for him between her legs. He joined them with one sure stroke. And froze.

There was pain. She'd always known there would be pain. Never had she known, never had anyone told her, about the heat, the fulfillment, the utter perfection of the completion of her being. Never would she have believed how right pain could feel.

"Kendra," he whispered, in a deep, awed voice. "Darling, why did—no, do not move. Not yet. Let me..." He arched suddenly, his head lifting away from her as he grimaced, attempting to fight the inevitable.

Kendra watched him struggle for control. As he battled with his body, images began to swirl around her. Along with the heat of her skin, the fullness of her own being, she felt his delight at being embedded deep within her, his length embraced by her heat.

"Darling, stop," he gasped, still struggling

for control, as thoughts and sensations began to rebound between the two of them.

She reached up, touched his face, his hair. With the contact, she perceived flashes of times long past, of sorrows and fears. Of confusion and questions about who he was, what he had done, what he was doing. This—this encounter, this loving—at least, was right. In the early evening coolness, he took away the pain from her leg and her heart and made her whole.

Threading her fingers into his hair, she tugged his face towards hers. She lifted her head, opened her mouth. When their lips joined, for just a moment, she felt a trembling in the very fabric of the universe.

Then he pulled his mouth away from hers, long enough to gasp against her neck before his hips flexed, his arms stiffened, and he gave himself over to ecstasy

# CHAPTER 6

The sensations ebbed away slowly, leaving tiny shivers coursing under her skin. In their wake came the questions she should be thinking about. Soon, she would begin to worry again.

But not yet.

"Not yet," he agreed, his lips moving against her neck.

He tasted her, a hot sweep of tongue, and whispered against her hair in the obscure language.

"You *are* reading my mind!"

"As intimate as we are." He flexed, reminding her that their bodies were still joined. "And as nearly as we could read each other before, does it surprise you?"

"At this moment, nothing could surprise me." She dared to touch her fingertips to his arching brow, the curve of his upper lip. "Later," she whispered, raising her head to reach his mouth with hers. "Later I'm going to have to worry about all of this."

Their lips met, a brief, glancing touch, and once again her universe swayed, tilted, and dropped her into a plethora of sensation. This time she didn't fight it. Letting herself fall back against the pillows, she opened to him. If she ceased to live tomorrow, she would at least have been alive tonight.

As the odd thought wandered through her mind, she felt Mykhael shudder against her. He muttered a denial against her mouth, the words strange to her ear but the meaning clear. Long fingers speared through her hair, tilting her head to just the right angle, holding her almost painfully. When she stirred, and would have initiated another round of love-making, he stilled her uncertain movements.

"No, my darling," he said, pulling his mouth off hers with a show of great reluctance. "Not right now. You're too new to this, and you need to rest."

He arranged their bodies, her head pillowed on his shoulder, her knee drawn up over his thigh. He dropped a chaste kiss onto her hair as he pulled the covers over them, holding in the warmth of their joining.

He smoothed his hand along her thigh, over her hip, and found the spot in her lower back that had hurt since she lost the ability to walk evenly on both legs. Kendra allowed herself to be soothed into sleep. Tonight they would share only warmth, not the cold fear and fury of their dreams.

❦❦

Almost dawn. Kendra woke to a feeling of absolute well-being. Her knees still pained her, one, as always, worse than the other. But for the first time in many years, she woke feeling warm on the inside. For the first time since she lay in a hospital bed surrounded by machines and strangers, clutching the notice of her grandmother's death, she woke feeling not lonely.

Mykhael's breath stirred her hair. His body rose and fell beside hers like the river below a canoe.

Selfish for even more of his warmth, she snuggled closer. So many exotic new sensations to experience, to catalog and save against the time when he would not be here, when she would again sleep alone in this narrow bed with only her memories to keep her warm.

"Sweet Kendra," he murmured, sliding long fingers through her hair. His lips brushed against her brow, lightly at first, then as though imprinting his touch on her. As he nibbled along her hairline, he whispered loving words in the language she still didn't understand.

"What is that you're speaking?" she asked, bold in the near darkness.

She didn't need light to know he was startled, as wary as any deer in the beam of a poacher's light. Daring even more, Kendra raised her head, resting her forearm against his chest, her chin on top of her hand. She touched his cheek, tentatively at first then with greater confidence. Under her fingers his skin was stubbled with the night's growth of beard.

Had she ever seen him shave? Kendra paused in her touching while she consulted her memories. Against her side, Mykhael seemed suddenly far away. She had vowed to not think about any of this. Not yet. Then, when?

"Is it Greek?" she asked, striving for a

calm, even tone of voice. "I've known some Greek dancers. They didn't sound quite like you do, but it could be a different dialect."

"I am certain it would be a different dialect, even if it were Greek." Mykhael moved his fingers absently in her hair then traced the shape of her ear. When she quivered, edging closer to his touch, he laughed to himself. It was a forced laughter, and the feel of his fingers on her skin seemed even more comforting to him than to her.

Kendra wondered how she knew. Even with this new ability to feel his emotions and even, sometimes, his thoughts. Only sometimes, and often not clearly enough to do any good.

"Is it Greek?" she persisted, soaking up his warmth as she lay along his length.

"Not quite." He drew in and released a deep breath in a heavy sigh, lifting her, ruffling her hair with his breath. "In moments of intense emotions: passion, fear, love, one tends to revert to the language of childhood." He fell silent, once more stroking through her hair.

"Which—which emotion was it?" she asked, holding herself still against his answer.

The soft laugh she felt against her side had little to do with humor.

"All of them, darling. Passion, obviously, fear of how much you could be hurt by all this. Love."

His arms encircled her, holding her still as she would have rolled away from him. She fought briefly, knowing the battle would be impossible, not wanting to hear any more of his words and the foolish hopes they brought to her.

"You don't need to give me soft words and promises meant to be broken, Mykhael. I may not be experienced myself, but I have seen much of what passes for love."

"In your world, perhaps." He eased the constricting hold of his arms, once more stroking her until she let herself relax, just a little, against him. "You are not letting yourself hear the truth of what I say, Kendra. Listen to all of me."

He was right. Wary of all that had gone on, she heard his words only on the surface. Now she relented, laying her head back on his chest, replaying in her mind what he had said.

Then she realized that his words had only

given her another puzzle to contemplate instead of answering her question.

"Mykhael," she whispered, feeling her breath as it teased the hairs on his chest. "What is the language of your childhood?"

It was not the question he had expected. She knew that by the sudden tension of his arms, the abrupt, forced stilling of his thoughts. Time held, for a moment, in a near vacuum. Then he breathed again, taking one second longer to frame an answer. His thoughts once more progressed. In the lightening darkness, he sought her face with his fingers, cupping her chin, holding her still against his chest.

"It is what your scholars call Akkadian."

Kendra pulled against his restraint, knowing he wouldn't hold her hard enough to do any harm. Mykhael looked away from her, his attention seeming to be on the increasing light easing through the bowed window. An exquisite tension thrummed through his body, transferring to her along all their points of contact. She struggled with what he was not telling her.

"No one speaks Akkadian any more, Mykhael. Even the scholars only read it. It's been a dead language for at least a thousand years." Her education had only given her the name of the language, not the details. But that was enough to bring a chill to her thoughts.

"A form of it is spoken in a remote area, but pure Akkadian has been dead closer to fifteen hundred years. I learned it before then."

"Mykhael," she began, framing her question carefully in her mind before she allowed the words to escape her mouth. "What are you trying to tell me?" No, that wasn't the right question. He needed to answer the precise question. "How old are you?"

"As well as I can calculate," he said, lifting her face with gentle fingers under her chin until he could look in her eyes. "Probably about three thousand years."

She could not doubt the sincerity in his eyes or in his thoughts. Mykhael believed absolutely in what he was telling her and wanted her to believe it as well. It wasn't the forced acceptance she'd felt when they first met, but something far greater. Mykhael needed for her to believe him, for her to believe *in* him.

Kendra swallowed, knowing he felt her

confusion, knowing he watched her throat work and was momentarily distracted by the sight of her, watching him. Fortunately, she could only feel his attention not actually see herself as he saw her. She strove for the right answer.

"You seem remarkably well preserved. Is there some formula for extended youth that has been lost through the years?"

Her answer, along with the grin she tried to give him, was unexpected. Another of the full, rumbling laughs overtook Mykhael, releasing some of the tension that had mounted to a near unbearable pitch between the two of them. He hugged her, a rocking, cradling embrace that joined them in happiness more than in passion, and she experienced one more level of consummation.

"You do not doubt me?" he asked, the wonder in his words and thoughts surrounding them with a soft glow that held back the encroaching day, saving for just a second longer the magic of their night together.

"Mykhael," she said, in a voice of extreme tolerance. "In the past week I've met a person of unearthly beauty who knew more about me than I knew about myself. I've experienced levels of courage and emotion I didn't know were a part of my make-up. I've remembered things about my childhood that had been lost to me for years. I've felt your thoughts and heard your worries. Nothing has been normal since I came back here. How could I doubt you?"

The glow spread, intensified, laughter enhancing their dark passion. Kendra couldn't understand what was going on between them and with them. She knew what she felt, and she knew, somehow, this was something she must have the courage to tell Mykhael.

"Whoever you are, why ever you are here, at this moment, I do not doubt you. I cannot."

A shudder raced through him, and his hold on her hardened. The breath he dragged into his lungs was ragged. He trembled against her. His eyes closed, but not before she could see the sheen of gathering moisture behind his lids.

"Mykhael," she whispered, anguished that she had brought pain to him with her foolish words.

"Not foolish, darling," he muttered through teeth that tried to hold back his words. "Unexpected, but not foolish. Your trust is a gift I could never have predicted and had not dared hope for."

Ask the right question, she reminded herself. If you want the right answer, you ask the right question. She braced herself, but in the end it was so simple.

"Mykhael." She settled her hand along his jaw, stroking a finger onto the pulse throbbing in his neck. "What are you doing here?"

He managed a smile at that, bittersweet but still a raising of the edges of his mouth.

"I must ask you something first, darling. Where in the world are we?"

"You don't know?"

"I was sent here. I will explain that in a minute. Where are we? You have nothing in this cottage to identify this location."

She allowed the tension building inside her to escape into laughter. If there was an edge to her laughter, a hint of hysteria, it dissipated as she took in the scowl darkening his sculptured features. There was no sign now of tolerant humor in his expression.

"You're telling me someone who has lived three thousand years, can appear out of nowhere, read minds, and control the weather doesn't know where he is?"

A reluctant smile twitched at the corners of his mouth. "I told you, I cannot control the weather."

"You know someone who can," she stated rather than questioned.

His answer was a small grimace, a tilting up of one shoulder.

"Perhaps, but it is not encouraged. Nature is to be lived with in harmony, not coerced into cooperation."

"You really mean that, don't you?" she said, a note of wonder in her voice. When his frown intensified, she rushed on. "I've known people who say things like that, but they only pay lip service to the philosophies. You actually live them."

"For most of my long and not always illustrious life." He looked away from her, sliding his fingers under her hair until he cupped the back of her neck. "'Lip service,'" he mused. "I like that. Is it a new phrase?" His fingers rubbed gently, seeking her warmth, offering her comfort.

"Relatively, I suppose." She wondered at the absolute calm of her voice, at her lack of any fear when she was confronted by what should have sent her gibbering into the corner. "Where have you been all your 'long and not always illustrious life'?"

For the first time, he sighed. It was a sound of intense sorrow, and there was no doubt in Kendra's mind that whatever was upsetting Mykhael was something she did not want to know about. Still, she didn't draw away from him physically or mentally. The turmoil in his mind came through as a swirling mass of dark red and matte black. "That is something we need to discuss, later. Our location?" he reminded, with a gentle shake to her neck.

"Sorry. California, near Sequoia National Park."

He only tilted his head, and the thought sensations coming from him became a swirl of memories being sifted through. Kendra waited as patiently as she could manage, but in the end could tell he still did not place their location.

"West Coast, United States?" Still nothing. "Western Hemisphere?"

Apparently this did the trick. No more confusion battered at her mind. He nodded.

"So that did succeed," he said, sounding satisfied. "I had hoped it would."

"I beg your pardon?" Kendra pulled away from the entirely too comforting feel of his fingers against the back of her neck. Too much unusual and strange was going on to allow herself to be soothed into complacence.

"The colonies—their experiment with liberty. It was such an amazing concept. I had hoped it would succeed."

"Mykhael," she warned, sitting up completely. The sheet fell away from her, and she felt the early morning chill of the cabin against her bare skin. Now was not the time to worry about such things. "You're making even less sense than before."

As she pulled away, he brought his gaze back to her. A sudden heat flashed from his eyes as he looked at her, taking in the slenderness of her body, the delicacy of her undersized breasts.

Kendra could feel hunger rising in him, his denial of her own appraisal of her appearance, then the conscious damping of his arousal. Never taking his attention from her, he groped over the side of the bed.

"Put this on." He thrust clothing—his knit silk tank top—at her. "Now. We need to talk, and I cannot when you..." He looked away, gulping, as she shook out the shirt and lifted her arms to drop it over her head.

It fell around her loosely, surrounding her with soft elegance and his scent. Kendra closed her eyes to better appreciate the feel of the costly material sliding across her sensitized skin, skimming the peaks of her tender breasts.

A muffled expletive from across the bed drew her eyes opened. Mykhael had moved back, his legs now exposed as he prepared to rise. She felt the force of his will, directed against himself. She also saw the effect of her unconscious exhibition on his body.

"If you expect me to pay any attention to our talk," she began, as dryly as she could. "I recommend you also clothe yourself."

⁊ᴑᴈᴑ

They settled, finally, in the window seat where he had already spent so much time. Extra pillows made the wide seat even more comfortable, and Kendra was able to stretch out, relieving a tendency to cramp. This exposed much of her legs beneath the shirt, but for once she didn't care if anyone saw her. Except for the scars. Livid, raw, they marred what had once been passably attractive legs. She wished then for a quilt to hide her legs, or at least the knees, the ugliness.

"To hide them, yes, but not because they are ugly." Mykhael sat, facing her, next to her legs, his thigh alongside hers.

For a moment he looked along the length of her legs, and the heat in his gaze almost scorched her skin. Then he pulled a lovingly aged quilt over her.

"We must talk, with as few distractions as possible."

*Then put a shirt on*, her newly brazen thoughts said. She nearly said it out loud. His linen pants hung from his hips, held up by a drawstring that dared her to pull it. But this was not the time for levity. The somber darkness of his thoughts made that very clear.

Bathed in the soft glow of the early morning light pouring through the windows, Mykhael reached for her hands. His touch soothed rather than aroused, and she could feel him drawing the same comfort from her.

"In the beginning of time, there were centers of...power, for lack of a better word, throughout this world. A few of them led to..." He hesitated again, obviously searching for a phrase or word she would understand.

"Other places, or other times?" she asked softly, trying very hard not to let her uneasiness show. He was so deadly serious, so anxious. As if this were the most important conversation he would ever have, and he had to get it just right.

"Both, actually. Humans were not the only higher beings on this planet. In fact, they are the newest addition, although the most prolific. As human population increased, others were crowded out.

"For many centuries all coexisted in relative peace, but it was obvious humans were going to reproduce at a faster rate than they could be educated or controlled, short of all out eradication. Not that that has not been tried, unfortunately."

"What do you mean?" Kendra strove to keep a strong control on her reactions. Only the feel of his hands, encompassing hers, gave her enough strength of mind to sit there and listen with at least an outward calm.

"Along with extraordinary differences between humans and—the others, there were also many similarities. Greed, corruption, and misuse of power are not limited to humans, Kendra. At times, I fear it may have been taught to you."

"Where is this leading?" And why do I need to know? she added silently. There was too much turmoil in his thoughts for the additional phrase to be heard.

"Let me tell this in my own way, please." He was silent for a moment, staring at the ceiling, or something else. "It was decided to leave, at least during the difficult time when humans were coming to maturity. The others left, leaving as much protection around the places of power as possible.

"Throughout the intervening years, many of these places have been violated. There have been crossovers, some voluntary, some welcome, some...not. Since, in the beginning, there was hope for human growth, intermarrying, or at least cohabitation, was permitted, even encouraged at times.

"Some humans carry a trace of Other blood. Although it does not follow any logical inheritance, in some, it is stronger. These humans often protect the special places."

"So Gran was..."

"A very wise and wonderful woman. This location is particularly important in the balance of power, and your grandmother protected it of her own free will, as have the women of your family for many generations. In the natural scheme of things, you would have been trained to take over for her. Unfortunately, she was taken away before her time."

"Did my father ever know?"

"He only knew his mother had always been a bit strange. Her strangeness embarrassed him many times as a child, and as an adult he was not always comfortable around her. He is a good man, by human standards, but by other standards not terribly intelligent." He glanced at her quickly, as though apologizing for the insult, then looked away again.

"You did well, learning from your grandmother, and it seemed the area would remain secure. Then the watchers sensed a disturbance in the area, a violation of the space. I was called to take care of the situation."

"Why you?"

"A heritage. Some are watchers, some are guardians, some are...enforcers. Alastor, my clan name, was misinterpreted with all the different translations throughout history."

"Alastor..." she mused, searching for an elusive nugget of information. Then the book opened in her mind's eye, and the answer appeared. "It was the duty of Alastor to ensure that the sins of the father were visited upon the son."

"Not precisely. It is the duty of the clan of Alastor to ensure that the sanctity of the places and balance of power is maintained at all times. When violations occur, a member of my clan is called, and we are given an image of the person responsible for the violation."

His eyes were even more remote, with that far away, almost sad, look she'd seen so many times before. A chilling premonition came to her and she lifted her chin, seeking the strength to ask the next question.

"Quit the games, Mykhael. Why exactly are you here now, in this place, at this time?"

He looked at her directly, and she saw the agony he had to be feeling.

"Darling, I've been sent here to kill you."

# CHAPTER 7

But...I was in the hospital. I never...it was Clarissa."

"I realize that, Kendra. Now. As far as my overlords, the Atrahasis, are concerned, a human who looks like you violated a special place of harmony. If she had written her name at Stonehenge, it would not be so serious."

"But—if these Atrahasis are so wise and all-powerful, why don't they know who violated their precious spot?"

He drew a deep breath, as though hoping the extra oxygen would make his words clear.

"Many who are now Atrahasis have become insular and self-serving. They saw the image of the person who violated this spot and gave me only that image. My duty was to deal with the person who most closely resembled that image."

"Even if it's not the right person?"

"As far as the Atrahasis are concerned, there are far too many humans on this planet. If the first choice is not the right person, they will simply choose another."

"The only good human's a dead human?" she offered, seeing a black humor in the situation.

He nodded, accepting her words, and allowed her to feel a touch of the anxiety plaguing him.

"There's no way out of it, is there?" What a twist of irony. Now that she had found a reason to embrace life, it was being wrenched from her.

"If you could bring your cousin back here, it might satisfy them." He offered it smoothly. Too smoothly, as though he had been waiting for just that question.

"They would relent if they saw how much alike we look?" Hope flared once again, though she knew there was more.

"No, dearest. If I dealt with your cousin, here, where the Atrahasis could be aware of the entire proceedings, then..."

"You mean con Clarissa into coming here so you can kill her, don't you? What kind of a person do you think I am?" Ignoring the rip of pain, she bent her legs until she could swing them off the window seat. Once clear, she lunged to her feet and staggered across the room.

⚬⚬⚬

At the door, she turned back, briefly, studying him as though trying to memorize his features. Her mind was closed to him, in that clumsy way she had taught herself, but her misery could be felt as a physical force.

When the door closed, far too gently, behind her, Mykhael slammed his fist against the aged hardwood, causing a fissure to open wider along its weak spot. If he felt pain in his hand, he didn't notice it. There was far more pain in his heart, and in the sudden blankness within his mind.

⚬⚬⚬

Kendra felt no peace in the garden, no comfort in the now orderly progression of growth. She hobbled along the cleared paths, seeking an answer not to be found among the herbs and vegetables. Since Mykhael's arrival, balance had been reestablished, and all the animals stayed in their own locations. What had seemed at that time to be a remarkable coincidence was now not so wonderful. With the support of the Atrahasis, why wouldn't he be able to control something as mindless as a slug, as silly as a rabbit?

No sillier than she was, she reminded herself bitterly. A rabbit would have to skin itself and throw itself into a frying pan to equal her stupidity. The sob rose, unexpected, from deep within her. Falling against a favorite old oak tree, she gave herself over to the misery that had seemed to be gone from her life.

Mykhael didn't come after her, as she half-expected. She felt him, along the edges of her conscious thoughts, but only as a presence, not as an intrusive force. In the end, her own discomfort drove her back into the cottage. No matter how comfortable his shirt might be, it fell only to her mid-thigh, and the ground was beginning to chill her bare feet.

He sat at the rough-hewn kitchen table, a steaming cup of tea in front of him. Another cup was placed in front of the chair across from him, and a quilt had been folded to serve as a pad for the chair seat. This act of kindness was almost her undoing. She stumbled to a stop, leaning on the back of the chair.

Mykhael half-rose, then dropped back into his chair. He wouldn't touch her, she realized, until she had come to terms with what he had told her. Such an exquisite understanding of her emotional state. What else could she expect from a man two—no, three—thousand years old?

Forcing back the threatening sob, she slid around the chair and lowered herself onto the seat. Still he watched, his gaze never leaving her face. Although he probably could have wrenched any answer he wanted out of her mind, he waited for her to speak.

She cast about for some phrase. There was so much she needed to know, so little she really wanted to know.

"These other women you have 'taken care of.'"

"And men," he reminded her in a patient tone of voice that drove her crazy. She felt his surprise at the question, as though he'd expected anything but this.

"Right. How, precisely, did you do it?"

"They died thinking they were in the midst of an intense sexual encounter."

"You seduced them and then killed them?" She couldn't keep the horror from her voice or her thoughts as she envisioned centuries of a heinous crime, enacted over and over again.

All in service to cold-minded superiors who saw no value in human lives.

"Thinking, dearest. Thinking. Most of the time, I never touched them. My control was legendary." He smiled humorlessly.

"What about me?" she asked in a tiny, frightened voice.

He touched her then, reaching across the table to stroke her hair, to trail a finger along her cheekbone, her eyebrow. "You? Kendra, you are either my greatest triumph or my greatest failure. I have not yet been able to decide which."

Long years of loneliness and current crushing fear combined to bring her once again to the point of hysteria. She felt so alone, sitting across the table from him, connected only by his finger on her face.

Obviously reading her blatant thought for the wish it was, Mykhael pushed back his chair and reached for her. She settled across his lap, her head encouraged to rest against his shoulder. She didn't question the comfort they shared from the contact. Mykhael had been sent to punish her for what Clarissa had done. If possible, he seemed even more distraught than she at the prospect.

"How much time do I have?" she asked, in a voice that barely reached his ear.

"I was given two weeks to take care of the problem," he said, his voice devoid of emotion.

Two weeks. Twelve days left. Although Kendra was prepared to embrace her fate, her mind refused to accept the time limit without argument.

"What if...what if you refuse? If you go back and say you couldn't find me. What if you never went back?" What if, she continued to herself, you stayed here with me? What then?

"The Atrahasis can find me wherever I am. If I do not take care of you, they will send another of my clan, who will enjoy causing great pain."

"You sound as if you speak from experience." He was so grim, so sad. His arms held her in comfort, but she sensed there was no comfort for him.

"The last time I refused was two hundred years ago. Some children accidentally damaged an altar, without knowing where they were. It was a foolish childhood prank. The one who replaced me not only eliminated the despoilers, he started a blood bath in France of epic proportions, and he loved every heinous minute of it."

Kendra had no trouble understanding what he was saying in such a matter-of-fact way. There were times when an extensive reading experience was a distinct disadvantage. But something more was not being said.

"What—what happened to you, Mykhael?"

"When one disagrees with the Atrahasis, one is consigned to a period of time away from the rest."

"What do you do there?"

"Nothing. You just are."

"What's it like there?"

He thought for a long time, playing idly with the ends of her hair. "Quiet. No sound, no light, no dark."

A horrible thought came to her.

"Did you exist while you were there?"

"Not really." He seemed very pragmatic about it, but when her arms slipped around his neck in an unconscious attempt to comfort, he enfolded her in his own arms. His cheek rested against her head as he absorbed her shudders.

***

With her attempt to understand Mykhael's experiences, Kendra's preliminary panic ebbed and her body reminded her how long it had been since her last meal. With a nurturing thought that food cured all ills, she began to consider meals to fulfill at least their physical needs. The psychic and emotional traumas would just have to wait their turns.

As this thought came to her she straightened, preparing to ease herself off Mykhael's lap. In spite of all that had gone on between them or perhaps because of it, she didn't want to meet his eyes. Not yet, anyway.

"Kendra."

His voice was soft as he helped her stand. Then he held her still in front of him, his hands caressing her waist subtly. When she did not look up, did not acknowledge him by glance or word, he raised one hand to stroke under her chin.

"Do not feel shame for what we have done. Our connection transcends any job I could have to do here."

"How can you say that?" she asked, puzzled

"Because it is the truth. I have not, in all my years, encountered anyone such as yourself, nor anything such as we have experienced between the two of us. We will find some way to deal with this."

"For now, let me just find some way to deal with today."

The rest of the day passed in a blur. Kendra dressed in warm sweats, washed his shirt and hung it outside to dry. As the sun began to withdraw its light from the clearing, she felt her meager store of energy fade as well. Not even her favorite nut butters could bring enthusiasm back to her, and it took all her backbone to prepare bread to bake the next day. Only knowing she would have no bread tomorrow if it did not rise tonight convinced her to use the energy.

Mykhael stayed by her, without interfering. He was available when she needed a stronger arm to stir the bread, to haul and lift and move. Nothing further was said about his task, his purpose. It was as though the mundane tasks of a semi-primitive existence held the unbelievable at bay, at least for now.

As moonlight graced the clearing with silver dignity, she gave up being brave and tough. Nothing more could be done anyway. For a moment, she considered asking Mykhael where he would sleep then consigned him to the status of a five hundred pound gorilla. Anywhere he wanted was fine with her, she thought, as she slid between the sheets of her cold, lonely bed. For some reason, the knit silk shirt seemed to be the only thing she wanted to wear.

As she reacquainted herself with the simple pleasure of sleep, the bed became far less cold and lonely.

Mykhael joined her with a minimum of fuss, turning her toward him and lifting her knee over his linen-clad thigh. There was little of passion and much of peace in the way he held her, his slumbering thoughts as comforting as the hand resting on her hip, steadying her leg. Mykhael dreamt of forest glades, rippling streams, newly opened flowers.

After the day of high drama, Kendra welcomed the peace. A perverse part of her, an unfamiliar impulse she'd never known before, expressed dissatisfaction. She'd experienced passion for the first time in what might turn out to be a short life. Would it be the last as well?

A chuckle entered her head, rich, sensuous, not echoed by any movement under or against her body. The tranquil scenes gave way to passionate imagery. The glades and streams and flowers all beckoned to her, welcoming her into their heated depths.

She raised her head, wondering if she could be mistaken, if her own half-formed desires clouded her perceptions. A mischievous sparkle showed under his half-raised eyelids. He was far from sleep, but when she would have asked for more, he stilled her restless movements.

Whisper-soft touches to her hairline, then her cheek, served to soothe and entice at the same time. He curled his hand around her neck, rubbing gently.

"No, dearest," he said to her silent plea,

"for many reasons. Never doubt that I want to, but you are weary tonight, and I feel much is ahead of us."

She rested her cheek against his bare chest, rubbing on the skin that stretched over muscle and bone. For a brief moment, he let her glimpse a bit more of his sensations, of how it felt to have her hair falling along his skin, her breath moving across his nipple. An errant thought strayed into her resting mind. What would it be like, to experience the frenzy of passion, exclusively in her mind?

The reaction from Mykhael was powerful enough to almost hurt her. He shielded her from the full violence of his thoughts, but not before she sensed his disgust at the mental perversion of the love act he'd once been forced to employ. There were other secrets behind the wall he so quickly erected against her. Ugly secrets he didn't want to face himself, much less lay bare before her scrutiny.

What kind of humans, or not-humans, she reminded herself, were these "Atrahasis," that they could take a man of sunshine and giving, and turn him into a darkened soul? Mykhael attempted to argue with her, offering denials of his own worth in the upper levels of his mind, where they were as clear to her as the morning paper. Whatever defense he chose to offer for the Atrahasis, it was not good enough for her. She intended to tell them so the first time she saw them.

The chuckle was real now, rocking her as strong arms closed more tightly around her, holding her against him. She felt approval in his touch and his thoughts, a recognition of how far she had come in her own self-worth, that she would even think to confront someone.

"Quite the warrior, are we?" he whispered, his breath stroking her face. "You may have the opportunity to test your resolution, sooner than you might like."

"Why's that?" she asked, coming to sharper thought at the dark edges apparent in his images and words. Feeling the texture of his chest hair under her cheek, she stroked her face against him, rather like a contented cat.

"This will be the second night I am not sitting where communication is easiest."

She pondered this for a minute then raised her head. "The window seat?" She looked over at the corner, now painted in darkened silver as the moon continued its reflective orbit. "Is that the psychic equivalent of a telephone booth?"

Again the quiet chuckle. "You gain rapidly in spirit, little one. That corner is the strongest place of power in this area of the woods, and allows for the easiest communication."

"Will they come after you if you don't stay in touch?"

"Not immediately, but, yes, after a few nights. Until I can report my task is finished here." He felt her shudder, and his arms tightened. "Sorry."

"Do you suppose," she asked in a very small sort of voice, "we could forget to mention why you are here? Just for a few hours, anyway?"

"I see no harm in that. You will spend the time asleep, so there will be no temptation on your part."

He painted a crown of small kisses across her forehead. The desire to argue drained away. Sleep would be best, for now. There was something on the way. Even she could feel it.

Kendra woke to bone-numbing cold, almost the equal of the surgical unit where her knee had undergone repair. Then, she'd opened her eyes to a sterile, empty room. This time, she was not alone.

A slender band of warmth along her side reminded her Mykhael still shared the bed with her. It was a sharing in the physical sense only. His every other sense was turned to the corner. As she stiffened, he tightened his arms then released her.

"I think it is time," he whispered.

At first it was only the sensation of cold. Then Kendra began to feel despair such as she had never experienced before in her life. Cringing against Mykhael's support, she wondered why she even bothered to draw breath. The world would be much better off if she simply ceased—

Mykhael moved abruptly, his hand coming up to grab her shoulder and shake her. Before he touched her, Kendra was already pulling away, tossing her head in defiance, refusing the images implanted in her psyche. Perhaps, if she hadn't already recognized

Mykhael's manipulations, she would not have been able to resist as strongly.

As it was, she was able to erect a clumsy mental barrier that could at least filter the intrusions. She envisioned it as a hodgepodge wooden fence, added to throughout the years. Nothing much to look at but it got the job done. Then the wood smoothed into a higher, more finished fence, with no gaps between the planks. Mykhael touched her only with his fingertips on her forearm, but his skill and experience fortified her barricade.

They rose together from the bed, his hand offering physical support until her legs developed strength of their own. By unspoken consent, they moved toward the corner window, where the moonlight began to take on a brighter hue.

Once there, standing next to the window seat, she unconsciously braced herself, raising her head as she would do before the curtain rose on a difficult performance. If nothing else, she could look like she was ready to do something worthwhile.

Mykhael stepped away a few paces. His face once again took on the remote expression she'd first seen. The only indication of life was the gradual rise and fall of his rib-cage and a slight flaring of his nostrils. Throwing back his head, he let his hair fall free as he moved his hands away from his body and bared his throat to whatever was about to approach.

The changes were gradual at first. A slight difference in the tone of silver edging through the windows. Then the light grew, deepened, darkened, and began to fill the room. Kendra wanted more than ever to cringe, to curl up in a ball, and let them do their worst. Anything would be better than this wretched waiting.

She realized this was what they wanted. This crushing sense of failure, of defeat before the act ever started, before the curtain rose. They wanted her to scream out her failure and abandon Mykhael to his punishment.

For herself, Kendra might have relented. After all, except for Gran and her dancing, nothing much in her life had held much pleasure. Gran was dead, and she could no longer dance. But in the last few days, she'd learned more about herself, life, and the broad schemes of the universe than she ever imagined. Because of Mykhael. Kendra could have broken if it were only her life at stake. She would fight any battle for Mykhael.

She felt a shift in the power growing in the room. Instead of concentrating on Mykhael, giving her only a cursory inspection, the focus became her own flimsy body. Along with the fear, Kendra felt a twinge of the humor she'd just discovered in herself. Maybe she wasn't totally insignificant. After all, they deigned to acknowledge her presence.

Soon, she wondered if it were such a singular honor. The force of the attention was such that she lost all contact with Mykhael. Adrift upon a frigid river of disdain, she struggled to remain upright, to keep her aching head above the dark raging power.

A beacon appeared off to one side of her consciousness. Weak, as though seen from very far away, or through a dense fog, the light ebbed and waned but never quite disappeared. When she focused on that, ignoring for a moment the buffeting cold power of the current surrounding her body, there was a moment, just an instant, of relief.

With a suddenness that left her staggering, the pressure ceased. Kendra shuffled, catching her balance in a quick series of half steps. She ended up leaning against the wall, facing the other corner of the seat. Mykhael stood as he had before, his attention on a point somewhere beyond the room.

Now thoughts formed in her head. Aimed at Mykhael rather than herself, they were strong bolts of power. He stood stoic under the attack, answering as the questions formed. It was made very obvious to her that she heard only due to the sufferance of the superior beings.

"She is not the one you seek"..."She is human, and close enough...she is without honor"..."She is—was a virgin."

Attention turned to Kendra, intense, brief. Her head felt as though it were inundated with the pressure. Then a smutty sort of snickering filled the room, and the barrage resumed.

"Perhaps, but not now, so who can know?"..."What would it matter at this point?"..."Can you not keep yourself under control, boy?" Again the snickering, as though schoolboys looked through their father's magazines. Then another voice, slightly different, stronger, yet less forceful.

"That is insignificant at this point. The assignment has not yet been carried out. Do you have an explanation?"

Again, Mykhael formed the thought that Kendra was not the person they sought, that she intended no harm to anyone, that she was—

"She's tired of being talked about as though she's not here." The mental thrust was beyond her, but a good clear voice carried to the back of a theater. Why not into a psychic debate?

Again, the full force of power focused on her. This time, the new voice prevailed, tempering the effect. The headache wasn't quite as blinding.

"You have something you wish to say to us?" At least he-she-it had the decency to form the question orally, although words hanging in an empty space were almost as unnerving as thoughts inserted into her head.

"Many things," she answered, striving to keep her voiced thoughts level and forceful. She at least managed to keep from breaking down under the pressure. "For now, I need to know how you can consider yourselves such superior beings, such magnificent guardians, when you do not recognize one human from another."

"There isn't all that much difference, you know," one smug voice informed her. "Take away the outer layer, you get the same basic mixture of avarice, malice, and insignificance."

"How long since you lived among humans?" Mykhael asked, his mental tone soothing to her overstressed brain.

"Not long enough, my boy." The shudder was particularly eloquent since it was felt rather than seen. To Kendra it sounded like every pompous windbag politician she'd ever had the pleasure of walking away from. This time, she had to stay, to deal with this windbag and his cronies.

"It seems our experiment is a failure," intoned another dry, self-important mind. "Pity. I had hoped the boy would be able to overcome his heritage."

Murmurs of consent filled the room and her mind. In the special area that was Mykhael, she felt a stiffening, then a masking of reaction. He'd been tried and found unworthy. Again. It was an ordeal Kendra understood so well, although it made no sense for

Mykhael to feel that way. When she would have rallied to his cause she felt a damping effect on her mind. Not enough to force her, or to draw attention. Just a mild warning.

"That is to be taken under consideration at a later time. For now, we must consider the recent events at this site."

It shouldn't have amazed her how they were able to decide the only important things were what they wanted to know about. Kendra thought angry daggers at the pontifical individuals she could sense in the room. She intercepted the echo of a chuckle from Mykhael, but nothing more. So much for cruising with the big guys. They couldn't even hear her.

"You find this amusing, boy?"

He sounded just like a master in a boy's boarding school. How trite.

"Mykhael was responding to me, not to you," she said out loud, before he could stop her or she could lose her nerve.

"Is she speaking again?" Exasperation sounded the same whether verbal or mental.

"You don't seem to be able to hear me when I don't verbalize. Since I'd like to get this over with, I thought I'd help you along."

"Do you 'understand' us?" asked the calmer one in a conversational tone of thought.

"Quite well, thank you." She was not reluctant to offer some graciousness, as long as they tried to be polite. A stir went through the crowd, more masked than it had been before.

"Where did you learn his name?"

"From him," she said, surprised.

"She heard my actual name while I verbalized the name chosen for me to use here."

This caused an even greater stir. Kendra began to wonder if these buffoons were really as frightening as she'd thought. Mykhael inserted a sharp warning. She was not to become careless. They were more frightening than she could imagine.

"Does any of this matter?" Kendra dared ask. She thought she might be acting brashly, but knew she'd lose what little nerve she had if she stopped to think about it.

"Perhaps," said the quiet one. "Not at this exact moment, but in the future it could be significant."

"Significant at this moment is the fact that this site was flagrantly violated, and retribution must be enacted to re-establish the balance of power." Another voice, less patient than any of the ones before.

Kendra wondered if blood had to be spilt to appease some esoteric deity. It didn't take Mykhael's shocked warning to keep that little nugget to herself. Instead, she asked the question that had been plaguing her ever since Mykhael revealed his role in the master plan.

"If this site is so critical that you feel you must kill to maintain the balance of power, why didn't you watch over it more carefully?"

The smugness increased geometrically.

"This planet is but an insignificant pebble on the edge of a meaningless galaxy at the far corner of the universe. Matters of more immediate consequences demanded our attention."

"If we are so insignificant, why do you bother to monitor this planet at all?"

"The places of power must be kept in balance throughout the universe. I see there are a few secrets Mykhael managed to keep from you."

Kendra reeled internally. The universe? These old farts controlled the whole universe? A chagrined acknowledgment from Mykhael confirmed the statement. She shook her head. Some things just had to be digested for a while.

"This is leading nowhere. The boy failed his assignment. Take care of this human creature, and we will return to our other problems."

"No." Mykhael said it quietly, but his voice allowed no argument. "This is not the person who desecrated this site. She has worked to maintain it as it was kept by her grandmother. It is her cousin who violated the laws."

"Then bring forward this cousin."

"You really don't know anything about humans, do you?" Kendra asked, adding a few angry phrases under her thoughts. "I will not serve as Judas goat for my cousin. Perhaps you higher beings don't concern yourself with petty matters of morality and honor, but we have learned we must live with the consequences of our actions. To lure her to her death would not be a humane act."

"All moot, anyway. Whole place is going to go up in smoke soon, just like that young man said a few generations back."

There was more to this thought than mere smugness.

Almost as if he congratulated himself on something.

"Nostradamus? Was he by any chance one of yours?" She sensed the shuttered thoughts that gave them away. "How interesting. Amazing how accurate predictions can be when nature can be manipulated for the whim of a few."

Their dissent was automatic but no one directly denied her accusations. The eerie light in the room faded for a moment, then came back stronger than ever.

"Enough of this. The power must be maintained throughout the universe. This site must remain in balance."

Kendra felt the power flow increase in the room. This was it. She would be killed, Mykhael would be punished. Neither act would be particularly pleasant. What a waste. And she never had a chance to tell him—

"Wait." Mykhael spoke, going against centuries of training and conditioning. "Punish me if you must, but it is unfair to harm Kendra. It is also foolish. She was intended to guard this area. If you destroy her, no one will be able to replace her. There will still be the problem with her cousin."

"And whatever she cooked up with that real estate hustler," Kendra interjected, daring much. "As little as you seem to understand humans, I don't think you'd be able to handle this situation without revealing yourselves."

The pressure ebbed, and she fell against the wall. She hoped they would come to a decision quickly. She didn't think she was up to much more of this.

"Your human side has made you weak, Mykhael, but what you say shows a modicum of sense." What seemed to be the leader ruminated, his thoughts crystal bright, almost painful to sense. "Very well. You had two weeks. You may finish that span of time. You will have to rely on your own talents to complete the job. If you and the human cannot resolve the balance of power to this area, we will take care of your job for you."

# CHAPTER 8

They were gone as suddenly as they had arrived and the interior of the cabin plunged into near darkness. From the amount of moonlight still pouring in through the window, Kendra realized how little time the confrontation had taken. Strange, how momentous occasions never fit the normal span of hours.

She pushed away from the wall, intending to prove how well she could stand on her own two feet. Before she could fall to her knees, Mykhael was there, his warmth and strength supporting her until they both sat on the window seat.

For the first time, she was aware that he trembled, that his brow was as damp as hers. The hand he raised to push back her hair shook, just a bit, though he steadied it against her cheek.

"Are they really gone?" she asked, in a

small, weak voice. Anything louder and she was sure her head would split into numerous pieces.

"For now. They will leave us alone until we have solved the problem, or the time limit is up."

Kendra tried to focus on the situation, on what had to be done to rectify the damage wreaked by her cousin. All she could think about was the pain in her head, the ache in her knees, and her fear of what had to be done. She trembled from more than just the bone-numbing cold.

"There will be time enough to worry about that." Mykhael stood, reaching for her. "For now, for tonight, you will let me guard your peace for one more night."

Ignoring her protests he lifted her and carried her the few steps to the narrow bed. Soon, she was surrounded by warmth, their combined body heat held in by the old quilts. After a while, the shuddering stopped, and she lay very still against him, her head comfortably pillowed on his strong shoulder.

"Not strong enough, I'm afraid, darling."

She no longer noted if she expressed a thought or if he heard it in her mind. For now, the mental touch comforted as much as the physical. When he burrowed his fingers into her hair, rubbing gently, she didn't suppress her sigh. For tonight, for a few hours longer, she would forget the meeting that had just taken place. Tomorrow, in the sunlight, was enough time to worry about it.

ᘒᘒᘒ

"There is much we need to talk about."

Kendra felt a cold emptiness blossom inside her when she heard his somber tone. Mykhael sat across the kitchen table from her, watching steam rise from the morning cup of tea he cradled between his hands.

"About Clarissa and the Atrahasis?" she ventured. For some reason, this morning she could feel nothing specific in Mykhael's thoughts.

"Partially. We need to speak about ourselves also."

Here it came, the way she had heard it would happen. Let's be friends, it was just one of those things, a spur of the moment happening that would be best forgotten.

"No." He moved one of his hands to still

the frenzied workings of her fingers crushing wrinkles into a napkin. "None of that. Believe in yourself and your own worth."

The bleakness was back in his voice, and black despair tinged his thoughts. Once again, Mykhael encouraged her to be the best, the strongest she could be. At the same time, he gave himself no hope.

"Your attempts at gentle explanations scare me far more than anything you could say," she said in a tone of benign exasperation. "Take your own advice, Mykhael. You have great value. I know that, even if you refuse to admit it."

He smiled, a warm, natural smile that lit his eyes briefly. Raising his hand, he touched her face then pushed her hair behind her ear. As the warm, slightly rough fingers traced the intricacies of her ear, she closed her eyes, leaning into his touch.

"My warrior," he murmured. "Throughout time, no one has defended me. Few thought it was necessary. Those who did could not find enough good in me to justify their defense. Until you, Kendra."

"You haven't been associating with the right kind of people, Mykhael," she said as primly as she could while sparkles began forming in her bloodstream.

"This play we are doing, this lovemaking. I am not sure how well I can actually do it for you. It has been so long since I intimately touched a woman in a physical way. I am very out of practice."

"You were lucky then, to meet one of the few virgins in the state over the age of twenty. I didn't notice any lack of skill on your part."

"There was little skill to notice. I was overcome. You entice me in ways you refuse to recognize. But to continue making love with you, as much as I want to, I do not know if I can. Not without risking hurting you."

"Why?" Such a convenient word. The battle cry of two year olds and confused novices, it satisfied Kendra's need to force Mykhael's explanations. She sensed he was not accustomed to explaining things. Also that few had cared enough to ask him why about anything. Kendra cared, perhaps too much.

"I know, darling. I know." He dropped his hand, took a sip of the now cool tea then stared into the cup.

"Long ago. Very, very long ago, I was a

soldier for a powerful warlord. I had no family to speak of and went into this man's service when I was young, five or six I believe. I killed my first man when I was ten, went to war the next year, and bedded my first woman shortly after that. We were a precocious lot by your standards, I suppose.

"By the time I was about fifteen or sixteen, I had killed more men and bedded more women than anyone else in my unit. When our unit leader was slain, the warlord made me unit leader. Some believed I was responsible for the death but could never prove it. Fortunately, we marched out of town shortly after that. I say fortunately because I had a number of irate fathers and husbands looking for me. It seems I might be a sire many times over. At the time, I was quite proud of that achievement.

"My employer sent me on a very long mission, mostly to let the dust settle. While I was gone, he died in a foolish duel over someone else's wife or daughter. I never did hear the whole story. It was not as though he did not have his own wife."

Hearing the bitter self-mockery in his voice, Kendra took his hands, squeezing softly, caressing him. Trying in all ways to tell him he was of value, of worth. At first, lost in his memories, he didn't respond. Then he stirred, drew a deep breath, and continued.

"Word came to us of his death while we were on our way back into town, along with notice the slayer had seized all of his victim's property. Including, of course, the warriors. I had no great loyalty to any one man over another at that time and welcomed the opportunity to win another battle. I sent back word we were owned by no man. He chose to lead the force that would meet us on the outskirts of town.

"The night before we were to meet, I walked away from my men as I often did. In the desert, I met a strange old man, who offered me anything I wanted, if I would work for him. I did not know this man, so I explained I intended to fight for ownership of myself. He only smiled, and disappeared.

"That startled me, but not as much as you might think. We still lived in contact with the Atrahasis. People appearing and disappearing was not unheard of.

"The next day's battle did not go as planned. We were overwhelmed when most of my men chose the other side. They took me captive and planned to make me the next gathering's entertainment. I understand most of the town eagerly awaited my defeat. I had made few friends.

"In the jail, again the elderly man approached me. Again he offered. This time, I listened. Whatever he wanted would have to be better than what I faced."

"What did he promise, Mykhael?"

"Enough killing to excite me and enough women to give me ease. Throw in immortality and you have a heady brew. A foolish young man's dream."

"Did they choose you at random?"

"No, but they did not tell me that at first. It seems the young woman who left me to the care of the streets had once been a favorite of one of the Atrahasis. When he moved on, he left her behind, large with his child. She tried to raise me, but pregnancy weakened her. She never recovered from his leaving. My blood was tainted, but enough of the Atrahasis blood ran in my veins, they believed I could be trained, like a fairly well-bred dog."

"Were you well trained?"

"For a time, perhaps a few centuries, I

went where they guided and did as they instructed. I killed people, razed villages, and started wars. I possessed immense power. One death became the same as all the others, until the smell of blood sickened me. Nor did I enjoy the game of seduction any longer."

"That's when you developed your 'technique'?" She strove to maintain an impersonal, clinical tone. This unveiling would aid Mykhael. She could tolerate whatever he needed to tell her.

"I was sent to discipline a woman who had intentionally desecrated an altar for her own, depraved reasons. She was beautiful, in an evil sort of way, and she tried very hard to seduce me. By then, I tried to kill as effortlessly as possible, so I let her think she *had* seduced me. I found I could manipulate the pleasure centers in her mind and give her the sexual encounter she thought she wanted. She died blissful. It was easy for me and painless for the people. I was able to continue for a while."

"When did you stop being an instrument of retribution?"

"Do you picture me with the flaming sword? It is a favorite image of some. I preferred something more subtle." He gave her an image of himself in ancient dress, younger in appearance.

Although an aura of darkness outlined the shape, there was a sensual pull in the way he stood, his eyes heavy lidded, one eyebrow raised.

"The lure of the forbidden," she said, unhappy when she sensed his dislike of the image.

"Most effective, and I pretended to myself that at least they died happy. Until even that was difficult. What right did I have to sit in judgment on these people? In later years, the desecrations were through ignorance, not malice. By then, the Atrahasis tried only to guard the most important areas, not all of the planet."

"Did they think if you did damage control long enough, humans would get the idea and behave themselves?"

"At the time, I wanted to believe that. Now, I wonder. Even then, some of the Atrahasis did not care for the human race. Too brash, too violent, too prolific."

"I doubt they can complain about violence, since they use it so casually."

"They consider it discipline, as one would slap a child to gain attention."

"Violence begets violence. How can you teach tolerance when the first reaction of the superior beings is to harm?" She tried to build up a head of steam to continue the discussion, but it was irrelevant at this point. "Whatever their reasons, I take it the Atrahasis didn't like their trained enforcers to slack off, by their standards. Did they blame it on the taint of human blood in your veins?"

"Precisely. At first, they attributed my stubbornness to the weakening of my blood by the human influence. I was not averse to carrying out an assignment, as long as I could believe the people were guilty of flagrant violation of the places of power."

"They didn't want a thinking soldier, did they?"

"As was explained to me, I worried too much about trivialities. If the Atrahasis did make a mistake, that was still one less human to worry about."

Kendra suppressed the shudder she felt erupting in her body. Now was not the time to become squeamish.

"France, late eighteenth century?" she

asked gently, looking into the cold tea in her own cup. A few glimmerings came through, of how he'd doubted. First himself, then those who directed him.

"France. When I was faced with a group of young people who had no idea what evil they had done, I knew I could no longer fulfill the dictates of the Atrahasis. When I refused, they said nothing at first, just sent someone else. They forced me to watch what he did before they consigned me to my punishment."

Mindless of any consequences, Kendra grabbed up his hand and held it against her cheek. In this way, she could at least give him the support of her belief in him. Mykhael smiled and cupped her cheek in his large palm.

"You would trust me, even now that you know what I have done?" His mind seemed to waver between wonder and mocking laughter.

"I only know what little you allow me to know, Mykhael. There is more, and you're letting it bother you far too much.

"I won't ask you to share it with me now, but one day..." She let the threat drift off, unspoken, while she turned her head to press a kiss in the palm of his hand.

Mykhael curved his fingers until he could stroke her jaw, tracing down to caress the pulse beating at the base of her neck. They sat quietly, connected by touch and thought.

❧❧❧

"I am afraid you have chosen the least among us for your champion, Kendra." Mykhael straightened from staking up a tomato, looking over at her, his expression somber.

"I don't recall any question of a choice. It seems you were here when I needed you, so there you have it. The observation could also be made that you have not chosen the pinnacle of human womanhood to protect and defend." Kendra eased onto the low garden stool, keeping her sore knee off to one side to avoid strain.

"That you still believe that bothers me, Kendra. You are far greater and more beautiful than you allow yourself to believe."

"When you meet my cousin, you'll know you've been locked away from humanity for too long. Clarissa is perfection. I am a pale imitation of her beauty." She pulled an insolent weed from the squash hill, tossing it over into the wild garden. Straightening, she wiped the heat from her forehead with the back of her hand and felt the dirt she left behind.

Mykhael did not answer. When she looked over at him, he met her gaze with eyes that smoldered intensely. The cool morning disappeared. Once again, she stood in a heated jungle in the middle of the night, grottos and deep flowers enticing her into their depths.

"Allow my greater experience to rule in this instance, Kendra. Your beauty is of the kind which never fades. When I see you next to your cousin, whatever you think she possesses in beauty will fade by comparison."

He seemed so sincere, she had no clever answer ready for him. She shifted, not look-ing away from him but not quite meeting his eyes. Then Mykhael turned his head, his expression becoming remote as he listened to something far beyond her range.

"Perhaps I will have that opportunity sooner than we thought. I believe your cousin has just turned onto your drive." He rose, extending a hand to assist her.

"How can you tell?" she asked as she took his hand to brace herself until she stood.

"The pattern of her thoughts, the arrogance and anger in her." He tilted his head, as if considering the impressions he received. "Her thoughts are disorganized, and it is very uncomfortable to attempt to understand her, but I believe she is coming to see you."

"She only comes up here when she wants something, but we already knew that." Kendra pushed at her hair, wishing briefly for a few hours of free time and the knowledge to use it to her advantage.

"Do not worry about your appearance, Kendra," he chided gently.

"I can say that I think only the inside of a person matters, and I believe it, concerning other people. Clarissa—" She shook her head, at a loss to explain. "She's like a rule unto herself. You'll see."

There wasn't much to be done about the dirt marking her jeans, the sweat flattening her hair, or the smudges she knew she'd rubbed into her face throughout the day. Had she just stepped out of a salon, Clarissa would still outshine her. The dark green sports car, erupting from a cloud of dust on the driveway, was new. So was the silk and linen outfit Clarissa wore with such panache. Designer label, naturally. White, of course. Symbol of purity in some cultures, a thought whispered in her mind.

"Sweetie, I heard you finally made it here, and I rushed right over here to help you out!" As always, Clarissa started speaking before the dust settled, before she could even unfasten the seat belt. "Why didn't you give me a call? You have my number, don't you?"

"Why did you tell that real estate agent you were me, and I wanted to sell the property?" Kendra hadn't been sure how she would approach her cousin. In the past, she would have been subservient, quiet, almost meek. Obviously, she was not the same person. Or was Mykhael interfering again?

The hint of laughter at the corner of her awareness assured her Mykhael was there, but not interfering. Not yet, anyway.

"I don't think I know what you're talking about."

"I met your real estate broker. He was quite surprised when I told him I had no intention of ever selling. Of course, by then he'd taken a closer look at me and knew I wasn't the person who'd promised him the property."

"It's all a misunderstanding, of course, sweetie."

"I don't think so, Clarissa. He was quite specific. You told him you were Kendra Weiss, the sole owner of this property, and you intended to sell as soon as possible."

"So, it was a joke. Just a little prank, like we used to play when we were kids." She shrugged, waving a perfectly manicured hand in the air. "I can't believe he took it seriously."

"If he'd had the papers ready to sign before I returned, would you have continued with your little prank? For that matter, who would have received the money?"

For the first time, Kendra saw her cousin at a loss for words, unable to react immediately. She also saw a haze beginning to form around Clarissa. At first it was a muddy brown then it lightened to orange and grew darker.

"I did it for you, you silly twit! You had every intention of hiding away up here, just like that strange old woman. Of course, I would have taken a small commission. With the money from the property you could get out of here, go anywhere your little heart desired."

"This is the only place I've ever wanted to live, Clarissa."

"Don't be ridiculous, sweetie. If you stay up here, you're going to molder away. You'll never meet any men worth keeping around."

"Deputy Hawkins came up here. He asked about you, by the way."

"Did he?" Clarissa passed her tongue across her lips, as though savoring a particularly tasty morsel of a feast. "I'll have to look the dear boy up."

Now the haze around her body was one of dark, sensual satisfaction. Kendra realized she was sensing her cousin's aura. She filed that realization away until later.

"You and Matt Hawkins?" In spite of her best efforts, Kendra couldn't keep the disgust out of her voice.

"There are times when a slightly less refined approach is...refreshing," her cousin said with a throaty purr. "Nothing you would ever understand, of course. In spite of my best efforts, you've avoided every man that came within miles of you. Or have you?"

Coming out of her self-absorbed reverie, Clarissa looked more closely at her cousin. Her sharp blue eyes missed no detail, from hair hastily pinned up to faded jeans and scuffed sandals. Something caught her attention, and she peered intently at the old denim shirt Kendra had pulled on to work in the garden.

Kendra looked down. On the front of the shirt was the print of a hand far larger than her own. She remembered stumbling earlier that morning, and Mykhael reaching out to steady her. He'd held his hand there just a second longer than he needed to, branding her with his heat. Kendra felt the warmth rising in her cheeks, but she refused to stutter out any explanations for her cousin's curiosity.

"Well, well, and what has my little cousin been up to, hmmm?" Clarissa strolled forward, an unpleasant smile barely lifting the corners of her mouth.

"Nothing that is any of your business, Clarissa. If you don't have anything better to do than tease me, I suggest you spend your time somewhere else. I still have a lot of work to do, cleaning up the mess you left behind."

"We straightened up before we left," she said, carelessly.

"You brought guests up here. You used chemicals and upset the balance in the garden."

"God, you're sounding like her already. Of course I used something on the damned bugs. They wouldn't leave us alone. As long as you're wringing confessions out of me, we also bagged a couple of those ridiculous rabbits and cooked a very tasty meal out of them."

Kendra controlled her stomach, but just barely. The rabbits had almost been pets. This was one thing she had not known. No wonder the Atrahasis had been so upset.

"Clarissa, no one has harmed an animal here for generations. Nor has anyone eaten meat."

"First time for everything, then. It's not as though I was breaking some stupid law, after all. Who is it, sweetie?"

Distracted by the path of her own thoughts, Kendra didn't at first understand the question.

"Who is what?"

"Silly twit. I thought you'd go to your grave guarding your cherry. Who finally got into your pants? You can tell me. I've told you about all my men. Well, most of them, anyway."

"I never asked about 'your men,' nor were your relationships with half the male population of California any of my business."

"You're telling me to butt out?" Clarissa laughed, a brash, ugly sound. "I don't think so, sweetie." She stepped close enough to threaten Kendra. "I'll find out who he is, make no mistake about that. When I do—" She looked again at the smaller woman, a sneer twisting her lips, no doubt at her unkempt appearance and insignificant feminine attributes. "When I do, I'll decide if I want more of him than just one night. Either way, I'll be sure to tell you all about it."

She pivoted on her heel, slid into the low slung car, and was gone. A hand raised above the cloud of dust, waving. Cheery, confident. Arrogant. Evil.

Kendra waited until she was sure Clarissa had really gone and wasn't planning to drive right back in and take over the place. As soon as the pressure left her mind she wheeled, heading for the clean coolness of the forest.

She made it as far as the first trees before she fell over, retching and choking. What little she'd eaten the night before and that morning came up in a rush, along with the last of her foolish misconceptions and lost childhood ideals.

# CHAPTER 9

Mykhael's arm slid around her as she settled back, her knees protesting the strain of the angle. He supported her, lifted her to a clean area near the stream, sat her on a log, and straightened out her legs. A cool, damp cloth moved across her face, closing her eyes, then continued down to her neck.

"Drink this," he commanded, setting the mouth of a water bottle to her lips.

She obeyed blindly, first rinsing out her mouth, then drinking deeply of the fresh water. Richer than any wine, it left her feeling refreshed, cleaner. When he slipped a leaf between her lips, she chewed without question. Mint exploded in her mouth, cleansing more deeply than any mouthwash.

Mykhael knelt in front of her, took the bottle from her, rewetting the cloth before capping the bottle and placing it to one side.

Again the cloth passed across her face, cooler now, damper. It continued, leaving a trail of moisture down her neck, then lower.

Startled, she straightened, opening her eyes. Mykhael was watching his fingers release a button on her shirt, then another. All the while, the cloth moved damply across her chest.

The shirt hung open, unbuttoned. Mykhael regarded her bra with a quirk at one side of his mouth. It was plain cotton knit, no padding, no lace. The fastener was in front, which had made it easier to wear when she had to change costumes quickly. The white bra stood out against pale skin and breasts swelling against the formerly loose confinement. Her nipples rose, reaching out to the water soaking into the material. Mykhael re-wet the cloth then passed the dripping end across the front of her bra. All the while, he watched the cloth's progress.

Kendra felt damp coolness on her over-sensitive breasts. She gasped, arching, lifting to the pleasure. Why didn't he open the damned bra? Kendra raised shaking fingers to the fastening, fumbling at what she normally opened so easily.

Mykhael pushed her fingers away, and she let her hands drop to her sides. Long, damp fingers traced along the edge of her bra, drifting underneath the cloth, teasing near her rising nipples. She shuddered, pulling her lower lip in between her teeth to control her reaction.

More. She wanted so much more. Finally, his clever fingers slid to the center front. Without fumbling, he opened the modern hook, releasing her breasts to the kiss of the morning sun. Kendra looked down at the blatant display with no shame touching her thoughts.

The wet cloth moved across her now bare breasts. Tiny bumps appeared on her skin, and the darker area puckered around her tender nipples. Mykhael sat back, cloth forgotten, and looked at her. Where his gaze touched blazed with a sensual hunger. Still he didn't move, and her confidence began to ebb.

Suddenly shy, Kendra sought to catch at the edges of her blouse, to cover herself. Mykhael dropped the cloth, stopping her hands before she could raise them.

He held both of her hands together in one

of his, out of his way. With his other hand, he pushed blouse and bra strap off each shoulder, taking even the shadow of cover away from her.

Then he released her hands, and lowered the blouse to her elbows. No farther.

She could have moved, shrugged her blouse back on, or off completely, freeing her hands for use. She did neither, and when his hands encouraged, she moved her elbows back further, lifting her breasts for his contemplation.

Keeping his fingers on her elbows, Mykhael moved just his thumbs, rubbing across her sensitive nipples with first the pad of his thumb, then his thumb nail. When she bit back a cry, squirming for more, he smiled a gentle, self-satisfied smile.

"Insignificant?" He broke the tense silence with the hoarsely muttered word. "I don't think so, dearest."

Then he leaned forward, and his mouth sought the breasts his thumbs had teased. When she would have raised her hands, longing to cradle his head against her, the blouse stopped her. He dispensed with the confinement in one stroke then slid his hands up her back, holding her still for the rampage of his tongue.

"What I want to know," he murmured, moving his lips slowly across her skin, "is where exactly have you been hiding this cherry? I would like to find such a treasure."

Gentle words painted praise across her body, rejecting any thought she could have of being less than beautiful. His breath warmed her to her toes, melting the icy knot in her middle. Her hands burrowed into his hair, seeking the living warmth of his scalp, giving back comfort for every delicate touch of his tongue.

"Could it be these morsels? So pretty, and they taste so sweet. Perhaps not. There are two of them." He raised his head, looking down at her damp breasts, then up at her face. A slow smile split his mouth. "Come here, Kendra."

He rose to his knees, nudging hers apart until he could nestle in the vee of her legs. Kendra shuddered at the heated promise of fulfillment and moved forward more herself. As their bodies nearly touched, Mykhael tugged at the belt closing of his top.

They shared a sigh when her soft breasts

pressed against the unyielding strength of his chest. Mykhael slid his hands up her back, cupping the back of her head and holding her still for the descent of his mouth. Slowly, their lips merged into a seamless perfection.

He eased her mouth open with the tip of his tongue, stroking her in a provocative reminder of their joining. Kendra edged closer, holding his face between gentle hands. As much as she needed affirmation of her value as a woman, Mykhael needed affirmation of his own worth. They shared each other while the world held its breath around them.

When he raised his head, it was only far enough to give each of them a chance to breathe. Kendra sought to regain the contact, easing her fingers into his hair, stroking his neck. He moved his head as though trying to increase the pleasure of her hands on him but only kissed her cheek, her chin, with light brushes of his lips.

"Mykhael," she breathed, seeking more. "Please. It's so lovely like that."

"Like what, dearest? Tell me," he urged with tiny biting kisses.

"To kiss you like that is almost like..." She hesitated, unsure of herself.

"Almost like the love act itself?" he waited for her hesitant nod before continuing. "In some ways, it is even greater than that." He nuzzled his cheek along hers. "Kissing is one of the few things that set humans apart from the animals. It can be more of a consummation than the physical act of love."

Before she could gather enough of her wits to reply, he once again joined their mouths. This time she met him eagerly, holding back nothing in her response. A new link opened between them, communication on an even deeper level. She felt his desire, dark and bright, still leashed but so potent. Mykhael wanted her, but this time he wanted her to be with him utterly, perfectly.

Before he lifted his head, she could feel his conscious effort of control, leashing his desire for just a short while longer. A new smile curved his mouth, belying the strain around his eyes when he looked down at her again.

"No cherries there."

Kendra nearly gave in to an insane desire to laugh. He shuddered with the force of his need. Against her eager, overheated femininity, she could feel his readiness. Still, he played the game, restraining himself to show her more about the joy of their joining.

"Stand up, darling."

He urged her to her feet, steadying her when her knees wobbled.

She felt the loose old jeans, the sensible cotton panties, slide down her legs. An automatic protest stilled in her throat. Mykhael had seen her scars, her imperfect body.

"You must help me here, darling. This cherry hunt is difficult. Perhaps you could give me a clue?"

He spoke against her stomach, breath hot on her over sensitive skin, while his hands shaped and praised her hips, her bottom. Kendra giggled, as much from stress as amusement, as she felt herself melt from the inside out. A rising tide of her femininity overtook her, swelling her breasts, clenching her womb, her womanly parts. Moistening her.

"Ah," he breathed in triumph. He urged her legs apart while his fingers searched through the damp thatch of hair at the apex of her thighs. "Pink, ripe, smells sweet. Tastes..." He nuzzled against her, searching for the source of her fragrance. "Magnificent. Could this be your cherry?"

"Mykhael," she managed, a bare thread of sound. Her head fell back, and she grabbed at his hair, his shoulders, as strength left her body in a rush. She fought for control, knowing he wanted to give, while she needed to share. "Please."

He heard her unspoken desire, gave back his raging hunger, while his tongue stroked against the most sensitive place on her body. Only the strength of his hands, cradling her bottom, kept her upright. He slid his arm around her, smoothing his hand along her leg, urging her to open more completely.

Kendra was losing every iota of control she'd ever possessed. Still she battled with herself, with her own overflowing passion. When Mykhael took all of her weight in his hands, she could no longer contain the fire growing between them.

As she finally gave in, allowing the heat to overtake her, he eased her down, wrapping her legs around his body, lowering her onto himself until the wave overflowed them both, taking them once again into their own private ecstasy.

Filling her. Completing them. Making both of them just a bit more whole.

☙❦❧

She returned to herself, to awareness of their surroundings, by gradual degrees. Mykhael pressed kisses along her cheek, leaning her back in his arms while he tasted the base of her neck. When she would have worried about where they were, outside, exposed to the world, he erased her doubts by covering her mouth with his own. It was a kiss of infinite sweetness, and it brought a new beauty to their joining.

"Tomorrow," he said against her lips. "We will go into the town, speak with this land person and whatever passes for lawful control. If we are fortunate, we will be able to resolve at least part of the problem." He shifted his weight, bringing them into closer contact.

"What—" Kendra hesitated, as she felt the spiraling rise of desire once more overtake her, feeding off his wants. "What about this afternoon?"

"If I exercise a tremendous amount of

control, I will be able to return you to the cabin." He raised her, just a fraction then lowered her again. "I think." Wrapping her in his arms, he held her very still, and there was a desperate blankness to his thoughts.

Kendra leaned back in his arms, trusting to his strength, reveling in the near loss of control she could feel roaring through his mind. She attempted her own image, of the two of them locked in an eternal dance of bliss.

"Damn."

It was the last coherent word she heard out of him for a long time. Bitten off curses in Akkadian, or whatever it was he used, filled the late morning, bringing new life to the forest. Some deep part of her knew their intense, nearly out of control loving was part of the healing for the deep woods. This, at least, the Atrahasis could not do, no matter how long they had lived.

She caught the echo of Mykhael's shocked laughter as he dragged her into the imagery of his release, plunging over a precipice together into a warm pond. Merriment filled the air with its own form of healing, its own consummation.

"You need to wear other clothing."

Mykhael's voice broke the pre-dawn quiet. Kendra raised her head just enough to meet his eyes and give him what he knew was a complacent grin.

"Why?"

"You like that word, don't you? Just like a child."

When she would have pulled away, pouting just a trifle, he tightened his hold. Her head nestled against his shoulder, and he could think of no better place for it to be.

"Mykhael, I've been going into that town since I was six years old. Trust me, they don't expect anything but old jeans."

"Have you been fighting with your cousin that long?" When he felt her quiver, he nodded grimly. "When she left yesterday, your cousin had many ugly thoughts going through her dark mind. She will want to discredit you, and what better way than to disparage your appearance."

"I would hope that they—"

"Not judge you by your appearance?" he cut in ruthlessly, while he soothed patterns across her back with his hands. "Perhaps they will not. Remember, however just they are, they are still human."

"Therefore subject to failure?"

"No, darling, but prone to judge by what they see. When you faced the Atrahasis, I doubt they 'saw' you, as a physical entity. Now that they are familiar with your inner identity, they will recognize you no matter how you appear. I fear the townspeople would not have that same advantage."

"How did the Atrahasis make such a huge mistake before?"

"In spite of your blindness, there are many outer similarities between you and your cousin." He threaded his fingers through her tousled cap of curls, watching the last of the moonlight turn the pale blond into finest silver. "It is a tendency of your race to identify by external appearances, and they sent me to deal with a certain set of physical attributes. Additionally, your cousin does not possess an attractive mental image. Any watcher who experienced that would not want to prolong the agony by describing it at length."

She arched under his touch, edging closer.

For the moment, she didn't seem disposed to talk, which was as well. An inveterate gambler for most of his life, Mykhael knew how severely the odds were against them surviving, much less succeeding. Evil had taken a deep root in this area, and even with the Atrahasis's assistance, they would have been in grave danger. Without their aid...He allowed himself a mental shrug. His had been an interesting life, and he could never say it had not been long enough.

At the end of a life that had begun to be too long had come this woman with the innocent trust of a child. So many people had harmed her, in so many ways, yet she continued to reach out, to place her hand in his, to defend him against the most powerful beings in the universe. Kendra even wanted to save her cousin, who was truly beyond redemption.

She nestled closer to him, letting him pet her into a state of near relaxation. After an active, intense night, the blazing sensuality influencing so much of their time together was at peace.

Temporarily.

Kendra seemed willing to let go for now,

let him control her enough to rest, to regain her strength and her belief in herself.

"In addition," he whispered, dropping a kiss on her hair, "I would like to see you in something more like a dress than a rag bag."

He could feel the wicked mischief in the smile forming in her mind. Kendra had a surprise for him.

৩৩৩

Kendra felt Mykhael's gaze on her as she dealt with clutch, brake, and the wretched lane down to the main road. Knowing his eyes were darkening with passion, she felt at once shy and triumphant. He'd been studying her intensely since she emerged, fully dressed, from the bathroom.

"Do you have many garments of this nature?" he asked in a polite tone that revealed none of the tension she could feel in him.

"Occasionally, I would dance as a 'wood sprite,' and this was one of my costumes. Of course, I'm not so spritely now." When had she begun to be able to joke about her injury?

Mykhael's smile approved her levity. "What do you call this?" he asked, reaching across to finger the full skirt of her long, turquoise colored dress.

"Green?" she hazarded, trying to decipher exactly what he wanted to know. "A dress?"

"No," he said, laying his hand on the leg beneath the material. Was it by accident that he stroked her thigh in the process? "The composition, the cloth."

"Oh, I think it's a cotton blend."

"And this?" His hand strayed up, knuckles brushing the loose men's shirt she wore over her dress. "A dress would cover your body. Why have you chosen to hide part of yourself?"

"You wouldn't let me wear a bra," she began. She would not blush. She would not.

"Absolutely not. Particularly not the ones you possess."

Her bras had strangely disappeared that morning.

"This dress—rubs on me." She shifted, feeling the unfamiliar cloth again abrade her nipples. "I show."

In spite of her resolution, she could feel the heat rise up her chest. She used the stop before the main road as an excuse to look away.

Mykhael wasn't fooled. In spite of her protests, the ineffectual blocking of her hands, he unbuttoned the overshirt. It was rolled and tied at her waist, but he only released the fastenings far enough to be able to peer inside.

"I see." A wicked smile tilted the corners of his mouth and lit his eyes. He studied the soft material draped across her chest.

Designed to be worn for dancing, the dress was modest, but her body refused to behave. She felt her nipples hardening against the soft material. His gaze heated her skin, caressing like a gentle fingertip. Still, he only looked, didn't raise a hand to touch her.

"You must keep covered, so no one else can see." With one last look, he refastened a few buttons before settling back in his seat. "I have worn cotton, but never this soft. Was it hand-woven?"

"I doubt it." She looked over at him while the car hesitated at the bottom of the lane, gathering energy for the trip into town, and she fought for her composure. "You wouldn't know about mass-produced clothing, would you?"

"There are many things I have never had a

need to know," he reminded her. The over-heated atmosphere in the car cooled noticeably.

"Sorry," she muttered, concentrating on the turn onto the road as though she had not driven it before. Now that Mykhael had reverted to polite stranger, she missed the sensual tease.

"I did not say I have no desire to know. In the past, I have had no need."

"Oh." What else could she say, without demanding he give her some sort of an idea about the future? Then again, they might not survive long enough to have much of a future. "I could lend you some books, just general history stuff, to help you catch up."

"Would you read them to me as well?" His attempted insouciance did not quite hide the defensive tone in his voice or in his posture when she glanced over. "Again, it was not a skill I needed for survival." He shrugged, not looking away.

Compassion warred with the desire not to shame him, not to give more significance to the fact that he was illiterate. In spite of herself, Kendra could not help feeling appalled.

"You read when you were a small child, didn't you?" he prompted, his gentle tone belying the strain in his thoughts.

"Yes, three years old or so. Gran used to listen to me and correct the most blatant errors. Otherwise, she let me discover words as I wished. It was the best possible education for me."

"You were a lonely child." There was no more sympathy in his voice than had been in hers, but she wasn't fooled.

"I didn't think so at the time. I had Gran, and the woods, and my books. My parents kept me with them sometimes. I felt very fulfilled. In fact, I used to feel sorry for Clarissa. Her family took her everywhere with them. She never had a chance to be alone."

"Do you think that excuses her behavior now?"

"Perhaps not. Clarissa was raised to think life would always give her whatever she wanted. I don't think she ever learned to work for something or do without."

She could feel his protest gathering in the air around them.

Desperately, she cast around for some distraction. "What about your clothes?" she asked brightly, as she eased over to the edge of the road to allow a tractor to pass. Fortunate she'd never cared for speed. "They seem very fashionable. Where did you pick them out?"

"When I was...summoned," he said, obviously searching for the perfect word, "I was given clothing to wear and carry, and an idea of what language and customs to assume."

"Orientation." She nodded. There seemed to be a lot of details to the Atrahasis's work she hadn't considered. "So you know about automobiles. I wondered, when you didn't want to come into town before." Not that he'd entered the cramped hatchback with any great enjoyment that morning.

"Yes, I was informed of this method of transportation." His face wrinkled in disgust. "Horses were a far better form of transportation."

"I doubt the horses would think so. Animal abuse was rampant when horses were the only means of transportation. Then, people had to deal with horses whether they liked them or not. Now, most horses are kept as show and breeding stock, or as pets. There is still abuse, but nowhere near as widespread as it was then."

"Sweet Kendra," he said in a tolerant tone of voice. "Are you trying to convince me this is a better world than it was before?"

"Not hardly. Abuse exists, perhaps on an even broader scale. For the most part it's more widely recognized but less tolerated. With television, radio, fax, telephones, it's more difficult than ever to cover up atrocities."

"Television?" he asked, stumbling over the unfamiliar word. "Radio?"

"Oh, wow, you wouldn't know anything about those, would you?" She hesitated. He needed to know, but how could she explain what she saw as just this side of a miracle?

"If you permit." He paused. "I could learn about it from the images in your thoughts."

"You don't do that already?" Her surprise was genuine.

He drew back, clearly shocked. "I hear surface thoughts, or what you broadcast to me directly. Nothing else. It would be a breach of one of the most important laws among equals. It is also too confusing for me to hear everyone's casual thoughts."

There were many questions she wanted to ask, but for now, she nodded. Bracing herself for the contact, she tried to concentrate on the little she knew about modern communication. As her attention divided, she slowed the car even more.

"Not like that, little one. Relax, and continue with your activity of guiding this machinery."

"Driving?" she hazarded, a smile pulling at her mouth.

"If you wish to call it that. Driving should be done with lovely horses and a carriage."

Stubborn man. As she consciously relaxed, Kendra allowed a stray thought about the leavings of lovely horses, plus the concept that she had many more horses working under her hood. His chuckle came from inside her mind as warmth spread through her thoughts.

It wasn't a deep, probing search. Instead, she felt only an occasional phantom stroke along some of her memories as he rummaged through the images that now formed so easily. Like a very polite houseguest, he only looked at what he needed to know. She presented visual pictures of the items in question, then some of the philosophy behind them, and the dearth of decent programming.

"I see," he said out loud, with a final mental stroke that left her squirming on her seat. "There is much less privacy today than ever in the past."

"On a public level. However, there are many more people than ever living in their own homes, or in private apartments instead of crowded into group living situations."

"How do you deal with the overload of information?"

"I can't. That's why there aren't even telephones at Gran's. When I was in school, she had one put in because the school office insisted. Turning it off was our favorite summer ritual, and the day I graduated we had it removed."

"How did your parents communicate?"

"They had to write letters. Most of the time, Mother did that, or they had their secretary take care of it."

Mykhael laid his hand gently on her shoulder, fingering the hairs at the base of her neck. Offering comfort, for the little girl who never quite fit in, from the young man who wasn't exactly what his people expected.

# CHAPTER 10

**M**ykhael's reaction to the town was not quite what she'd expected. Instead of disparaging the tiny old buildings or sneering at the oil-stained parking area, his thoughts seemed pleased.

"It is very clean. These pathways you have. There is no mud?"

"Concrete sidewalks. We have mud when it first rains, then everything washes into the gutters and down the sewer."

She pulled into the shaded parking lot by the old post office, once a train depot. The old Victorian building had always charmed her, although the postmistress upheld the stereotype of curiosity.

"Don't let Mrs. Edwards get to you, Mykhael," she said as she coped with door, skirt, and walking stick. Then he stood beside her, offering help and a comically lecherous look at her legs.

"Who is this Mrs. Edwards, and what will she get?"

"She's been in charge of the post office since I was a little girl. What she doesn't know about someone now, she'll find out as soon as she can."

"Post office?" he queried, holding her elbow gently while they navigated the shallow steps.

"Ummm...place where the mail is sorted. I know letters aren't all that new a concept."

He nodded, stepping aside as two of the town matrons passed them. The blue-haired women clutched letters in their wrinkled hands, but their attention was on the conversation they held with a person inside, out of sight. Until they turned and saw Mykhael.

Kendra could almost hear their dentures click when the aggressively red lips snapped shut. She exchanged greetings with the women, one of whom had taught her freshman English. The women nodded to her, but never turned their eyes, amplified by thick glasses, away from her companion.

For his own part, Mykhael seemed unaware of the attention he attracted, from these two women, and the others inside the building. He held the door open for Kendra, touching her elbow until she had edged past him and stepped securely onto the polished wood floor.

"The mail seems to be piling up here. Glad you stopped in, Kendra." Mrs. Edwards never took her attention off Mykhael.

"That's unusual. I hope I haven't missed anything important. Usually, once a week is more than enough." She took the proffered bundle, sorting through the various messages as she spoke.

"A couple letters from friends of yours, one from your parents," Mrs. Edwards began, obviously not at all embarrassed at her knowledge. It wasn't as though she steamed open the mail, after all. "Something from that Tucker person, too. That big piece there."

"Tucker?" Kendra separated out the large manila envelope, juggling the rest of her mail until Mykhael relieved her of the shifting stack. "I don't think I know anyone of that name."

"Smarmy sort of guy, moved into town a couple months ago. Set himself up as a real estate dealer. Shyster, you ask me. Has most of his mail special-delivered. There's regulations against that, you know. Your cousin palled 'round with him a while back, while you were in the hospital. Damned crime, you ask me."

All this came out in a rush, while she sorted her cash drawer, never taking her eyes off Mykhael. He remained oblivious, holding the mail, and looking over Kendra's shoulder at the envelope.

"What's a crime?" Kendra pulled out a slick four-color brochure, richly illustrated with photographs of old buildings and deep forests. The skimpy text proclaimed in large letters this would be the ideal site for the weary executive. Puzzled, Kendra opened the thick piece of stationery attached to the outside of the brochure by a clip that also held a business card.

"You gettin' hurt like you did, and your cousin tryin' to start trouble. You back here for a while?"

At this Kendra looked up. Mrs. Edwards' face bore the same scowl she'd always offered the world, and her small eyes still darted about, gathering information about everything and everybody.

But there was an expression of genuine

interest on her face as she waited for Kendra's answer.

"I hope to, if I can make enough money to cover the taxes."

"You let me know if you need a part time job. Might have something available here."

She spoke gruffly, then turned away to wait on someone else. Kendra hesitated then thanked the older woman politely before making her way out to the car.

Once in the undersized vehicle, Mykhael stopped Kendra before she could turn the ignition key. His hand covered hers while he slipped the mail under the seat. "I cannot think well while this machine is making so much noise. What has bothered you?"

"She was serious about a job. I could sense a kind of warmth under all her bluster. Has she always been like that, and I missed it before?"

"If so, you were not meant to know it, Kendra." Once he realized the cause of her distress, Mykhael showed no disposition to dwell on it. He trailed his fingers along her arm, cupping her elbow before releasing her and sitting back. "Explain about this job."

"You know, Mykhael, there are times you

can sound like a dictator of some petty little country."

"To be unit leader for a warlord, it helps to be despotic. You worried about a job?"

"I can feed myself pretty well out of the garden, but I need real cash to keep the property taxes current and take care of incidental expenses. Since dancing was all I was ever trained to do..." She didn't bother to finish the thought. No use fussing about what she couldn't change, after all.

Mykhael did not comment, and his attention seemed to be far away. Then he straightened, drawing a deep breath.

"The money your cousin arranged for on your behalf would be welcome?"

"Of course, but since I'd never sell even a part of the land, that was never my money. I'll just have to find some other way to make ends meet that doesn't require too much physical effort."

"Do not discount yourself so quickly, Kendra. Let us continue to speak with people, so that we can be back to the woods by evening."

It was a day of revelations for Kendra. Instead of being their normal selves, casually interested in her, the townspeople seemed genuinely concerned with how she fared by herself. When they met Mykhael, most of them seemed happy she would not be living alone. Although there were many curious sidelong glances, especially from other women, no one made any kind of a snide comment.

Mr. Thornton, manager of the grocery store, explained it to her while he was supervising a clerk setting up a vegetable display.

"You spent a lot of time here as a kid, and old Mrs. Weiss was a part of the town. She used to let us all know where you danced, how you were doing. It was quite a shock, her dying like that, even if she was piling up a lot of years. Put the riper bananas in the front," he directed in an aside to the young stock clerk. "You'd think they never saw food outside of a frozen dinner." He paused to rearrange some melons.

"You're more a citizen of this town than your father. It would be easy for you to just sell out to Tucker. We might have a few more jobs in town, and a lot more traffic. It really isn't worth it, in spite of all the good things he's trying to sell us on. We appreciate the fact that you don't want to sell, and we'll be around when you need us."

Mr. Thornton went back to his fruit as Mykhael walked up, a bag of cherries in one hand. Mykhael's smile was so filled with the promise of mischief, and so much more, Kendra had to smile back, foolish and not caring.

She was in good company. The other women shopping paid more attention to her companion than to what they bought. There would be some interesting dinners in town the next few nights. After they fitted groceries into the back of the car, Kendra pulled out the brochure and business card, studying them again while she gathered her resolution. Enough stalling. It was time.

Tucker was easier to find than she'd thought. As she searched out the address on his card, she spotted him unlocking his office door. He spied her at the same time and stepped forward to greet her.

"I see you received the packet. Have you had any time to look over my proposal?"

"That's what we need to discuss with you, Mr. Tucker. Among other things."

Once they were settled in his obsessively

homey office, complete with doilies on the armchairs, Tucker didn't seem eager to start. He studied Kendra, his gaze examining her shape under the flowing green dress. When he looked overly long at the overshirt, Mykhael shifted, straightening in his chair and staring until Tucker changed his attention to a stack of brochures on his desk.

"Now that you've seen the prospectus, what do you think of our little retreat?"

"What I've seen are some pretty pictures and a lot of vague descriptions," Kendra began strongly. Now was not the time to be insecure. "Exactly what would you propose to build, providing you owned my property?"

"Only the best, most up-to-date international businessman's retreat ever constructed. I plan to put a turn-of-the-century lodge in that clearing with every possible modern convenience. Including a helicopter pad, so the town won't be bothered by too much coming and going."

"They also wouldn't benefit from shoppers. In fact, it looks like, in spite of all you're saying, the only people to benefit from this venture would be you and your partners."

"And you, Miss Weiss. Don't forget that."

"How could I?" Kendra forced a smile, feeling slightly ill even thinking about allowing this man to step foot on her property, much less actually selling to him. "Would you be building anywhere near the existing structure?"

"Let me show you." Tucker reached eagerly for a leather-bound photo album on his desk, dropping it once when his fingers shook too much to lift the weight. He carried it around the desk to hand it to her then moved to her side.

Kendra balanced the album on her lap. When Tucker edged closer to her, she reminded herself how important it was to control this meeting. Still, it took all her resolve to not lean away from the man. She wasn't sure if Mykhael helped her resist, and this time she really didn't care.

"We thought we would put the main lodge right here." Tucker opened the album to a series of eight by ten photos of an area deep within the woods. "Up against the granite, it could have a great view. Then some cabins off to the side here, maybe scattered throughout the woods for hunters who want to feel like they're really roughing it."

At the thought of someone hunting in the woods her stomach threatened once again to rebel. Kendra squashed down the feeling and made appropriate comments to encourage Tucker. They would need as much information as possible if they wanted to defeat this man, and her cousin.

"Up here, maybe a spa, or a swimming pool. I played around with the idea of a heated pool that could be indoor-outdoor, so there could be year-round swimming." Warming to his subject, Tucker began to flip the pages, obviously looking for the choicest photos.

"That ratty old cabin would go, of course. Then also—here it is—the heliport would go in here. If we dam up this little stream and make a Koi pond, that would be a nice touch for some of the more sophisticated guests."

Kendra could not suppress the tiny sound that issued from her throat. The photo depicted, in absolute clarity, the area where she and Mykhael had made love the day before. At the sound, and the panic she could not shield from her thoughts, Mykhael rose and took up a position at her side. Tucker straightened, backing away a step.

"When did you take these pictures, Mr. Tucker?" She was proud of her level tone of voice.

"They were taken a couple of weeks ago."

"You do realize these photos could only have been taken within private property—no trespassing postings, don't you?"

"I wouldn't know about that. I didn't take the pictures. In fact, I've never been in these woods."

He sounded sincere. Too sincere.

"How would the photographer know what areas to shoot, if you weren't there?"

"They took plenty of pictures, so I could choose without going into the woods. Trust me, I've been everywhere in that damned place I need to."

"Who is your photographer?" She had a sinking feeling she knew.

"I'm not at liberty to give you that name."

"When do you think you will be able to?"

"What difference does it make?" The unctuous note was disappearing from his voice. Fast.

"I need to know exactly who will be charged with trespassing, along with your charge of perpetrating a fraud."

"What fraud? Any dealings I had with your cousin were in good faith."

"The fraud of presenting photos of a place you will never own as the site for a complex that will never be built."

At this bald statement, Tucker drew himself up to his complete five feet, seven inches.

"What the hell are you talking about, woman? I have a contract and deposit recorded against the sale of this property."

"With my cousin, Mr. Tucker. Clarissa doesn't own the land. I do."

"Your cousin acted in your behalf, since you weren't capable of acting for yourself."

"What story are you using now?"

"When you were in that hospital in Phoenix, you sent your cousin up here to take care of things for you. She entered into the contract with me on your behalf, since you were not capable of making a decision for yourself at that time."

"Why wouldn't I be able to make my own decisions?"

"You were—you know—under supervision. Because of your breakdown."

Kendra felt a cold stab of disquiet. Now what was Clarissa up to? Even without substantiating data, an accusation of mental instability would be hard to disprove. Especially since she'd never followed an ordinary path. Then a warm tendril eased through her panic, and she drew a deep breath to calm herself.

"I was in a hospital in Phoenix, Mr. Tucker, but my problems were physical, not mental."

At his condescending look of disbelief, Kendra pushed the photo album off her lap, letting it fall to the floor at her side. Extending her legs, she raised the full hem of her skirt, until her knees were exposed.

In the bright office light, it was not a pretty sight. Obviously new scars ran along and around her knees, the after effects of an attempt to undo the damage caused by another group of self-centered males. Tucker stared, gulped, then backed away.

"Surgery and therapy. Physical, not mental." She shook down her skirt, and reached for the walking stick. Mykhael rested his hand under her elbow, offering unobtrusive support. "Whatever you and Clarissa have cooked up, you better realize I don't intend to let her win this time."

Keeping her head high, her back straight, and her speed dignified, Kendra exited. Any momentary elation was tempered by the realization that this was just the beginning.

"True, but it is all you need to do today, little Amazon," Mykhael murmured in her ear as they approached the dilapidated old car. "Once we are back at your cabin, you can admit to the groans you suppress now."

This mind-reading stuff wasn't terrific all the time, Kendra confessed to herself. She also admitted she was more tired than she had been in years, and more worried. Still, it was done for now. Once they were back at the cabin, she could forget about all of it for a while.

A tightening of Mykhael's fingers was her only warning before the cold ugliness washed through her thoughts.

"Just exactly what the hell do you think you're doing, Kendra?"

Clarissa's voice, as she'd never heard it before. Cold rage dripped from every syllable, no doubt reflected in her cousin's lovely face. Not so lovely, Kendra realized as she turned to face the oncoming woman.

Hand-painted silk draped effectively

across Clarissa's body, emphasizing her proportions. Someone in the small town had obviously worked on her hair and nails, as both were salon perfect. Next to her, Kendra felt just a trifle ragged. Even so, there was no beauty underneath the make-up. Clarissa looked angry, and old.

"Good morning, Clarissa," she said, as sincerely as she could manage. "We were just leaving. Sorry there's no time to chat."

"You'll find time to spare, once I—Hello, do I know you?"

In her rage, Clarissa had not noticed Mykhael until he moved forward a step, shielding Kendra. Or, perhaps he hadn't let himself be noticed. Whichever, there was no doubt she saw him now. A slender hand, perfectly manicured, extended with feminine limpness in his direction.

"I don't believe we've been introduced. I'm Kendra's cousin—"

"Clarissa," interjected Kendra, edging around Mykhael to intercept that red-tipped hand. She could feel his waves of disgust, and his desire to handle Clarissa himself. "This is Mike Alster. He's been helping me get Gran's garden in order."

"I just bet he has." Clarissa was very good at innuendos. Only someone who knew her well could catch the venom. "How is he with fruit?"

"Such as cherries?" asked Mykhael mildly, sliding his arm around Kendra. "I am very good with cherries. But that is nothing you have known about for some time, is it?"

Clarissa whitened, her mouth pinching with anger, and the last vestige of beauty drained from her face. After a moment, she got herself under control and even managed a tinkling laugh. "You're quite right there, dear. But there is something to be said for experience, don't you think?" She leaned forward as she spoke, managing to display her considerable charms.

Only the brief tightening of his fingers betrayed Mykhael's disdain.

Then he relaxed, and his hand subtly caressed Kendra's waist while he surveyed her cousin.

"Perhaps there are some people who prefer to travel on a well-used road. I have always found far more satisfaction in finding my own way. If you will excuse us?"

He turned away as he spoke, opening the

car door and helping Kendra into the driver's seat as though he lifted her into a gilded coach. When he stepped away, heading for his own seat, Clarissa moved in.

"I have to hand it to you, Kendra. Once you finally decided to join the ranks of real women, you did it in an impressive fashion." Insincerity dripped from every syllable, while Clarissa never took her gaze off Mykhael. "I just hope you're not too broken up when he doesn't stick around. His kind never does, you know."

"I must defer to your far greater experience. For now, he's been invaluable helping me put the property in condition."

"You're going through with the sale?" Shock warred with relief in her voice. "Kendra—"

"Clarissa. You know I could never sell that property. I'm planning to live there full time."

"You have to sell, dammit. I need the money."

"Sell something of your own, Clarissa. The property was left to me so that it would never be sold." Kendra started the car, keeping the smile on her face when Clarissa stepped away from the black cloud of exhaust.

"Wills aren't valid if the person writing them can be proven incompetent. Think about that, little cousin." Clarissa's words trailed after them, out of town.

☙❧☙

Kendra felt very proud of her control. She drove exactly in her lane and kept the speed well within the posted limit.

If her hands clutched the wheel a bit tightly, well, she'd never been completely comfortable driving.

The shaking started in her knees, traveling quickly down to her feet, and she eased off the accelerator pedal just a bit more. Then her lungs began to quiver, pushing the air out of her body until she wondered if she'd ever be able to breathe again.

"Kendra!"

Mykhael's voice held a sharp note she'd never heard before. When his large hand gripped her shoulder, she realized he'd called to her more than once. Her reactions had become dangerous.

A clearing to the side of the road offered safety. She wrenched the wheel, coming to an abrupt stop in the shade of a stately old oak tree as the shaking took over her hands.

The old hatchback coughed, then stalled, and they were left in the comparative quiet of the forest. Kendra's head dropped forward onto the steering wheel, kept from harm only by falling onto her hands. Mykhael sat quietly beside her, but there was as much warmth in his thoughts as in the hand that soothed her back.

Kendra raised her head, fighting the shaking and a nausea centered as much in her mind as in her stomach. A cool breeze wafted across her cheeks, and she realized they were damp with tears. Sniffing, she scrubbed at her face with the palms of her hands.

"Do you feel ill, Kendra?" Mykhael intruded quietly on her struggle to maintain composure.

She hesitated then shook her head. "Not like yesterday. Maybe I'm getting more used to dealing with this aspect of Clarissa." She gulped, fighting the additional nausea her memories raised. "It was worse this time. There was something else."

He looked over at her, alert in manner and thought. "How do you mean that?"

Instead of answering, Kendra opened the car door and slipped out before he could stop her. Stone picnic tables made the roadside clearing a casual gathering spot. She perched on one of the tables, staring at the toes peeking out of her sandals. Mykhael joined her, his presence a welcome warmth against her side.

"Evil," she said in a choked voice. He didn't respond, and after a minute, she raised her head. "I felt something very evil back in that town. Not at first, but, later—"

"At Tucker's?"

"There, yes, and with Clarissa. And also—Mykhael, no one in that town ever noticed my presence before. Not like they did today. Nor do I think Gran actually talked to Mr. Thornton about me. To one of the kids, maybe, if they were brave enough to come see her. Not to an adult."

"Your thoughts are too jumbled for me to make any sense of them, Kendra. What are you trying to say?"

"Mykhael." She raised her head, looking at him with what she knew was desperation.

209

"Are the Atrahasis you know the only ones capable of controlling people?"

He tilted his head, examining her as though she were a new species of wildlife. Soothing thoughts came from him, and he lifted a hand to push an errant lock of hair behind her ear. Mykhael obviously wanted to say something to her and was not sure how she would receive it. Kendra schooled herself to patience, ignoring his attempts to calm her while she waited for his answer.

"You cannot assume external control just because someone seems to change, Kendra. It is the nature of humans to change as circumstances dictate. You have changed drastically, and many of the people in the town reacted to your change. If they seemed to like you more, perhaps you asked more for their liking. You were not extremely friendly before, were you?"

She shrugged, wondering why his careful, reasoned reply left her feeling so bereft. Whatever Mykhael thought, there was something very wrong with the damned town. She just couldn't figure out what.

# CHAPTER 11

Kendra set the last ceramic plate in the dish strainer, wrung out the dishrag, and laid it over the edge of the counter. When she would have lifted out the dishpan, Mykhael appeared at her side to dispose of the soapy water.

The entire evening had been like this. Quiet, with them sharing chores and dinner. Speaking minimally, because there was so much to talk about, and so little to say.

That afternoon, she'd gotten back into the car to drive them home. Mykhael had refused to hear any more about conspiracies in the village. She would have continued to argue, but his attitude was very clear. His many more years of existence were proof that he knew far more than she did about anything. That, and him being a man, of course.

She sighed. Two thousand years to change, and he still couldn't rise above his instincts. So much for the evolution of humanity.

"You are angry with me." It was a statement of fact, delivered in a quiet voice.

For a moment, she thought about being polite, about giving him the answer he wanted to hear. Ladies didn't complain, after all. Of course, she was no lady.

"I guess I'm disappointed, more than anything else." She hesitated then plunged on when he tilted his head, indicating interest. "I thought we had a deeper understanding than most people have with each other."

"We do. I have known this for many days, now."

"Then, why do you treat me like a mindless bimbo?" She didn't shout, but she came very close to it.

"Kendra, whatever a bimbo might be, there is nothing mindless about you. At times, I wish there were."

"This afternoon, at the roadside. You insisted my imagination was running away with me. I guess you expect that in a female, after all."

"Your worries about the town?" His brows rose when she nodded. "Dearest, no matter how evil the Atrahasis may seem to you, even they must follow certain restrictions. They cannot influence the way people treat each other. They can only interfere when it has a direct connection with one of the places of power. No other time."

"Are you sure?" she asked in a very small voice.

He crossed the room in a single gliding step. In spite of her protests, he slid his arms around her, holding her still while he looked down at her.

"I am sure you have many values of which you are unaware. I am sure the townspeople have always cared about you, and you only just realized it. I am also very sure people would care even more, if you would let them."

Are you people? she wanted to ask. Even her newfound, Mykhael-enhanced courage would not let her. Nor did he seem to hear the question within her. Or, did he?

"I am also very, very sure I would like to sleep with you tonight, in that ridiculous excuse for a bed. I want to hold you, to feel your breath brush across my chest, and your heart beat against mine."

Her heart was beating now, in a rhythm just this side of impossible. She could sense the excitement building in him as well, anticipation of what could come to be. Memories of what had already been.

Gently, oh, so gently, he brushed the hair back from her face. Cupping her chin, he bent his head slowly, slowly.

Tilting back her head, she gave herself up to the moment. When his hands stroked along her back, molding her against his body, she shifted until his hardness imprinted on all of her. When he began to move them toward the bed, and the obvious conclusion to the moment, she balked.

"Not yet," she managed to say, against his lips. When he raised his head, looking down at her with a question in his feral eyes, she stepped back. Her senses screamed at her to stop being so silly, to melt against him, and have at least a short time of oblivion. "Not this time," she said, as much to herself as to him.

"What are you talking about?" Even aroused and breathing hard, he managed to sound indulgent, humorous.

"You're doing it again, Mykhael. Every

time we start a serious discussion, you avoid it. You kiss me or distract me some other way." In spite of the blood raging hotly through her veins, she stepped away from him.

"Is this what you mean by 'treating you like a mindless bimbo'?" He managed to only hint at a sneer, though she could feel his anger clearly.

"Partially, yes." Drawing a quick breath, she headed toward the window seat, talking as she hobbled. "Ever since I met you, when you weren't directly manipulating my thoughts, you maneuvered me into situations where I could barely think. And you knew it."

Mykhael followed her, but sat on a chair drawn up to the dining table. His face was a study in concentration, though few of his thoughts seemed pleasant. Kendra waited for him to react verbally.

This was important. They had to face it if they were ever going to go beyond a simple relationship.

"You must understand, my dear modern miss. I have very little experience with women who act as equals among men."

"No Amazons in your personal history?"

She managed a tiny smile as she asked, a sort of hint at an apology for being difficult.

"Amazons, of course. Warrior women, who fought as men and kept men as possessions to be used and discarded. Not women as the equal of men. You are not being difficult, Kendra." When she flushed then tossed her head in mild defiance, he smiled. "Your worries fill my mind. It is not a problem," he hastened to add. "You are still reluctant to talk with me. This helps me to understand what you worry about."

"That matters to you?"

"That matters to me very much." He did not embroider, either in thought or gesture. Instead, he sat, watching her face, her hands.

"Do you see me as a woman who wants to be an equal?" she asked, remaining consciously calm.

"I think," he began quietly, looking at her in the dim light, "We first need to define our terms. You speak of women who want to be equals among men. That sounds very rigid. I see instead a woman who wants to be a partner to a man. Not his equal, any more than he is her equal. They are different, as it should be, as it is right."

216

"Have you known many women as partners, Mykhael?"

"The list of women I have known is too long to remember. Although much of my existence has been with the Atrahasis, I did associate freely with many people in my youth. Those women have nothing to do with you." He raised a hand, stemming her protest. "Not because you are different, worse, less or more worthy than they. Their ways were the way of their mothers, and as such they would never be able to change, to adapt as you have."

"What were their ways?"

"That was so very long ago." He hesitated, as though debating how much to tell her. His surface thoughts were muddled, chaotic. "I could detail their daily lives, but it would have no bearing on what we discuss."

She waited, while he clasped his hands around his upraised knee, contemplating something far beyond the room. Patience had never been her strong point, but it seemed to be the most important characteristic she could develop in herself. The answers would come, if she merely waited for them. Turning her head to look out the window, Kendra counted the moths grouping outside the glass, attracted to the lantern's dim glow.

"Of all the times I have gone amongst humans, or those of mostly human descent, I can remember no time when so much attention was given to the concept of being equal. There were societies dominated by one sex or the other, and every race has taken turns at being the superior. Partners among people, either individual people or entire civilizations, is a curious concept. It seems to be exclusive to you and your people."

"You haven't experienced people working toward a common goal anywhere else?"

"Not myself, nor have I heard it discussed. You must remember, my dear Kendra, I have been out of contact for a few hundred years. Nor am I considered one to whom anyone tells stories of the most recent discoveries."

This casual statement revealed another facet of Mykhael's life, and his personality. He might have been conscripted to live among the immortals. They might even consider him worthwhile to do their dirty work. But he was not considered enough of an equal to share information with. A small part of the ice melted from around her heart.

"You never had any friends?" She sounded appalled, which was odd, when you thought about it. Friends were as common as patience with her.

"As many as you have?" The note of gentle mockery was back, so much at odds with the shadows chasing each other across his face. "When I was quite young, before the Atrahasis chose me to work for them, I had a few acquaintances among the warriors. Not many, since the death rate was too high to risk friendships.

"After that, I only saw people for brief periods of time, whenever I was needed. After the first few assignments, I found it was easier not to develop friendships. One never knew which people might need to be eliminated in a general cleansing."

Kendra studied him briefly then turned back to the window. Silly little moths, throwing themselves against the unforgiving glass to be just a bit closer to the light. He went on, his voice low, self-mocking.

"The people I did meet became less than real to me. I dealt with them as little as possible otherwise. Knowing their thoughts disturbed me."

"Weren't you curious about them? If you only went among humans when your particular ability was needed, you must have spent a lot of time away from them. Weren't you ever tempted to just take a quick peek into their heads and find out how they thought, what progress they made since you last knew them?"

"As I explained to you, that sort of curiosity is never encouraged. It is a violation more heinous than anything else to use your mind to take the thoughts of another person."

"When you used your ability to discipline those people, you weren't using your mind?" She asked, looking at him directly as she attempted to understand.

"Not to read or extract their thoughts. I placed the memory of sensations in their minds, but I did not linger, and I did not seek knowledge from them."

He shut off the casual mind chatter he'd maintained with her.

The abrupt difference confused her. Then the contact resumed, just a comforting background sensation that let her know he was nearby, thinking of her.

"What you hear from me is the same that I

hear from you, unless I search. With most, it is very difficult."

"You seem to do it easily enough."

"With you, yes. Not as a general rule. Do you remember the night the Atrahasis visited?"

"Who could forget?" She realized he was changing the subject, perhaps because he wanted to be rid of depressing thoughts.

"True. Most of your headache was not caused by exhaustion, or over-work, or pain. They were trying their best to read you and not getting anywhere."

"But, I could read part of what they thought. I got impressions, anyway, just as I guess I always have with you."

"I know. That is one of the reasons I was chosen for the jobs." He hesitated, rising to pace around the room. He stopped near the fireplace, glancing over the collection of photographs. "Due to the taint in my blood, I have never been considered among the most important of the defenders. When I ceased to revel in spilling blood and causing widespread ruin, many of the others ceased to trust me.

"When the problem occurred at your

grandmother's woods, a few of the Atrahasis wanted to send someone who would work thoroughly and present a definite message to anyone else who might think about harming the area. The leader felt it would be more efficient not to create so much notice."

"So they brought you out of solitary, or wherever, gave you the clothes and a picture of who you were supposed to discipline, and sent you down?"

He nodded, still not looking at her. She could feel a grim darkness in his thoughts that had been missing, or perhaps hidden, before.

She hurt and feared on so many different levels. Poor Mykhael, not able to deal with one part of his heritage, shunned by the other part. Poor Kendra, who'd kept herself uselessly locked away from the rest of the world. For what?

Two incomplete souls, lost in their own world, locked away from any other. There was some sort of a message here, maybe even a solution to many of their problems. She was too weary, or her mind was not yet ready to understand.

Straightening her legs, she stood, using the wall for a partial support. Mykhael watched, but didn't step forward. This she had to do on her own, she realized. He'd made so many first moves. Now it would be her turn. She hesitated, halfway across the room and asked the question plaguing her for so long.

"When you go back, will you be accepted as a worthwhile member of the exalted group, or will you continue as an outcast?"

He shrugged, and it seemed as though it truly did not matter. "I am not exactly certain. At one time, that was my greatest ambition. Now, I find my existence has taken a new direction."

She stepped forward the rest of the way, stopping close enough to him to feel his heat.

"What direction? What are your goals now, Mykhael?"

Hesitantly, he lifted his hand and touched the side of her face with infinite gentleness. For a moment, it seemed as though he would speak, defining their relationship in concrete terms. Instead, after a moment, he dropped his hand to her shoulder, supporting her unobtrusively. "I cannot speak most of them clearly as yet. You, Kendra? Do you know your ambitions?"

"They have also changed, long range at least. Although, if we don't solve the Atrahasis's problems, long-range is a deceptive term. Short range, I believe I'd like to take you up on your offer of a while ago."

"To sleep in your bed together?" A new, soft smile softened the lines of his face. "You would not be treating me as a bimbo, would you?"

She considered it as she took his hand, leading him unresisting toward the cot. "Perhaps. But if we are both mindless bimbos, we will match perfectly, and nothing else will matter, will it?"

She was not allowed to walk the last few steps.

&#x2767;&#x2767;&#x2767;

"Mykhael?"

Her voice lifted tentatively into the darkness. They had dozed, intertwined in the too-small bed, and the intimacy was far deeper than most people of wide sexual experience ever knew. Now their lungs and hearts moved in unison, and she knew he was no more asleep than she. His hand stroked along her back, letting her know he was awake enough to listen.

"If we don't succeed in solving the Atrahasis's problems, and they do decide to eliminate me—" She felt his instinctive tension, his denial. "No, hear me out, please. I don't know when I'll have the courage to say this again. When that day comes, if it does, I must ask you one thing. If that decision is made, please, do it quickly. Don't worry about finesse, or implanting erotic memories. Just take me away quickly, while I sleep. I don't fear death as much as I fear dying."

He did not answer in words, but his arms closed around her as though he would protect his greatest treasure from harm. Fine trembling moved against her skin, and he buried his face in the curve of her neck.

Then his hands began to stroke her body. There could well be an end to both of them, and when the time came, he would deal with it as he had to. That was later.

The image he gave her left no room for doubt. The future would take care of itself. Tonight, he intended to celebrate life, and this moment.

# CHAPTER 12

The disturbance came first as an unsettling along her nerve endings, a jarring of the senses more felt than actually heard. Kendra opened her eyes to the lightening green-gold of predawn, and knew something was very wrong with her world.

As with every night this week, her head rested on Mykhael's chest, her ear directly over his heartbeat. The few times she'd rolled away, thinking he would be more comfortable without her weight on top of him, his arms had tightened, pulling her back. Even in his sleep, Mykhael kept her close to his side.

They'd waited, eagerly at first, for something to happen, some sign the forces which had disturbed the forest were returning. After a while, they fell into a routine of quiet days spent in the garden and in the surrounding woods, and nights spent in each other's arms.

It was a calm, perhaps dull existence. The

226

lack of excitement seemed to help strengthen the bonds between them. She knew, somehow, it would take something far more to test and prove whatever they were to each other, whatever they would always be.

"What is it, little one?" Mykhael's voice rumbled under her ear as his arms tightened, pulling her up to touch his mouth to hers.

It was intended to be nothing more than a brief early morning greeting. Passion, never far below the surface, rose up to take over the kiss. In spite of her misgivings, and the unease even now pricking at her nerve endings, for a moment Kendra sank into his personality, and they were one.

Her lips parted against the urging of his tongue, and she tasted the elemental reality that was Mykhael. Sleepy early morning thoughts mingled in slowly building passion. Vague, then clearer images began to form in her mind. Nebulous thoughts, that this was the only way either one of them ever wanted to wake up.

Need overcame restraint, and passion took over their waking. For a while, the odd unease was forgotten in the renewal of themselves. Kendra gloried in her love for

Mykhael, and the world, the future, all other existence, was forgotten.

Later, in the garden, she felt again a hint of apprehension. This time, Mykhael was at the edge of the woods, securing the fence that kept some of the deer out of the house garden.

For a moment, she was tempted to call out a warning. But the feeling was too nebulous and was gone even as she thought to speak. Besides, Mykhael didn't believe there was anything wrong beyond the obvious problem with her cousin's greed.

She tried not to let the fact he didn't believe her intuitions bother her. Everyone was entitled to their own opinion. Mykhael was so convinced the evil came only from within the people themselves, he refused to even consider anything else.

Not that it was hard to believe her cousin would be self-serving and borderline evil. Kendra's early memories were filled with her cousin's spiteful games. Clarissa had never done anything for herself if she could con someone else into doing it for her. Nor had she ever taken responsibility for any wrongdoing.

This disturbance had a different taste to what she now ascribed to the feel of Clarissa. It was as though the earth shifted, far beneath the surface. Kendra had been in earthquakes, but never here. This section of the forest stood on bedrock, nowhere near any known fault line.

She remembered many talks with Gran and the assurances that there would never be an earthquake here. No, it wasn't quite that, more like—

"What is wrong?" Mykhael asked, from only a few feet away.

Only then did she realize she held the rake in a death grip. Consciously, she loosened her hands and took a deep, calming breath. Her attention focused on Mykhael, and she realized as if for the first time how dear his features had become to her.

Then a cloud moved across the sun, and a shadow fell across his face. In the shadow she saw more than just his handsome features. As though exposed by an X-ray machine, she saw beneath the skin, to a starkly bleached skeleton. To the evil he'd lived in so long it had become imbedded in his very bones.

"No," she moaned, dropping the rake and

stepping toward him. Her hand raised, reaching for but afraid to touch the shadowed area. Again, she felt trembling in the ground far beneath her feet.

Then the clouds drifted, the sun brightened, and she saw only his face, now drawn into a frown as he reached out to her. He grasped her elbows in his large, secure hands.

"What is it little one?"

"I saw...I felt..." Closing her eyes, she shook her head abruptly. "Did you feel the tremors?"

"Tremors?"

"The earth moving. Did you feel it?"

A wide, wicked grin split his face, and he drew her closer.

"Not recently enough. The earth moved for both of us this morning, did it not?"

"Mykhael! Be serious! Just now, you didn't feel anything?"

He shook his head slowly, not releasing her arms.

"Nothing. This is not an area that would be disturbed by earth movement, is it?"

"Not that I know of. Gran always said..."She hesitated, searching her memories for the exact quote. "I think—Yes! She said this site would never be plagued by earthquakes of a natural origin. At the time I didn't understand her, but now, I wonder."

"Kendra, I felt nothing," he said gently, as though humoring her. "Are you sure you did?"

"Well, of course I am!" She wrenched away from him, grateful her knee had benefitted from the somnolent days. She could almost walk on her own again. Walk away from him.

"You don't believe me, do you? You haven't believed anything I've said." Disappointment made her voice tight, and she ended on a small sob. She turned away, speaking over shoulder as she ventured into the now productive garden. "I don't know why I even bothered to tell you, since you have little, if any, respect for the opinion of any woman, particularly one like myself."

"One like—Kendra, what are you talking about?" Mykhael stood where she had left him, his hands clenching. He didn't reach out with hand or mind, and she stopped after a few steps. Looking back, she saw him now in a beam of weak sunlight that illuminated the confusion, the concern, on his face.

The loneliness. All at once, the fear gripping her left, and she stopped, raising a hand to her mouth. What had she said to him?

"Mykhael?" she whispered, taking a small step backward to lean against a tree. "What's happening?"

This time he did step forward, his hands reaching out to touch, to support. "Tell me," he urged, closing his fingers around her upper arm.

"I felt a tremor again, deep inside the earth. Just like the one this morning that woke me. Then, when the shadow touched your face..." She gulped and let her words trail off. He would never believe this.

"Tell me, Kendra. Share your fears."

"It stripped the flesh from your face, like it was stripping the humanity from you. As though—as though I was supposed to fear what you'd become, through the centuries of working for the Atrahasis."

His expression stilled, and he tilted his head. This time, the frown marring his perfect brow was one of concern for her, not lack of belief or worry about her loss of sanity. His hand raised, brushing the hair back from her cheek, encircling her neck to offer a gentle massage. "And do you fear this, little one?" he asked in a gentle, subdued voice.

"Of course not. I know you too well to believe such a thing. That's why I worry there is more influencing the situation than just greedy humans."

"You trust me. With no good reason. Even when I trivialize your concerns and imply you are, what was it, a 'mindless bimbo'? you trust me. You are a gem among women, true to your name."

"Kendra? I told you, it's the feminine version of my father's name."

"'Kendra' is the name of a prophetess or a wise woman. Your last name, Weiss, is altered from the original. Your far removed ancestress would have been 'Kendra the Wise,' or the Prophetess, Kendra."

"Sounds more like a carnival side show," she muttered, wanting to deny the calm certainty in his voice.

"This is not a time for jests, Kendra. If we face more than I first believed, you will have to take on the mantle, if not the power, of your ancestress."

"But you—"

"I am a warrior. I was conscripted by the

Atrahasis to find and destroy those who do not fall within the accepted guidelines of life. I cannot heal. I can only harm."

The anguish in his voice was real, and she hurt for the truths he was forced to utter. Truths as he saw them, anyway, which was enough of a reality for him to believe what he said. For herself, she felt fear, and a resurgence of the long-held doubts about herself. Kendra, who was never quite enough of a daughter to have a girl's name and not quite acceptable enough to her parents to be taken along on their travels. She'd dealt well enough with the name, and certainly life with Gran had been filled with richness and warmth. Nevertheless...

"Nevertheless, my dear Kendra," Mykhael murmured, bringing her to him until she could rest against his shoulder, her troubled face raised to his, "Nevertheless, you are a result of your upbringing, as am I. We must face these trials with whatever weapons are at our disposal. This would be ourselves."

"The Atrahasis?" she asked, in a very little voice.

"Have left it up to us to handle, with no intervention from them."

"Even though things are different now?"

"I am not completely certain things are different. If there is another influence, they would know immediately. They should know, no matter how busy they might think they are on other situations."

"We truly are an insignificant pebble on the far edge of the galaxy, aren't we?"

"They would like you to think so. Few of the Atrahasis care much for humans. I think they look forward eagerly to the time when they once more have control of the planet."

There was nothing more to be said after that.

❧❧❧

Since their trip into town, she'd avoided leaving the clearing. There was enough to do, and she saw no purpose in wasting her time among strangers, no matter how well they'd treated her before.

A further concern was growing in her. It was obvious she and Mykhael would be facing a showdown of some sort with her cousin and possibly some of the Atrahasis. After that, his job would be done. Would he leave then? She never quite had the nerve to ask him.

⌘

Sheriff Danvers drove up one day.

"I was hoping to catch you in town, but you seem to have made yourself scarce."

"You know I've never gone to town much, and with my leg, the drive is just too tiring. I can grow just about everything I need right here."

"That's the truth. This is sure a pretty place. I remember when I was a little kid, I used to come up here in the summers and get preserves or fruit from the old woman who lived here."

"From Gran?" She was frankly stunned.

"Naw, I was just a little shaver, and she was old then. Must have been your Grand-mother's aunt."

"I never really thought of Gran as having family before her. I know she had to have had family, and of course she was married and had children of her own. I just don't know much about them. I guess I'll never know, now."

"We never seem to get around to asking until it's too late to get the answers." He looked around in contemplative silence for a moment then drew a deep breath. "I didn't mean to come up here and dredge up old memories. Must be a sign of getting old. How you getting along?"

"Well enough. My knee is more flexible than it was, and we pretty much have things back to the way they were before Clarissa stayed up here." At mention of her cousin's name, the sheriff's pleasant face drew into a scowl. He looked as though he smelled something bad in the vicinity.

"That was partially why I came by today. Where's your friend? He still around?"

"Michael?" she asked, pronouncing his name carefully. "He was here a little while ago. We saw some rabbits acting strangely. I think he wanted to check them out."

"Mmm," he grunted, a noncommittal response to go along with the blank look on his face. "How much do you know about this person, Kendra?"

"Why do you ask?" She kept her answer calm with a great effort. No need to arouse any more suspicion than necessary.

"There's been talk around town." A wide grin suddenly split his weathered face. "Hell, my wife's been doing some of it herself. She says he's the prettiest thing ever set foot in this neck of the woods."

"He should be back soon." Kendra felt her mouth begin to rise in a smile of its own. "You can make up your own mind, if you haven't seen him before this."

"He never seems to be around when I can get out of the office."

"We haven't left this area since our last trip into town. There's just too much to get done here."

"You've got it looking real fine now. I remember how it was when we found the old lady up here. Looked like some kind of a storm had hit, plants thrown every which way, fences knocked down. Wouldn't have mentioned it, except there hadn't been any storms for quite a while before then."

"I didn't know. I was in the hospital when Gran died."

"That's right, you were. You ever press charges against those creeps who left you under that set?"

"How did you know about that?"

"I make it my business to know about everyone in my town, what kind of trouble might come their way. When I heard you were hurt, I contacted the Phoenix station that handled your case. They said they had one of them in custody but you weren't too eager to identify anyone."

"Those deputies tried so hard to help me, and I was such a coward." She shook her head, watching a rabbit ease out of the forest, intent on a lettuce snack. "It took too much out of me to even talk about it, much less pick them out of a line-up."

"You aren't the only one. That's pretty common, especially when you've been roughed up and left trapped like that. No need to call yourself a coward over that."

An echo of agreement came as soft stroke along her mind. Mykhael offered encouragement and support while he made his way back to her. Something, an overlay of another problem, shaded his message.

"I appreciate you saying that, Sheriff." Apparently the lawman hadn't noticed her briefly divided attention. "I admit I've been feeling kind of low about it. It's not as though I've ever been much in the courage department. Anyway, whoever hurt me left Phoenix, without collecting their final paycheck."

"That ever strike you as odd?"

"The whole episode struck me as odd. There were a lot better looking woman in that dance troupe, and most of them would have been willing to play whatever games the men wanted. Granted, those men were big in the ego department, but they seemed to be awfully interested in one mousy little female."

"Some men don't want their women too willing," he reminded her, a heavy sound in his voice. "We see enough of that, even out here." He looked her over, apparently noting the fit of her loose work clothing, her wind-tousled fair hair. "Besides, don't you go selling yourself short in the looks department. You're no pin-up type like your cousin, but you're still a fine looking young woman."

"I could not state it better myself."

Mykhael spoke from the edge of the garden. He stood there with a rabbit in his arms, looking completely harmless.

Kendra forced the grin away from her face. It wouldn't do to ruin the impression he wanted to make.

"Michael, this is Sheriff Danvers. He was just sharing some updates on what's going on in town."

"Ah, yes." Bending gracefully, he set the rabbit on the ground then watched it hop away before he looked directly at her. "News from town. How kind of the sheriff to bring it himself."

An edge underscored his words, a new tone Kendra had never heard before. She offered Mykhael a tentative smile, seeking to understand the reason for his annoyance. He returned the smile after a moment as he stepped toward her then turned to face the sheriff.

Danvers studied them from under the rim of his Western style hat, a quintessential lawman of the modern frontier. He obviously didn't miss the way Mykhael braced his shoulder against hers, offering unobtrusive support. After a moment, Kendra relaxed her defensive posture, trusting her weight to Mykhael. They'd gone too far together for her to do anything else.

"You mentioned something about Kendra's cousin?" Mykhael asked, his voice pitched low and quiet.

"I just wondered if you were aware what she was up to now."

"I haven't been in town," Kendra reminded him. "And Clarissa comes out here as rarely as she can."

"That's why I came by. Seems she was trying to have you certified as unfit to make your own decisions."

Kendra gulped and raised her hand to her mouth. Mykhael captured her hand, holding it in a secure grasp. The physical touch joined with his mental comfort to soothe her and bring her back to herself.

"We heard something about this from Mr. Tucker, the real estate man. I hadn't realized she did more than talk."

"Talk's as far as it's gone for now, at least in my town. Unless she can get herself some high cost lawyer who can convince the judge otherwise. That might be difficult, since the judge and I play cards every Wednesday night. He remembers you from when you were a little tyke, dumped here by your folks while they were off gallivantin' around the world."

There was no mistaking the scorn in Danvers's voice. Kendra felt a gentle squeeze from Mykhael's fingers, and she managed an almost real smile.

"Thank you," she said simply. "I hadn't realized anyone noticed, outside of Gran."

"We may not talk much around here, but we notice 'most everything. With Hattie Edwards as postmistress, the whole county's bound to know everything about damned near everyone. Whether they want to know or not." Danvers lifted the hat from his head, ran his fingers through his hair, then resettled his hat.

"Anyway," he went on. "Your cousin didn't get too far with that, but I wouldn't put it past her to try something else dumb."

"Would your deputy be helping her, Sheriff?" Mykhael asked, the edge back in his soft voice.

"Ex-deputy. He outstayed his welcome long ago. Helping Clarissa try to cheat Kendra was the last straw.

"That's another reason I came by. I told Hawkins yesterday to turn in his badge and get out of the county. His gun was county issue, so I confiscated that. Wanted you to be aware he might not be in a good mood."

"I hope he doesn't decide to even the

score on his own," Kendra murmured, a trace of her old fears sneaking into her thoughts.

"I doubt it. I gave him a lot of other reasons for firing him, including dereliction of duty and general poor behavior. Unless someone tells him, I doubt he'll figure out what got me riled this time."

He studied the two of them, as if taking note of Mykhael's arm around Kendra's waist and her total relaxation. After a moment's hesitation, Danvers touched the brim of his hat.

"Well, I'd best get. Sam Lawson'll be driving by every now and then, just keeping an eye on things. He won't come up the driveway unless there looks to be a problem."

"Thank you for stopping by, Sheriff."

"No problem. You take care of yourself now, you hear?" As he spoke, Danvers looked between her and Mykhael. There was no doubt what he wanted to warn her about.

"You need not worry, Sheriff. I will take care of Kendra," Mykhael reminded him, his voice smooth.

Danvers nodded then looked around once more.

"Sheriff Danvers?" Kendra stepped forward, her hand raised. "You said something about finding the house when Gran died. I understood she died in her sleep."

"No doubt about it. Doc Whittaker said her heart just couldn't take much more. It just surprised me, seeing the place in such a mess. She would never have allowed that."

A light touch of the fingers at her waist warned Kendra not to pursue this any further. Instead, she stood quietly with Mykhael while they watched the sheriff drive out of sight.

# CHAPTER 13

S am Lawson showed up as they were finishing breakfast the next day. A tall, raw-boned young man, he seemed at first reluctant to leave his vehicle. When Kendra approached, he opened the door, but stood awkwardly next to it as she came up to him.

"Is there a problem, Deputy?"

"Could be, ma'am. Sheriff asked me to swing by here." A bird called a morning greeting from one of the trees and he started, pulling the cowboy hat from his head. He gulped, his Adam's apple bobbing.

"Would you like to come in for a cup of tea, perhaps?" This nervousness seemed strange in such a strong young man, but Kendra had seen the same reaction from time to time in town. As though the old stories of "The Witch-lady in the Woods" were still told around campfires.

246

"No ma'am," he said quickly, actually shrinking against the opened door. "I'll only be a minute. Someone found a dead deer a couple miles north of here. It'd had its throat cut, but no one slaughtered it, and there's no sign any animal's been near it. Sheriff thought you or your friend would want to know."

"I am most certainly interested." Mykhael came out from the trees as he spoke, approaching with his usual grace but a much reduced speed. "Could you take me to this place?"

Lawson paled below his outdoor tan and wheeled, dropping his hand briefly in the direction of his gun. When he identified Mykhael he relaxed visibly, even stepping a few feet away from his truck. Apparently he had been exposed to the stories, maybe even heard Clarissa's recent version. Kendra felt impatient, but not too irritated. The young man meant no harm.

"If you're going with him, Mike, I might like to ride along. There're some herbs in the woods up that way I don't have the opportunity to harvest very often." She managed a serious tone but was hard put to not break into laughter when the deputy took a step back toward his truck.

"It's kind of a hike from the road, ma'am. Sheriff said your leg's been bothering you."

Kendra thought briefly about tormenting him just a bit more. Where had this sense of mischief come from? Then she felt Mykhael's laughter as he reached her side, his face set in serious lines.

"The good deputy is right. You should not over-strain your knees." He allowed the laughter to reach his eyes as he leaned forward to brush a chaste kiss on her cheek. "Behave yourself," he muttered, before turning back. "Whenever you are ready, Deputy."

Lawson had the door closed and motor turned over before Mykhael could reach the passenger side. Dust rose in a plume, hanging in the cool morning air before falling in new patterns on the ground.

Kendra turned away, not allowing the Deputy's attitude to bother her. Mykhael would need to go through the woods at his own swift rate of speed. Even as she'd become as healed as she would ever be, Kendra could never keep up with him. It would be better for him to go alone anyway. Most of the people in the town had tolerated Gran, but there would always be some who chose to believe rumors and superstition. For them, she would seem to be a reminder of stories they had passed around about the witch in the woods.

The animals brought the first word of trouble. Not by any fantasy-like communication, but with a general air of unease. Deer scurried across the clearing in the middle of the day, intent on their journey rather than worrying about being seen by any predator. Rabbits ceased nibbling lettuce to group along the edge of the clearing, long ears twitching back and forth while they conferred among themselves.

Kendra wondered if she was giving her own interpretations to the animal behavior. She'd spent much of her life around these woods and never seen these sorts of actions. This behavior might be consistent with a forest fire, but she smelled no smoke and saw no ashes upon the gentle wind. Until she knew more, she'd busy herself with the garden. This way, she would be available. For what or whom, she didn't know.

She diverted one of the streams into an irrigation channel Mykhael had helped dig. It had been an unusually dry spring, and the summer promised to be even less forgiving. The vegetables had welcomed the extra water, growing prolific under their care.

A rustle in the trees at the far edge of the clearing pulled her attention. One of the does moved hesitantly forward, shadowed sunlight dappling her sleek coat. A sense of urgency took over Kendra, and she straightened quickly. Instead of dashing away, the doe stood her ground. Trembling, but very still, she seemed to await the approach of the human. Kendra tentatively reached out with her mind.

She wasn't sure how to do this, so she thought about being a deer, about moving around in sunlit meadows, browsing on new growth. The freedom of being able to run through the forest balanced with the fear of natural predators. Yes, the big cats, the wolves sometimes came looking for a meal. At certain times of the year, the bears would eat anything in front of them. Still, if you were fleet, and alert, you survived. When one of those predators took you down, it was because your reactions had lessened, and it was your time to go.

The other predators, the two legged ones who stank of noxious burning fumes and fermented grain, they were truly to be feared. They took only the strongest, the fleetest, the family members in prime. They struck from far away, often staying out of sight and sound and scent until after death came. Then they would appear, befouling everything they touched, sometimes taking only the head and perhaps a small portion of the slain family member, leaving the rest to rot.

It was these the doe feared now, Kendra realized, as she edged forward, drawn by scenes of peaceful meadows threatened by foul-smelling predators. It was only when she was just a few feet away from the rigid doe that she realized she was receiving vague images from the large-eyed, frightened creature.

The doe shied violently as Kendra stopped, shock and fear stiffening her as she tried to come to grips with what was happening. This was different by far than anything she'd ever experienced with Mykhael. Perhaps because she was as far removed from the doe as Mykhael was from her, in mental development.

It was a depressing thought, one which didn't help now. The deer was gone in a rustle of dried grass, the scent of crushed leaves hanging on the static air. Kendra pondered why the shy doe had broken with instinct and heritage to approach a human. Perhaps one of the Atrahasis, but herself?

But the deer had, obviously, for a very good reason. Kendra contemplated waiting until Mykhael came back or leaving him a note. An earlier attempt at communication had given her a headache and a feeling of great distance. She was on her own.

Checking that the water bottle hung at her hip, she tightened the buckles on her sandals and followed what she hoped was the deer's path into the old forest. Her walking stick helped steady her and assisted her speed.

She soon realized it was not as difficult as she thought it would be. It almost seemed as if the deer were laying a path for her. What she would have laughed off a few weeks before, while crossing her fingers and looking over her shoulder, she now accepted as a viable possibility. When the path led around a slight rise rather than directly over, circumventing a difficult spot in the trail, she knew something beyond her former knowledge was at work here.

She entered the darker part of the forest with great caution. Even as a bold younger person, secure in her own imagined immortality, she'd rarely ventured this far. Recent memory brought up the first glade Mykhael had taken her to, where he found the herbs for her knee. That also had not been part of her youthful explorations. She tried again to reach Mykhael and felt again the suffocating shield enveloping her thoughts.

This wasn't right, she thought. Maybe she should just turn around and go back. Right after she found out why the forest ahead of her was brighter than the rest of it. Compelled by something new and somewhat frightening, she moved forward. Her stick could be used as a weapon.

"Not much of one," said a mellifluous voice to one side of her as she edged around a granite outcropping.

She wheeled, raising the walking stick then lowering it to support her suddenly protesting leg. Now that she was here, she realized how far she'd walked, how fast, on barely healed knees. Refusing to give in to the pain, she searched out the strange speaker.

He leaned against a rock at the edge of the clearing. Brilliant blue eyes laughed at her from a face that held equal parts of classic beauty and roguish charm.

Shiny black hair flowed around his head, lying on his shoulders. As with Mykhael, it made him more, rather than less, masculine. If possible, he was even more gorgeous than Mykhael.

"I wondered what could have caused Mykhael to make such a fool of himself. I see once again he has done less than is expected of him."

His sneering glance let her know how little she impressed him. Kendra allowed herself to be very slightly amused. This was a minor reflection of the degradation she heaped upon herself. She discovered no one could hurt her more than she had hurt herself and was momentarily distracted by the observation.

"Should I know who you are?" she asked as if not really interested.

"Beg pardon, madam." His bow was low, mocking. "Gabriel, of the clan Alastor."

She nodded but did not identify herself. After a moment, he scowled. "And you are?" he asked, imperiously.

"Kendra Weiss," she said, as though he should already know her name.

"Pardon my ignorance." He apparently controlled his aversion with an effort. For some reason, he seemed to want to make a good impression on her. "I have heard of you, of course, but we were never introduced."

"You've heard of me? From whom?"

"Various places," he said, with an encompassing wave of his hand no doubt meant to show the unimportance of where he learned about her. "Not, however, from my little brother."

"Your brother?"

"Half-brother, actually. Mykhael and I share more than clan name. Our sire was the greatest fighter, and lover, in all of history. I like to think I take after him in many ways."

"I see," was all she could manage to say. Mykhael, related to this pompous testimony to male ego?

"At least in the lover department,

Mykhael shares many of his characteristics. Of course, in him it is sorely diluted, since he is also of tainted stock."

He rose, strolling toward her with the practiced ease of athlete and seducer combined. Just the right flick of his head at the proper moment brought her attention to his chin, to his muscular shoulders and torso rippling with power. Thick black hair enhanced his chest, narrowing into the opening of a pair of jeans, zipped but not buttoned, that covered him like a second skin.

He stopped in front of her, long fingers resting suggestively on his hips. A deep breath rippled along his chest, his washboard-hard stomach. The smile he offered her was mysterious, provocative. Images formed in her head, heated, sensuous scenes of a couple entwined in the eternal search for sexual fulfillment. As the images became clearer, she heard the zipper edge down, one tooth at a time.

It was a very good act. But it was only an act, and Kendra realized how much she had learned, how much she had grown from knowing Mykhael. This was an amusing sideshow. Mykhael was for real. This person reminded her more of her cousin than anyone she had met before. An image of Clarissa, in all of her artificial perfection, formed in her mind. She shook her head, trying to free herself of the distraction.

An impressive scowl crossed the stranger—Gabriel's—features, giving her a glimpse of the ugliness she'd sometimes seen in Clarissa's face. She was reminded of the fearsome image she'd seen in Mykhael's face one afternoon. This time, when Gabriel tossed his head, it was with defiance, and a slight wind held his hair back away from his face while he stared at her arrogantly.

"Such a pitiful, drab excuse for a female. Appallingly lacking in imagination, I see. I cannot believe even Mykhael would stoop so low. Then again, two hundred years of forced abstinence can make even one such as you appear desirable. You know about that, of course."

"I believe he did mention it briefly, yes."

"'Mentioned it briefly,'" he sneered. "I have no doubt he wailed about it for hours. He certainly complained loud enough at the meeting of the Atrahasis. It would not have been so bad, him refusing to do his job, if he

257

had not acted irresponsibly before. You can only defy authority for so long, before they treat you like the child you are."

He paced around the clearing, his stride that of a predator. Occasionally he would step closer to her but for the most part he moved around as though too restless to stay in one place. Or as though he were trying to do or say something difficult. She noticed also that he stayed within the shaded clearing.

"Do you know what will happen to him if this latest foolish quest of his fails?" he demanded, stopping again in front of her.

This time, he tried to intimidate rather than entice. A thick black eyebrow crept up toward his waving hair, almost as if it had a life of its own. To Kendra's over-tired imagination, it seemed like a wooly caterpillar, heading for cover in the brush. When she merely watched, rather than responding, Gabriel started to pace again.

"To start with, he would lose the few privileges he has managed to retain. He has displeased the Atrahasis too often. At the very least, he would return to the state from which they took him for this work."

To that, Kendra had to react. To think of

Mykhael, so aware of all that went on around him, who loved the sun and growing things, once more locked in a gray limbo. She was saddened, and she also feared.

Gabriel must have picked up on her reaction. Like a panther he leaped toward her, stopping now close enough for her to feel the heat of his breath. This time, he deigned to touch her, a fleeting, disdainful brush of his hand against her shoulder. She felt a brief, numbing chill from where his fingers pressed.

"He would not have the comfort of even such a pale imitation of a female as you are. No voices to speak with him in the gray darkness. Just himself, and his thoughts, for as long as he retains his sanity. You should ask my little brother why he stopped eating flesh. It is yet another sign of the weakness of his tainted blood."

He whirled away from her, and she had the impression he would prefer a cape flying around him as he moved. At the edge of the clearing, he turned back. Fists braced on his hips, he regarded her through narrowed eyes.

"I, of course, would once again have to clean up after my little brother." He smiled, an evil leer that did nothing for his face. "Last time was so much fun, and I had so little actually to work with. Other than the natural evil that lives in the minds of you humans."

"Yes, I understand it is one of the traits we share with you. Of course, we are not able to display our evil as well as you, due to the taint in our blood." She spoke blandly.

This time when he leapt toward her, it was with his hand raised. Kendra did not flinch. Fear for herself had somehow disappeared from her thoughts. There was no room. She worried instead about Mykhael.

"You would like me to mark you, so that you could take the proof back to my brother. Bitches such as yourself are all the same. You taunt and tease, then when someone calls your bluff, you claim attack."

"You speak from experience, Gabriel?"

He laughed, a low, mirthless sound that brought no joy to the clearing. "Great experience. I am not, perhaps, as prolific a lover as my brother, but I certainly do understand human females."

"For that alone, you are a magician among males."

Again, her barb went past him. Kendra wondered if he did not listen, or if he simply did not care. Whichever, the day began to grow darker, and she had a long walk back to her cabin. The compulsion which brought her here was gone, and she was beginning to tire.

"If you have nothing of any more interest to tell me, I'll leave you now. When I see Mykhael again, I will tell him you are here. I am certain he will be interested."

"You will tell him nothing." Gabriel reached out to grab her arms. A chill radiated from his grip, numbing her shoulders and stilling the defiance in her brain. His fingers flexed, in an ugly imitation of a caress, and he smiled. "If Mykhael irritates the Atrahasis any more, they will not wait until the end of the days to punish him. This time, they might choose to punish his body as well as his feeble mind.

"Even your meager human mind can envision the unending agony of torture when one is nearly immortal? If the punisher is sufficiently skilled, he leaves just enough for the body to regenerate before the next session." He shuddered in genuine ecstasy, his eyes narrowing as he contemplated the thought.

"Perhaps first I will sample what it is that will cause the downfall of my damned brother. There is always the possibility you are worth of an eternity of misery." He leaned closer, head tilting as his hands drew her into the heat of his body.

Kendra controlled the bile threatening to choke her and blocked the erotic images he attempted to force upon her mind. She allowed herself to sway toward him, knowing any resistance on her part would merely increase his perverted interest. A chuckle, degrading rather than amused, rose from his chest. Obviously, Gabriel saw her as another easy conquest.

In the instant before their lips touched, while her mind revolted from his images of them in a series of increasingly impossible positions, she reacted. Twisting away from him, she brought up her oak walking stick and used it like a sword, aiming for the center of his male ego.

It seemed the pain was as great for an immortal as for a human, if not even greater. Kendra allowed herself a very brief instant of self-congratulation, an even briefer spell of misplaced sympathy for the agony she could feel in his body. Then she fled, forcing her legs to work beyond the restrictions of pain.

Behind her, the gorgeous man with a soul as black as his hair screeched for her to return. When she did not obey, he piled curses upon her until she was far beyond hearing.

❧❧

She heard gravel shifting under the Jeep's tires just as the pasta came to a boil. Dinner had taken more of her attention than usual, and she could spare only a quick wave to Deputy Lawson as he turned and went back down the hill. It almost seemed he sped up when he saw her hand.

Mykhael appeared very tired, but that could have been as much from dealing with the deputy as from the day itself. He nodded in her direction as he turned first into the bathroom. She could hear him splashing and sensed he was trying to wash off more than a day's collection of dust and sweat.

What, precisely, she could not say. Only by maintaining strict control of her thoughts could she hide her own meeting on that day. This kept her from knowing more than Mykhael would want to tell her.

He emerged with water glistening in his hair and on the chest hair exposed by a fresh shirt, left open. Dinner was on the table, pasta, nuts, and vegetables, with bread and hot tea. For a moment he hesitated, studying her already seated, intently applying honey to her bread. Then he shrugged and took the seat across from her.

"How—" She hesitated, clearing her throat of a stray crumb. "How did it go today?"

He seemed intent on serving himself, on savoring the warmth of the tea. Once this was accomplished, he turned his attention to her. For a moment, she knew he wanted to ask questions of his own, but he followed her lead.

"Well enough. We found a number of deer, most of them untouched save for their death wounds."

"Not even trophies taken?"

"No, nor were they killed for food."

He spoke with a determined efficiency, though she knew the thought of eating the lovely animals brought as much revulsion to Mykhael as it did to her. She remembered something Gab—no she mustn't let herself even think his name—the other had asked her.

"Mykhael, have you always been a vegetarian?"

He stared at her while his jaws worked efficiently on the pasta. A bite of dark bread disappeared behind his strong white teeth as he contemplated her and her question. She knew he was wondering about the reason behind it. If he weren't so weary himself, he would have already been probing her curiosity.

"Not at all. It is not an efficient diet when one is on a march, and I reveled in meat when I could get it. Later, after the killing, the deaths, I could no longer eat the flesh of another animal, whether it was raised to eat or not. A personal quirk."

"Do some of the Atrahasis eat meat?" she asked, genuinely shocked, and sidetracked from her curiosity. "I would have thought—"

"Most of the older ones have chosen not to eat flesh. Some of them eat whatever passes for a diet on the planet of their origin."

Intergalactic dietary habits. She had to think about that one for a while. Later, when she did not have so much to hide.

"Your dinner is excellent," Mykhael said, serving himself another large portion. "You do not eat much for yourself."

Startled, she looked down at her plate. The attractive arrangement of pasta, nuts, and vegetables had been pushed from one side of the plate to another, but very little had entered her mouth.

In spite of her actual lack of hunger, she forced a bite.

"What did you do today, Kendra, that has you so upset?" He asked it gently, his green eyes showing the concern his thoughts were trying to give her.

"Worked with the garden, watered some vegetables. Your irrigation ditch is proving to be invaluable. I don't know when we've had such a dry summer."

"That is all, little one?"

The endearment, his quiet voice, were almost her undoing. She wanted to throw herself on him, to beg an explanation for all the awful things that other had told her. She could say nothing. At the risk of Mykhael's eternal life, she could say nothing.

"I went for a walk. I thought perhaps if there were a plan to harm the animals, there might be some signs closer to the cottage as well."

"Did you find any?" He probed as he asked, and she stiffened her resolve. She could feel the anger begin to rise. Mykhael did not like what he could not understand.

"None. Perhaps the others were random, not related to our problem with the land." Perhaps, she realized, they were intended as a decoy.

Mykhael would not have wanted her to spend the day slogging around with a deputy; she would have been here alone. The thought chilled her, distracting her control for a brief, dangerous moment.

"Kendra!" Mykhael pounced on the chink in her guard. "What happened today?"

"I just told you. Since you had better things to do, I did things around here."

"What kind of things?" He was probing deeper as his voice hardened. As though he were interrogating her.

"Back off, Mykhael," she warned. "I'm not some prisoner you have to grill. I don't have to answer you if I don't want to."

"You can have no secrets if it has to do with what is going on in the woods." He leaned toward her, his show of dominance no longer subtle.

She rose, pushing back her chair, substituting violent action for the strength of will she knew was fading fast.

"I spent the day enjoying being alone," she snapped, choosing the one thing she knew would shock him enough to halt his scrutiny. If he would relent for just long enough, she would be able to guard against him, and protect him. "We have this odd concept in our backward society. It's called privacy."

Mykhael rose, towering over her. Exhaustion showed in every line of his body and in the lack of control he had over his thoughts and speech.

"You want to be alone, woman? Very well. You shall be alone."

A wind whistled through the cabin as he whirled, heading for the door. He hesitated briefly, looking back at her with scorn in his bright green eyes. His hair lifted, impatient to be gone.

"When you decide to cease your foolish human games, you may attempt to contact me. I might consider returning."

He whirled, the door slamming. Kendra

felt the breeze of his departure suck the life from her soul. At least for now, he would be safe.

❦❦❦

The dream came again that night. It had never left her, but she'd been able to fight it, when Mykhael was there. Now she was so very alone.

There were faces to the voices this time. Taunting, floating in and out of her knowledge as she lay pinned beneath the great weight. Gabriel's unearthly beauty joined with the coarser faces of her attackers.

No one but she knew her attackers had stayed that night. She'd heard them in the darkened theatre, threatening unspeakable acts. Once, she'd called out to them, begging for their help. In her pain, she'd offered them whatever they wanted, if they would only remove the weight from her legs. They'd only laughed and come up with more lewd suggestions.

Off to one side, she sensed a presence, perhaps Mykhael, perhaps another, watching grimly.

Not joining in the torture. Not protecting her, either.

In spite of her restless sleep, or perhaps because of it, Kendra woke even earlier than normal. Her bed was cold and empty. She would have to become accustomed to that. She'd always known Mykhael would leave one day. It had simply happened earlier than she might have wanted. For his safety, he must stay away.

Intent on not thinking about him, she busied herself with mundane chores. It was not a day of sunshine, and the shadows formed around her, startling her when she turned quickly. She made it through the day, somehow, and on into the next night. Was this the way the rest of her life would progress?

Refusing to let herself wonder if it was worth it all, she reviewed her library. Perhaps re-reading Mark Twain or Bret Harte would produce enough mental stimulation to flavor her dreams. If not, exhaustion could help avoid the usual dream. She barely slept long enough to know if either ploy succeeded.

Late that night, or very early in the morning, she gave up her pretense of rest. If she were to face Gabriel on her own, she wanted as much help as possible. The Atrahasis had said before they were on their own, but one of them might relent.

Wondering when the last of her sanity had deserted her, she rose from the tangled sheets and made her way over to the window seat. Any sort of a formal meditation posture was impossible, but she could at least make herself comfortable while she tried to negotiate with the big guys.

Not quite sure how to go about this, she tried to reach them, tried to cast her mind as she once learned to throw her voice. All she got for it was a crushing headache and a feeling they were laughing, somewhere right beyond her reach. Still, there was no sense of unwelcome in the window seat. Grudging acceptance, perhaps, as one invites an unwanted cousin along on a picnic, out of family manners and the fear there won't be any watermelon for kids who acted rude.

Now, in this moment of quiet, Kendra remembered about her grandmother. Gran had always encouraged her to think about things, to examine all the facts about something before she made any decisions. "Seek the Pattern," Gran had taught her. "There is always a pattern in everything. Coincidence, happenstance, luck do not exist. All life is part of a larger pattern."

So. The pattern. Fact: after years of dancing in odd places all over the world, staying out of trouble by avoiding dangerous situations, she'd waltzed into jeopardy with little thought. Compulsion, but little thought. As a result, she'd been injured and laid up for over a month.

Fact: during that month her grandmother, still spry and young in spite of her years, had died in her cabin, of unknown causes. Not until recently had she been told there was anything suspicious about the death.

Fact: while she could not move around, her cousin, who lived for herself alone, offered to come up and tend to the cottage. Perhaps with an ulterior motive. Kendra remembered Clarissa in the hospital. She'd been uncomfortable, but there'd been no evidence of deceit in her demeanor. It seemed only later that she conceived the idea of selling the property.

Fact: Tucker, a realtor from the cutting edge school of real estate, suddenly decided to set up shop in an area where nearly all the land was privately owned by people who didn't need to sell or was government controlled, protected by miles of red tape.

Fact, she reminded herself grimly: In the midst of all this, she was visited by the most beautiful man she'd ever met, who admitted, when pushed, that he would have to kill her.

Fact, she continued in the same somber line of thought: this man, this immortal being, had said he cared about her. He'd never said anything beyond that. If he were to show up again, what would an immortal say? "Hey babe, it's been fun, but you're bound to get wrinkles, and I am, after all, due for a renewal on my companion quota?"

Kendra stopped herself before her sense of humor began to encourage suicidal thoughts. Leaning back in the window seat with her legs braced against the far wall, she sifted through the facts as she saw them.

Throwing out her doubts, fears, and hopes about Mykhael, she concentrated on the unusual occurrences of the last year. Luck, either good or bad, was also not something Gran believed in. Luck was merely a manifestation of how your environment reacted to you.

If luck were not a factor, then conspiracy must be. Something—someone, some force, had caused her to be incapacitated at a time when her grandmother needed her. Gran would've come to the hospital, but she'd died while Kendra was still under the control of drug-happy doctors. Clarissa's offer to tend the gardens, and her subsequent damage, made sense if you accepted the existence of bad Atrahasis as well as good Atrahasis.

If some of the Atrahasis knew about her and her cousin, could they have manipulated and maneuvered until events happened the way they wanted?

Kendra felt like one of the Claymation figures in a stop motion animation, being posed and poked and prodded, moved a fraction of an inch at a time. All to suit the whim of some slightly bizarre creator. No control over her own actions and no chance to see the script, so that she'd know how it would all end.

If she told anyone about this, it would be padded cells and tapioca for the rest of her life. She was even tempted to put herself into isolation. Too bizarre. Too, too bizarre.

So, she asked herself, attempting to use

the logic her father lived by, what about the fact that she could read images from the animal's minds? Or did she only think she could read those images?

Carrying that to its logical conclusion, did Gabriel and Mykhael actually exist, or were they also figments of an excessively fertile imagination?

Mykhael existed. There were too many ordinary, simple memories of him for her to think he was a fabrication. Not to mention the changes in her own physiology, she reminded herself. If Mykhael existed, so did Gabriel. There was always an ultimate balance, the conclusion to the equation.

Strange, how her grandmother gave birth to a world-renowned mathematician. By his standards, stranger still that he'd sired a dreamy, introverted daughter who read the minds of animals and thought in circles instead of straight lines.

"Sorry, Dad," she muttered, managing a grimace—smiles were in short supply right about now. "Guess you gotta go with what you get." Or something like that.

For the first time in many years, Kendra felt at peace with herself. As though she'd been, for so long, incomplete and now had all the pieces to the puzzle.

"If I get out of this intact," she vowed, swinging her legs off the bench, "I'm going to have a long talk with you, Dad." Terrific, now she was talking to herself. Acting out, with no one there to applaud or dismiss her.

She headed back for her bed. Whatever the next day would bring, more sleep would definitely help out.

∽∾∽

Late morning brought Sheriff Danvers back up the hill.

"You feelin' all right, Kendra? You look a might puny."

"Bad night's sleep," she said with an attempt at a smile. "My knee still bothers me sometimes."

"Best stay off it today, then. Mike around?"

"Oh. No, he's not." She felt his impatience, the solid strength of him as a lawman, and she feared for Mykhael. "What happened?"

"Your cousin and Hawkins disappeared

night before last. Her room and his house are trashed. No one heard anything. No one's seen that real estate guy Tucker, either. When did Mike leave?"

"This morning," she said calmly. "He had to go out early this morning. He wanted to check for any problems in this area." After a lifetime of honesty, it was surprising how easily the lies came to her.

"Damn." He hesitated, absorbing the information. She knew he believed her, for the moment. "Well, you might want to come into town, then, if you're going to be alone up here."

"He should be back any time now, Sheriff. I'll be all right."

He didn't want to leave her alone, but she sensed far more than one stubborn woman was on Sheriff Danvers mind now. Too many odd things were happening in his normally quiet county. Danvers was a man of routine who preferred boredom to excitement. She knew he wouldn't enjoy this latest turn of events.

Danvers left eventually, promising to send a patrol car by from time to time. She heard them on the road throughout the day. There was even the odd beat of a helicopter passing overhead now and then.

Kendra felt the crushing weight of fear, slowing her reactions, shadowing her every step. It was not her old fear, but a new one. She feared for Mykhael, for what could happen to him if he dared defy the Atrahasis any longer. For herself, it was all moot now, anyway. Her life had gone along well enough, and there was little future for her.

Evening came earlier than it should have, darkening the clouds massed around the clearing. Giving up her chores in weariness, Kendra went inside to prepare her dinner. No reason to waste fuel on lamps this evening. She'd eat dinner, bathe, and go to bed. Perhaps now she could sleep.

Dinner did not look appealing, even nut butter and honey spread on dark bread couldn't bring hunger. She ate because she must. Silence grew in the cabin as she spooned soup into her mouth, chewed on bread, drank tea. All of it tasted like dust and ashes.

The door opened as she considered ending this last exercise in futility and just going to bed. There'd been no footsteps, no echo of thought. Mykhael simply appeared in the opened door. He'd obviously stopped to bathe on the way in. Once more, water beaded the hair on his chest and head. He'd used his shirt as a towel and now dropped it on the counter as he reached into the cupboard for a bowl.

There was a dark blankness where once she'd felt his thoughts, a barricade made up of anger, frustration, and hurt. Even so, she felt something ease within herself. Suddenly, she was very, very tired. She knew, now, she would sleep soundly. Without speech, she gathered up her dishes and left them in the sink.

Mykhael ate at the table, finishing the pot of soup, the loaf of bread, in grim silence. She watched his shadow against the wall as she lay in her bed. Their time together was done. She'd ensured that with her hurtful words. Even so, he had not abandoned her yet. This thought followed her into sleep.

The dream was inevitable. After all, she'd lived with it for so many months. Even with Mykhael in the cabin, she could not control the excess of hate that had caused her pain. Now, Gabriel's image did more than watch, more than taunt. He was there with the rest of them, touching her, pinching her, laying his cold, cruel hands on her body.

An insidious thought snaked into her memories, slithering along the tendrils of her dream fears. Asking, probing, searching. It seemed at first just another part of the evil she'd lived with and fought for so long. Then she knew it was not. In her sleep, she felt his anger and knew the instant he realized what had happened.

"I will kill him," he said in a low voice that ripped through her nightmare. "With my own hands I will spill his worthless blood."

"No," she moaned, coming awake with a start. "You cannot kill him. If you do, you never will be accepted and you will be returned to the place of grayness and tortured throughout eternity."

"I will kill him," he repeated, scooping her out of the bed, onto his lap. "You, I should beat for not telling me, for making me think..." This was said with a tender, indulgent sort of anger, as he held her close, safe against his body.

At first she resisted, stiffening herself against her own wants, fear for him making her stronger than ever before. She succumbed finally, leaning into him with a feeling of coming home. Their eventual parting would be more difficult than ever, but she could not resist the lure of safety, of comfort, and something far more, his hold offered.

"Kendra, when you shut me out, when you sent me away, I was so angry with you." He spoke into her hair in a low, almost contemplative tone. "I spent these days in the forest, wandering aimlessly, trying to find a reason for your coldness. Late this afternoon, I was in a clearing near a granite outcropping. Would you know this area, and perhaps why I sensed a strange presence there?"

She shuddered but refused to respond. He would find it all out eventually, but not yet. She was too tired to fight him. She felt his weariness as though it were her own and knew she had hurt both of them.

"I did not sleep these last nights," he whispered, agreeing with her but speaking out loud. "I could feel your pain, your fear, but I could not reach you. Even today, I felt you."

He shifted her in his lap, holding her closer.

"Not, however, the way I wanted to feel you."

There was much emotion in his words, in his touch. No passion, no desire. Not as there had been before, anyway. There was something more here than she'd ever before experienced, but she could not quite give it a name. Perhaps she did not dare.

"Let us rest together, dear Kendra. In the morning, we will talk about what happened with you. There will be no more secrets between us."

He shifted, easing her onto the bed. Safe in the cradle of his arms, she felt sleep overcome her. They would talk, about the last two days, about the problems. Not about this new feeling she had, this closeness. Not yet.

# CHAPTER 14

Is Gabriel actually your brother?" Kendra leaned against the tree, accepting an apple and cheese out of Mykhael's backpack.

"Half-brother." He pulled out his own snack, set the water bottle between the two of them, and brushed against her shoulder while sharing the tree as a backrest. "I am certain he made that very plain."

"Yes, he did. He said you share a father who was quite famous in his own right."

"Ah, yes, Xerxes. Our sainted sire." He sank his teeth into the apple, taking a minute to enjoy the flavor and crunch before he went on. "It has been many years since I thought of him. I only met him once myself, but I heard many stories of him. Mostly from the mothers of his children. For the most part, his children tended to be lovely daughters, which must be some sort of a cosmic joke."

"Do you know Gabriel well?"

"Our paths cross, but only when they must. He was born, I believe, a few centuries before my sorry appearance on this earth."

"How old are you? In actual years, I mean."

"I have tried to calculate that, more than once. Taking into consideration how old I was when I became an enforcer, I believe I would be somewhere in my third decade. An age of maturity in my former life. I notice there are much older people now."

"Much. Forty and fifty are considered only starting to get old now. Especially if you are approaching that age yourself."

Their laughter sifted into the trees, landing on a cedar-scented draft of air and spreading throughout the forest. Kendra let her head drop back until her hair fell free behind her and the sun stroked her neck with welcome warmth.

Peace settled over them, a peace so fragile neither of them was willing to risk disturbing it. She knew she could not keep more news from him. Not when it could affect him. She would tell him later.

The opportunity came that evening, as she was making more bread, always a good time for discussion.

"Sheriff Danvers came by yesterday. He told me Clarissa and Matt Hawkins and that Tucker person are missing, and their rooms and houses were trashed."

"Trashed?"

"Items broken, things thrown on the floor. As though someone either put up a fight about leaving or was looking for something. He said it happened sometime during the night before. Then he asked about you."

"Did he come up here because Clarissa is your cousin, or because he thought I may have been involved?"

"It's hard to say. I think he was disappointed when I told him you left that morning."

"You did not need to tell him that."

She shrugged, never looking away from the bread dough that had risen in her large bowl.

"I saw no reason to tell him where you were. It's not as though you would harm my cousin."

The silence in the small room was deafening, but she didn't lift her eyes from the punch, fold, press of bread making. Then she turned the dough out onto her floured bread board and began the usually soothing process of kneading, pushing, turning. Forcing air out of the bread dough and sense into her life.

"Kendra, lie to me if you feel you must, but do not now begin to lie to yourself. I have killed before, and if the need is there, I will kill again."

She lifted the dough, slammed it back down. Folded it over, pressed and lifted again.

"But you did not harm them yesterday." She said it with little inflection, although she could not quite hide the hope. For all that Mykhael spoke of killing, she knew he paid a high price every time he took a life.

⌘

"I did not. Had I known where they were, I might have considered harming them." He watched her at her busy work, wondered how much she could take before her fragile control shattered. "There is a good chance your cousin, at least, is with Gabriel."

"Why would he..."

He could see before she finished the thought, Kendra knew the answer and blushed, hiding her face by turning back to the bread.

"Yes, there would be that reason." He watched the color rising in her face and enjoyed the innocent discomfort she felt at her thoughts. "Many other reasons as well. Gabriel could need your cousin, and those other people, to help him."

"I thought he could handle anything on his own. He certainly gave me that impression."

"Anything that he would have encountered in his own time, yes." He sensed her confusion, her attempt to understand exactly what he tried to say. "Put simply, Gabriel cannot handle the science, or weapons, of this time."

"No guns." She thought for a minute then glanced over her shoulder at him. Flour decorated her nose and chin and some of her hair had fallen into her eyes. Doubts and questions warred in her eyes. She had never looked more vulnerable to him, nor more kissable.

"As one of mixed blood, the problem is

not as severe for me. Remember, I was able to ride in your strange little vehicle. If necessary, I believe I could handle a gun, although I have never tried."

"But Gabriel definitely could not, so he would need someone to help him out." She thought out loud while wiping her face against her shoulder and getting flour on her cheek. He began to feel the effects of two nights away from her even more clearly.

"They might not help of their own free will, but yes, he would use them. It is only hypothesis, however. Since I did not see them, I could not know for sure."

"I did wonder. I had thought that, even if you were angry with me, even if you shut yourself off from me, I'd know if you'd done something like that." She divided the dough, shaped each lump into a loaf, dropped each loaf into a pan. Covered the pans with damp towels and set them aside to finish rising. "Foolish of me, I suppose."

"I knew you were upset and dreamed badly that night. I felt your uneasiness all day yesterday. It would not be impossible for you to also know what I did."

"Just unlikely." The counter was wiped to

an unaccustomed sparkle, the dishes set in the sink to wash with the dinner dishes. "I know you wouldn't harm anyone without cause. Although Clarissa is not a person of goodness, I cannot believe she would have bothered you enough to kill her yesterday."

"She hurt you, as she has hurt you many times in the past. That alone would be enough reason to cause her harm. Hawkins as well."

"Mykhael, I am not worth the life of any other person. No one is. If my survival can be bought only by the sacrifice of another, I do not want to survive." Chores finished, she stared out the window at the busy bird feeder.

လ၁လၵ

Either her hearing had left with her common sense, or he moved more quickly than she remembered. Before she heard the chair scrape across the floor, Mykhael placed ungentle hands on her upper arms and was turning her. She stiffened, even more when he lifted her, setting her on the newly cleaned counter. Green fire flashed from his eyes, and he held her face between his hands, keeping her very still.

"If you refuse to see your own worth, I will see it for you. It is my choice to defend you, and your worth. Your cousin, and her mindless friend, are of less value than the slugs you could not keep out of your garden."

He stepped forward, spreading her knees so he could stand pressed up against her feminine secrets. His face descended, mouth seeking out hers in a kiss that was almost not gentle. At her stiffening, her muffled protest, he softened his approach. His tongue slid out, running along her teeth, seeking entry.

With a moan of self-disgust, Kendra gave in, lifting her arms to rest along his shoulders. They would have so little time together, and she knew he'd do what he felt he had to, both to protect her and to fulfill his duty.

With her surrender, he softened, nibbling along her lips, over to her cheek. Pulling her closer, until she had no doubt about his involvement, his concern.

"It is a lonely life, to spend the nights apart without cause."

"There was cause. If you had stayed, I would have ended up telling you about Gabriel."

"You told me anyway."

She tried to pull away, disgusted with herself, but he did not allow it. Large hands soothed along her back, kneaded her thighs.

"My half-brother intended for you to become upset and tell me immediately. Then I would go to the clearing in anger, and he could goad me into a battle."

"You would have done that?" She leaned back as far as he would let her, seeking to see into his face. The resulting movement brought their lower bodies into closer contact.

"Be very still." He held her tight against his body until the moment of immediate urgency passed. "If you had come back from a visit with Gabriel with your thoughts racing and your mind panicked, I would not have stopped to discuss the weather."

He lifted one hand, pushing the hair back behind her ear, cupping her chin, trailing his fingers down her neck. "If he had touched you, beyond the cold, angry grabbing he tried, I would not have been able to control myself. He knew that."

"Why?" She knew it was a childish sound, but it was the only one she could come up with.

"You...matter to me." Sliding his arms

around her back, he pulled her even closer. As if he didn't want her to see what was in his face, and in his mind. "Gabriel would know that. You would also hold some attraction for him, yourself."

"Me?" Her voice was a muffled squeak, somewhere in the region of his neck.

"You. Your freshness, your innocence. It has been many long years since Gabriel was close to one such as you."

"I'm no one special, Mykhael." What an image to live up to! Maybe she could just tough it out. Or take the modern approach and ignore the whole thing.

"Let me be the judge of that, shall we?" He spoke against her lips then closed the distance between their mouths. The kiss was leisurely, and frankly erotic in its message. "In the meantime, we could make up for sleeping apart like a couple of fools."

"We can't," she whispered. "We'd be here forever."

"A wonderful way to spend eternity." His hands foraged along her sides, encircling her waist, moving up to graze against her breasts.

Eternity. The concept dashed ice water over the heat of his touch. Trembling, gulping for control along with breath, Kendra raised her head.

"If we don't resolve this situation to suit your Atrahasis, you'll be spending eternity in a much different fashion."

"Gabriel exaggerates. He always has." Cupping her breasts, he brushed his thumbs across her nipples, enjoying the feel of her under the loose blouse. "Consider, also, that I could not enjoy eternity at the expense of your loss."

She moaned, twisting her body against his touch. The contact coursed along her nerve endings, making her feel overfull with sensations. Wresting control of her reactions away from him, she drew a deep breath and tried to pretend she couldn't feel him.

"What is the possibility you were chosen for more than your ability to deal with lesser beings?" She concentrated on breathing while she tried to form rational thoughts.

"What do you mean?" His breath heated the skin on her neck. "Enforcement is my duty."

"Are you the sole enforcer on this project?"

That got his attention, if only briefly. He

raised his head, tossing back the dark red hair that often seemed to get in his way. "Explain yourself, Kendra."

"You were yanked out of isolation, given a cursory briefing, then thrust into a world that had changed radically since the last time you drew breath. It's not an efficient way to get results, if you want results. Is there any chance someone wanted you to come here and fail? By sending you here, did they pretend to be taking care of the problem?"

"That is unheard of," he insisted.

"You told me humans didn't invent cruelty. Would the same hold true for dishonesty?"

He tilted his head, passion forgotten temporarily. When she would have pushed away from him, his hands clamped again on her thighs, holding her body against his, though his attention was obviously far away.

"Why do you ask that?"

"Look at it logically." She ignored his muffled groan as she straightened, rubbing against him while she counted off points on her fingers.

"First of all, you have been, in your own estimation, considered among the least of your clan. According to some of the Atrahasis, this is an important location. Why would they use you and not a more favored enforcer? Then again, the Atrahasis can't seem to decide whether or not this is an area of significance."

"It is critical. That much I do know. This area has been critical to the balance of power since before humans appeared on the planet."

"I—see." She took a moment to digest that. "Well, even more so then. If you're not among the elite, and have not been kept up to speed, why in the world would they send you to clear up the problems of such an important area? Do they lack sufficient help?"

"Numbers have never been high, but there has always been assistance for any undertaking." He looked at her directly. "Are you trying to tell me that they want this area to fail?"

"Perhaps they want you, or someone who supports you, to fail. If you were to come here and refuse, for some reason, to perform your duty, that would be sufficient reason to use ultimate force. Whatever that would be."

"Weapons beyond your imagination, if they want to use them."

"Weapons of mass destruction," she

whispered, feeling a chill race up her spine. Bumps raised on her arms as she contemplated the sort of mind that could conceive of that. "But why would they want to? If they hate humans so much, I'm sure the race will do itself in, given just a few more centuries. That's not long in Atrahasis terms."

"Not at all. But not all Atrahasis hate humans. Perhaps this all happened at an opportune time for those Atrahasis who wanted to control some more power." He looked at her shocked expression and uttered a short, humorless laugh. "Do not look so surprised, my dear. The Atrahasis are not above petty squabbling. They just do it on a cosmic scale."

"Absolute power, corrupting absolutely. I wonder how many of the philosophers knew of the Atrahasis."

"Perhaps they just knew of men."

Confused, Kendra slumped, trusting her weight to Mykhael's chest. She could feel the frown pull at her brow, but she was too tired right now to worry about wrinkles. The way things were going, the world wouldn't last long enough for her to develop age lines.

"Could they have sent you out here then

set it up so you would go off on your own, and they would have an excuse to pull the plug on you?"

"To plan in that fashion, they would have to know about you. I would not have arbitrarily decided to refuse my assignment without cause. When I was sent here, it was to eliminate the danger to this area, and you seemed to be the best candidate."

"They really didn't know I was here? I mean, as opposed to Clarissa."

"Few of the Atrahasis have paid attention to this planet, beyond cursory inspections from time to time. Most of those who express an interest don't like humans enough to try to find the good in any of them."

"I'm not—" Her automatic protest was stifled by his fingers against her lips.

"You are good, in so very many ways, Kendra. You are good within yourself, and you try to see the good in others. This is not the way I remember Earth."

"You ran with the wrong crowd." At his look of disbelief, she continued. "There are many people on this planet right now who do care. They worry about pollution and disease and the harm people do to each other."

"They also worry about self-worth and personal gain," he pointed out, his voice wry. "Many of them worry only about their own projects, not the effect they could have on other people. Selfishness, in the guise of selflessness. Very dangerous, Kendra."

"I don't have a good argument for that. But are the Atrahasis any different? After all, they would be happy to eradicate half the humans in the area in hopes of ridding themselves of the one or two bad ones."

"I was like that once myself."

"What happened?"

"Two hundred years is a long time just to think. It's amazing how different things are when you have time to think them through. Then." He smiled down at her. "I was awakened, given my assignment and sent to meet a frustrating, bewitching little slip of a woman. Life hasn't given me a moment's peace since then."

"You say that well. Obviously you didn't forget much in two hundred years."

"I perfected my approach. I also learned what matters."

Pulling her forward once more, he lifted her off the counter and carried her over to the lantern. The contact between their lower bodies heated, intensified. "Turn out the light, Kendra. It's time to go to bed."

# CHAPTER 15

Kendra pushed aside the hanging vines, listening with her ears and mind to the forest around her. The early morning mist made vague outlines of the giant trees, and she could sense the constant forest life. Small animals scurried, thinking of food and safety, in blinding bursts of illogic. Deer settled in their daytime hiding spots, content with a night's browsing. Caution sharpened their thoughts, and she could almost discern complete scenes.

Unknown images still teased the edges of her awareness. There was a feral quality to these minds, a greater sharpness, with less tolerance of her probing. She made no effort to contact or understand them, but she did make mental notes.

She hesitated, leaning on the ancient stick. A day's walking had done little harm to her knees, but she saw no reason to take any chances now. Healing was already far beyond anything promised by the doctor.

They'd left the cottage shortly after dawn, heading into a deep part of the forest, where Mykhael had found some signs of trespassing. The hike was long but not too difficult, and after the first hour, she found herself enjoying the exercise.

A night of uninterrupted sleep had certainly done her a lot of good. With Mykhael's arms around her, she'd fallen asleep instantly and slept soundly all night. They both woke early that morning, sharing sexual thoughts in a gentle intimacy. Before this could go further, Mykhael rose from the bed, declared a beautiful day, and advised her to dress appropriately.

The day had been one of walking through the forest. Mykhael told her to come with him, and to listen.

Nothing more than that. From time to time, he went off on his own. Usually, she knew where he was without thinking about it. Just before his arms slid around her waist, she knew he'd returned.

"Anything?" His breath ruffled the hair at the base of her neck, and her nerve endings.

"If you'd tell me what I'm supposed to hear, I'd know if I've heard it yet." She tried to not let her voice show how he affected her.

"If I knew what it was, you would not have to listen." His hands remained safely at her waist, but he flexed his fingers, caressing her subtly.

"Is there some sort of logic in that remark?"

"Why this sudden fascination with logic?"

"Are you about to say females shouldn't worry themselves about logic?"

"I sense I have trespassed on dangerous grounds." He quelled her twisting easily, nuzzling under her hair until he could find her ear. "I am saying I know there is something desperately wrong with this area, but I do not have the ability to discover the problem."

Tiny shivers rippled along her back from her increasingly sensitive ear. Still she managed to turn and look up at him. In spite of his light tone, there was no sign of teasing in his face.

"I can't believe you have no ability to sense this yourself."

"In the past, I occasionally guessed what would happen before it did, which was one of the reasons my troop succeeded when others died. I have some ability in that area."

"I know you have more abilities than that. You always know what I'm thinking, what's going on around us."

"I have always been aware of my surroundings. That is another tool of survival and is far stronger now than ever before. Your thoughts are often very clear to me, but I do not have your ability to sense unknown thoughts or images."

"I wasn't aware I had that ability."

She could not totally believe him, but he had no reason not to tell her the truth.

Her awareness of the underlying life of the forest had sharpened dramatically in just the last few days.

In an effort to help, she concentrated fiercely.

"Do not force yourself, Kendra. Just relax, and let me know what you experience."

"Upset. Confusion. A sense of loss because—Mykhael, many of the animals are no longer in the forest. The ones left are unsettled."

"Which animals?"

"Most of the images include browsing or

gathering food, so I would guess the deer and rabbits. With so many of them gone, the few remaining worry about the predators."

"Do you sense the predators?"

"Only very faintly, and they fade in and out."

"They have not yet made a commitment. The others knew of your grandmother, and perhaps of you from when you were young, and had already formed an opinion. The predators only think of man and his problems when it interferes with their own concerns. Eventually, they will decide if our battle is of consequence. What else?"

Remembering his admonishment, Kendra relaxed and allowed the edges of her awareness to move away from her in ever-increasing waves. The images returned were increasingly familiar. Until she encountered something different. With a gasp, she jerked her mind away.

"What is it?" Mykhael's fingers bit into her arms, holding her still when she would have jumped up and fled the turmoil in her head.

"Badness. Evil. And I have sensed it before."

Mykhael shook her gently, bringing her awareness completely back to him.

"Easy now. You are not accustomed to this searching. What sort of evil, and where did you sense it before?"

"An ancient sort of corruption. Before, I can't remember. I only know it for total evil. It means to do me harm again, later. Right now, it seems somehow satisfied."

He nodded, as though what she said agreed with something he already knew. "Perhaps for the moment it has fed its need. Which direction?"

Trembling, her mind cringing from the effort, she pushed out her awareness until she could point. "That way. I feel it strongest over there. Mykhael, what do you know about this?"

He didn't want to tell her.

She felt again the faint barrier that had remained, even as they slept.

Then he sighed.

"You need to know, before we meet anyone else. Yesterday, while I was wandering, I found that ugly little man who wanted to take your home from you."

"Tucker?" She had no trouble understanding what he was saying, but she feared what he did not say. "What happened?"

"By the time I found him, it had already happened. His body was on one of the outcroppings of rock at the bottom of the ravine. He had died sometime during the night."

She felt the blackness come over her and reached instinctively to brace against his shoulder. Only then did she question both his story and her automatic acceptance. Mykhael's hands held her up, fingers biting into her upper arms. She felt the proud anguish in him. That she could even briefly doubt hurt him, but he would never defend himself. Men. Even the immortal ones. She remembered the night before.

"That was why, last night—"

"I cannot shield myself from you during intimacy. You needed to rest safely."

"And you needed to forget the evil you have seen." At his abrupt refusal, she smiled, though she could feel tears pooling in the corners of her eyes. "Mykhael, however you once were is no longer of any significance. You have become far more."

Mykhael leaned toward her, brushing his mouth against hers so softly. Speaking with his actions because words meant so little. Then he straightened, turning his head to look the other way.

"I believe your friend Danvers is coming into the forest, from the other direction. He could soon meet up with my half-brother."

"Mykhael, he's a good, honest man." She hesitated, wondering how to approach the rest of the question. "Could you head him off? He won't know how to deal with Gabriel."

"You think you do?" Mykhael's smile was one of masculine amusement. Then he sensed what she tried to keep from him. "Your cousin is with him?"

Kendra raised her chin defiantly, but nodded.

"You do not trust me?"

"With myself, or anyone else? Absolutely. With Clarissa? Can I?"

He sighed, looking to the tops of the trees. A slight, self-mocking smile raised the corners of his mouth. "Perhaps not."

Kendra raised her hand, laying grubby fingers against his cheek. He leaned into the touch, as though gathering comfort from the words she wasn't sure she could ever say to him.

"I will intercept your sheriff friend. My half-brother is not with your cousin at the moment. It is possible he will still be somewhere else by the time we meet. Nor is this a time of strength for him."

She frowned a question, tilting her head.

"Gabriel is a creature of darkness. Moonlight does not bother him, but even gloomy afternoons are difficult for him to concentrate. He also has much occupying him at the moment. I think he expends effort in trying to control his group of mortals."

"Dealing with Tucker must have been difficult for him."

"Dealing with Tucker would have been an appetizer for the feast he expects to glut himself upon."

# CHAPTER 16

The mist was back. Cold, gloomy, seeping through her clothes, into her body, into her very joints. If she listened closely enough, she could almost hear the mist talking. Or maybe it was an echo of conversations far away. Sounds carried strangely in mist. Perhaps it was an echo of conversations distant not only by space but also by time. Almost, she could believe those speaking did not use any language she had ever heard. Instead, the voices were guttural, harsh with consonants and few vowels.

No animals could be heard or sensed. Even straining until her head was ready to burst, Kendra could not sense even snakes, with their devious, sliding, self-centered thoughts. The last few days had brought an exodus of the animals, but this emptiness was unprecedented.

Forming an image of Mykhael in her head, Kendra tried to reach him, to share what she had found so far. Again, she met with a blank wall. He was occupied with something, trying to keep a secret from her. That was all. Certainly, he was all right. She would have known if something had happened to him. Wouldn't she?

Pushing those thoughts to one side, she closed her eyes. Now she cast for different quarry. Not the vague, half-formed thoughts of the animal minds. Something far more advanced, far more malicious.

Nothing. Which in and of itself was a problem. There should have been some echo. After all, Clarissa was supposed to be somewhere within a few miles of this site. Gabriel, also.

She refused to think of him, believing, perhaps childishly, if she didn't think of him, he couldn't find her. Her cousin, on the other hand, she wanted to find.

Feeling momentarily weary, she rested one hip against a downed tree, leaning over to adjust a bootlace. A disturbance in the trees in front of her drew her attention.

Clarissa swaggered forward, tossing her

head and leading with her hips to display her many charms.

"So, little cousin. You've come out of hiding at last. Did lover boy get tired of you already?"

Kendra studied her cousin, wondering how she'd ever thought this woman beautiful. There'd always been a certain exterior charm, and she dressed to enhance every positive factor. Now there was an obvious underlying darkness, as though evil leached away much of her beauty.

"Clarissa. I wondered where you were." She kept her voice level.

"Enjoying myself, darling. I do want to thank you for introducing me to Gabriel. He is every bit as exciting as you said."

"But I never—"

"Not in so many words, of course. You told him about me, and he was so eager to meet me, he came to my hotel room and swept me away."

"He also swept away your friend Tucker. You do remember him, don't you?"

"That little geek?" She uttered a brittle laugh. "He was amusing for a while. He did possess a certain simple charm. Nothing that could satisfy long-term, of course, but he served his purpose quite well. Where's your little playmate, dear?"

"He's busy this afternoon." As she spoke, Kendra continued to try to communicate. Still no images from the forest around her. Up close, there was a new feeling to the air. As though a dark cloud descended around herself and her cousin.

Clarissa's thoughts had always been self-centered. Even as children, before Kendra realized she sensed as much as she actually heard from her cousin's speech, she knew Clarissa existed for herself alone. In that fashion, she'd always been as easy to read as a first grade primer. Now, it was as though a veil covered her most basic thought images.

"Clarissa, how did Tucker get onto that ledge?" She hoped her abrupt question would pierce the fog surrounding her cousin's mind, allow her to grasp something of what was going on.

Clarissa smiled, as though remembering something very pleasant. "He amused us for a while. Then Gabriel decided he'd become boring." She smoothed her hands down her sides in practiced maneuver, intended to bring attention to the curves of her body. All Kendra could notice was the broken nails and rough skin on her elegant hands. Something was very wrong here.

"Clarissa, are you all right?"

"Better than I've been in years," she purred. "Why wouldn't I be?"

"You just look so different."

"That's the glow of satisfaction, sweetie. Something you'll never know about."

Kendra ignored the barb. They wouldn't be alone for long. She had very little time to try to get through to her cousin.

"I've known you most of your life, Clarissa, and I've never seen you step out of your room with even a chip in your nail polish. Now you're missing two nails, and your hair looks like you slept in a tree." As she spoke, she tried again to reach her cousin's mind, to impress upon her the difference in her appearance.

"Under one." But the satisfaction and confidence wasn't quite as blatant. Clarissa looked down at her nails then plucked at her stained, ripped clothing as though suddenly realizing what she wore. "Oh, my God, what happened to my clothes?" She felt at her hair, tangling what nails were left on her fingers in the matted mess.

"This is awful! How bad do I look?"

"Bad enough. Rissa." Kendra intentionally chose the childish diminutive she hadn't used in years. "What happened to you?"

"I don't know."

Now she sounded lost, almost pathetic. Kendra steeled herself. Pity wouldn't get the job done. Not right now.

"Think. What do you remember last?"

"I was in my motel room. Matt was mad because I wouldn't let him spend the night, but I was tired." She spoke slowly, as though from a great distance. "We'd gone out to dinner with Tucker, to talk about getting the property transferred in spite of you. I had some Tequila Sunrises, and I was feeling pretty good. We decided to use the unstable idea, prove that Gran didn't know what she was doing, leaving the land to you instead of her son. Your dad was going to help, since he didn't want you living out here all alone."

The magnitude of the deceit was too much for Kendra to absorb. With an effort, she set that to one side. Instead, she laid her hand on Clarissa's shoulder, hoping the personal contact would give her cousin strength. She looked frail, as if she'd aged many years overnight.

"You do understand, we only wanted to do it for your good, don't you, Kendy?"

"I understand that's what you wanted to believe."

It seemed to be enough assurance, for the moment. Clarissa pushed her matted hair back from her face. "I know I went to sleep in the motel. When I woke up, I was in the woods, with this gorgeous hunk." She paused to consider her memories. "Maybe not quite as much of a hunk as that one I saw you with. I'd have to see both of them together."

Kendra forced herself to remain calm as Clarissa's thoughts wandered into a realm she had no interest in exploring. Lewd images forced themselves on her subconscious in spite of her care. She shook her cousin's arm, urgently.

"Clarissa, get to the point."

"Sorry. I guess I spent the rest of the time in the woods. I don't know what happened to my nails and my hair." Once again, her voice raised in a pitiful wail as she began another inventory of her appearance. Then she stopped. Her head lifted, and she turned her face to look at a point just behind Kendra. It was a slight warning, but it was enough. Leaning on the cane for balance, Kendra pivoted, stepping away from the path and placing her back against a large, elderly tree.

Somewhere in his existence, Gabriel had learned about dramatic appearances. One minute he was a mere disturbance in the air, an irritation to Kendra's nerves. Then he was there, between her and Clarissa.

Before, Gabriel had wanted her to think he was merely an overgrown, mischievous boy. Peter Pan with hormones. The danger she sensed in him then had been muted, layered over with charisma and shallow friendship. It was obvious he no longer saw her as a potential conquest.

"Enjoying a chat with your little cousin, my love?"

He didn't reach out to touch Clarissa, but Kendra could feel the sensual stroking of his voice and mind against her cousin's unguarded psyche. Clarissa flushed, gulped a deep breath, and stood once again erect, displaying her charms.

Gabriel looked between the two of them,

blatant arrogance on his sculptured features. He didn't bother to hide his triumph from Kendra. Instead, he flaunted his mastery, letting her know without words how insignificant her efforts were.

"There is in your culture a story of the city mouse and the country mouse. That would seem very fitting at this moment."

"I don't believe you've actually read this story, have you?"

His angry flush told her she'd guessed right. Gabriel had also not bothered to learn to read. Unlike Mykhael, he preferred to hide his lack. Then he sneered, letting her know how insignificant he found her opinion.

"According to the story," she continued in a conversational tone. "The city mouse was as out of place in the country as the country mouse was in the city. It was meant as a parable to encourage acceptance of what you are and tolerance of those different from you."

She pushed away from the tree, stepping to one side so she could see Clarissa more clearly.

"Clarissa blossoms in the city. She's meant for a world of beauty salons and weekly manicures. To keep her out here like this is tantamount to cruelty."

This time, the other woman didn't respond. She was obviously deep in the enthralling net of Gabriel's weaving. Her lips moved in a silent conversation with the players in her fantasy.

"Clarissa." Kendra took a step forward, leaning on the cane a bit more than she needed to. Somehow, having her Grandmother's walking stick as a support helped more than just her footsteps. "You do not need to stay out here in the woods. You're a person in your own right, with your own thoughts and dreams. Don't let him do this to you."

"How charming. It is unfortunate she can neither hear nor understand you." He shifted, just enough to intercept her. "You must be feeling lonely, with my brother gone so much, trying to pretend he is an actual human."

"Your brother is far more human than you will ever be." She stepped away, not letting him any nearer, in a subtle dance of power and resistance.

"For which I thank all the powers that are and have ever been." He narrowed his eyes, concentrating a larger portion of sensual control on her. "You do not have to be lonely, Kendra. It would be amusing for you to find out how a true immortal makes love."

"I doubt you could make anything but pain and fear."

"For some, that is a great aphrodisiac."

"For some, perhaps. Not for me."

He hesitated, pushing harder at the mental wall she erected against his intrusion. When the pressure came close to pain, Kendra stopped resisting him overtly. Instead, she let her thoughts wander to earlier, happier times, in the garden with her grandmother. She remembered a spring morning when they set out squash plants, started weeks before in the cabin.

It had been a sunny, clear day. Warm rain the night before had proclaimed the start of spring, and they rose early, not wanting to miss a second of the day. She remembered the rich, fertile ground between her fingers, the smell of newly sprouted mint planted to cross the pathway so that they could always have perfume when they walked. Gran had told her stories—

"Enough!" Gabriel uttered curses in a language even stranger sounding than Mykhael's. He took a step forward then stopped himself. "This time. I will let you win for now. Do not become too confident. In the end, victory shall be mine, all the sweeter for your inconsequential triumph today."

"Why?" Kendra heard herself asking the same simple question that never failed to irritate and amuse Mykhael. Gabriel was not amused. "Why do you involve yourself in these matters?"

"Your meager mind could never comprehend the scope of my plans."

Try me, she wanted to say. Instead, she remained mute. No need to give him any more reason to gloat. When she didn't press the issue, demanding explanations, he turned away, smirking. The consciously superior expression on his face hid a fleeting uncertainty.

"Come, my love." He held out a graceful hand to Clarissa. She roused enough from her near-trance to stumble forward. "We must leave your cousin for now. I feel a need to be alone with you."

With their hands linked, Clarissa seemed to grow in strength and in the appearance of beauty. Then Kendra realized the effect was projected by Gabriel. She thought of how Clarissa had looked before, and the glamour fell away.

"Gabriel?" Clarissa sounded lost, uncertain. Obviously Gabriel had merely extended his talents to include the doubting as well as the trusting cousin. With Kendra's resistance, he lost control. But only temporarily.

A force near pain ripped through Kendra's mind as Gabriel shut her out. She looked away for a moment, squeezing her eyes against the pressure. She glanced back as her cousin slipped away, once again a confident *femme fatale.* A fleeting last image of them was one of extreme lust and anticipation.

As they left, she heard a new noise off to one side. Only then did she realize how isolated their encounter had been. Almost as though it occurred in another place and time.

Mentally, she chastised herself as she took stock of what she could sense.

Mykhael was coming closer, along with some other people.

She sensed a few animal minds, predators, waiting.

She felt nothing more than a glancing

communication before they turned away from her, still not ready to make a decision.

"There you are Kendra. Mike said he saw you over this direction a while back." Sheriff Danvers was with Mykhael, along with a small grouping of deputies and some of the more active hunters in town. All of them looked like they were at the end of their energy. Kendra knew Mykhael had known where she was all along, although there was a question in his thought.

And a warning. She decided at that instant against mentioning the last meeting, at least to this group. "I thought I saw something of Clarissa's over here."

"Clothing?" Danver's exhaustion fell away as he straightened.

"A blue scarf she likes to wear. But it was a bird."

"Probably a jay." Danvers exhaled heavily, bracing his hands against his back and stretching before he looked around at the group. "Men, what say we call it a day? By the time we get back to our rigs, it'll be near dark, and we can't do much good then."

A general stirring and muttered acknowledgments answered him.

"I'll drop you two back at the cottage. Save you a walk."

"That won't be necessary, Danvers. We'll camp out here tonight and get a fresh start in the morning." Time spent among the rugged outdoorsmen had given Mykhael an easy control over language. He blended effortlessly with the rest of the hunters.

"You too, Kendra?" Danvers was dubious.

"I'm looking forward to it. I haven't camped out in years." She felt the muffled laughter from Mykhael but didn't dare look in his direction. Odd, being able to find amusement even now.

"Well, if anyone can take care of you, I reckon he can. Let me leave you two a gun. We don't know for sure yet how Tucker died."

"There is no need." Mykhael spoke abruptly then tempered his response with a small smile. "I have all the protection I need with me." He indicated the backpack he wore across his shoulders.

Danvers looked dubious, but the rest of the group was beginning to head down the darkening trail. Finally, the sheriff shrugged.

"Suit yourself. Take this at least." He

pulled a cellular phone out of his backpack and handed it to Kendra. "Star one will get you right to the station. Someone'll be there all night."

She smiled her thanks and wondered where they could keep the instrument out of the way. Good as Danvers was, any dangers they might meet that evening would be beyond his care. Apparently, he felt his duty was done. With a call to the missing men, he headed down the mountain.

"Come." Mykhael held out a hand, indicating a vague path among the trees. "We need to settle ourselves before the night is fully here."

⋘⋙

Kendra stared into the warm glow of the fire. Mykhael had found another private clearing, one she was sure hadn't been there earlier that day. They'd reached the clearing and set up camp in silence, broken only by minimal talking about dinner. Strangely, the evening chill wasn't evident here, and she'd shed her warm jacket, using it as a pad against the tree behind her back.

Now Mykhael sat on a sleeping bag on the other side of the fire, far away from her in more ways than just physical. There seemed to be little welcome from him. Kendra wondered if she would have been better off going back to her house with Danvers.

He looked up, a smile in his eyes, turning up the corners of his mouth.

"You had a difficult day." It was a statement, not a question. "And now you want to talk about it, but you aren't sure what I want."

"That sums it up fairly well." She tried to imitate his casual tone and managed to at least not give in to her need to unload all of the day onto him.

"Why don't you come over here?"

It was an invitation issued in a dark velvet voice of temptation and longing. Without hesitation, she rose and walked the few feet around the fire, to sink down next to him.

Silence once more fell in the clearing, broken only by the subtle pop of the fire and a few beats of a nocturnal bird's wings. Kendra felt as though her every nerve ending was exposed. Then Mykhael stirred, turning his head in her direction.

"Talk to me." He settled his arm around her waist, offering warmth along with the comfort. "You've been thinking of many things these last few days, and you need to discuss them. Share with me."

She thought of her solitary attempt to communicate with the Atrahasis. The attempt itself had been an abysmal failure, but her later thought processes had done much to solidify her faith in herself and also to raise questions about Mykhael. But those questions had always been there. She decided to start with the rest of her vague suspicions.

"This thing about Gran worries me. All I knew was that she had died in her sleep. I was never told of any problems here."

"Perhaps no one wished you to worry."

"My family believes adversity strengthens character. Telling me Gran died under awful circumstances would be seen as an exercise in maturity."

His arm tightened around her waist, and he bent forward, turning her head to look directly into her face.

"They would do such a thing to their child?"

"Mykhael, I'm nearly thirty years old. Not

much of a child any more. My family believed in raising us ready to handle anything that came up."

"Did your cousin's family also have this philosophy?" It didn't require an ability to read minds to know he didn't think so.

"I believe they tried, in their own way. But she was always so feminine, so delicate, even as a young girl. It would've been difficult to expect her to withstand a lot of pressure. I wonder if they would recognize her now."

"You saw Clarissa?"

"I spoke with her and Gabriel. I barely recognized her. She's always been so meticulous about her appearance, and now, she's a mess. It worried me."

"Does she seem happy?"

"She seems to think she's happy. That's not quite the same thing, is it?"

"You ask questions philosophers have discussed for years." He slid his other arm around her shoulders, pulled her closer, resting his chin on top of her head. A sigh ruffled her hair, and she felt contentment begin to ease into his mind, his body. "Perhaps you mean to say that someone has told her she is happy. What do you think?" The hum of increasing awareness in his body told her he'd put aside the matter of their relatives for the moment.

"About Clarissa?" she teased, letting herself ease into his hold. Just a little. What could it hurt? He punished her with a tiny biting kiss at the base of her neck.

"About happiness. About the illusion of happiness."

"About the fact that, right now, in the middle of a dark forest, surrounded by unnamed evil, in the arms of a man I'm not quite sure I know, I think l might be closer to happiness than I have been for years?" She turned as she spoke, looking up into his face. As always, the beauty of his features took her by surprise. Then he smiled, tenderly mocking, and she forgot to breathe for just a moment.

"Something like that." He breathed the words against her cheek as he brushed tiny kisses across her face.

"If happiness is an illusion, then you are, for me, a master of illusion." She sensed his defense, his need to disclaim, and rushed on. "Only for tonight. You would not have me here if it were not safe. For tonight, let us practice our talents with illusion."

Soft laughter stroked her mind as he lay back on the sleeping bag, pulling her with him. A few gentle adjustments and she stretched full length over him, relearning the intimate contours of his body. Her hands somehow ended up under his shoulders, held without harm.

"For tonight, in this place, we are safe from harm. Gabriel must regain power before he can deal with us. Your resistance today would have lessened his strength."

He stroked his hands down her back as he spoke, easing her more fully into him. Strong hands cupped her bottom and he flexed upward, joining them in a frustrating imitation of intimacy.

"Mykhael," she warned, squirming to free her hands. The friction moved her dangerously along his body. She felt her lower body clenching in anticipation of joining with him.

He laughed, his chest vibrating against her breasts then rubbing against her as he lifted first one shoulder then the other one to release her hands.

Kendra braced against his shoulders to lift

her upper body away from his. He stopped her from moving completely away with his hands at her waist. Then his legs separated, and wrapped around hers.

Perhaps she could have struggled, but there would have been no dignity in it. Instead she relaxed, resting her forearms against his chest.

His eyes promised mysteries in the firelight that pushed shadows to the edge of the glade. A feeling of safety and well-being overtook her, and she felt her fears and inhibitions fade away as she sank against him. With one small hand, she stroked the sculptured plane of his cheek. Never looking away, he turned his head, placing a kiss in the center of her palm.

A shudder ripped through her body as she felt his tongue probe delicately at her fingers, thrusting wetly between them then retreating. Again. Then he traced a path along her middle finger. Up then down then up again before his mouth opened, and he took her finger between his teeth.

Kendra felt the serrations of his teeth, the heat of his tongue. The eager wetness of his mouth, opening, lifting, asking for hers.

Throwing caution to the wind she lowered her head.

A slight tilt by both of them and they achieved a perfect, seamless union.

The blood sang in her ears, and Kendra remembered what Mykhael had once said about kissing. Only humans kissed, and for a few fortunate humans, a kiss transcended any other expression of emotion. Almost.

She felt the roughness of his fingers under her shirt, along her bare back, massaging gently. Feeling distinctly feline, she arched into his touch, stroking his body. A satisfying groan vibrated against her sensitive nipples, and she relaxed her elbows, lowering herself more completely.

"You like that?" she purred, lifting her head just enough to whisper the words into his mouth.

"Should I show you how much?" Humor buoyed the deep passion in his voice as his hands shifted down to her waist then up again, this time pushing her sweatshirt off her body. Had she wanted to resist there would have been little chance, but there was no resistance in her. The sweatshirt ended up under Mykhael's head, and he slid his hands along her rib cage, lifting her, staring down at the skin he had exposed.

"Lovely. A treasure beyond all imagining."

Removed from the warmth of his chest, her nipples began to harden. He pursed his lips and blew a stream of air gently against her chest, watching the tiny bumps appear wherever she felt his breath.

"Come closer," he urged with deep voice and gentle hands, until his mouth could close around her nipple, until his tongue could stroke, his teeth nibble while she writhed and whimpered.

Driven by instincts she had only recently discovered, Kendra clawed at his shirt, working the buttons with trembling fingers. A knit silk undershirt stopped her for only a minute before she pulled at that also. Underneath the shirt she felt a few hairs pull, then release. The small pain seemed only to galvanize him into a deeper, stronger suckling.

He pushed at the waistband of her jeans, unfastening the buttons when she raised her hips to accommodate him. Then bare skin rubbed against rough linen, an erotic stroking he did nothing to alleviate. Frustrated, she plucked at the drawstring of his trousers with fingers that only functioned nominally. The knot finally released. Breathing fire along her chest, he moved reluctantly from one breast to the other.

"There is something to be said for strange looking garments. At least they remove easily," he murmured just before closing his mouth around her other nipple.

When she would have raised herself, completing the union in the only way she could figure from her present position, his legs once more captured hers. Wrapping them around the outside of her, he hooked his heels over her ankles and held her still.

Kendra groaned in frustration, reaching for his head to keep his mouth where it was. Her fingers threaded into his hair, nails scraping along his scalp. She felt his hands searching, seeking with a frustrating slow-ness, opening her more fully to the night.

She could feel him, the probing, vibrating length of him, as eager to finish this madness as she. Squirming, writhing, she tried to lift herself, to impale herself upon him. Still, he kept them separated.

Now his body flexed, and he stroked himself along her ultra-sensitive tissue while one of his long fingers sought out the hidden cluster of nerve endings. A strained groan lit fires against her breast. Mykhael was nowhere near as controlled as he wanted her to believe.

Relaxing, she let all of her weight fall against him and entrusted him with full control. Something deep within her knew they would soon face challenges beyond their ability to handle. This could well be their last night together. For now, she would not think of it, would not rush whatever he wanted of this night together.

He relented, adjusting her. His arms closed around her, holding her safe against him, completing the union of their bodies, their souls, their selves. Kendra could hear gentle, satisfied laughter echoing between them, lifting into the night, and beyond.

# CHAPTER 17

The deer are unhappy." Kendra made the observation the next day as she lowered herself onto a fallen tree. "You can sense them that clearly?"

Mykhael continued across the clearing, stopping only when he was beneath a sycamore. He had been restless like this all morning.

"Not really. I can sense unease and know it is a deer. There is a different...feel to the emotion. Rabbits think, or sense, more quickly. The way they do everything. Deer think in spurts. Their thoughts are not clear, and they come in all at once. As if they take the time to think between mouthfuls of food."

"The progress of your communication with the animals is impressive."

"If that's what it really is. Mykhael, what if I'm just fooling myself? My imagination has worked overtime before. I could want to communicate with the animals so much I convince myself I can."

"You speak again with your own lack of self-esteem. There is no reason why one person should not communicate with animals, just because another one cannot."

"You're sweet." She leaned over as she spoke, re-tying the laces of her hiking boots to offer more support.

"That would not be the consensus of most who have known me." He looked away, isolating himself mentally.

"It seems to me—" She stood, testing the fit of the boot. Then she stepped toward him, using the cane only as a matter of habit. "You suffer as much as I do from a severe lack of self-esteem."

"I am cursed with the memory of centuries of worthless living." He still spoke without looking at her, but she could feel what he believed to be the truth of his words.

"A riddle for you, Mykhael: Who is of more worth, a man born and raised to be good, who does good deeds? Or a man born to be selfish, raised without guidance and love, nurtured in hate and violence, who is unfailingly kind and supportive to someone who has trouble getting her own act together?"

He turned as she approached. A small smile twisted his sculptured lips when he reached for her hand. At the contact, a memory of the night before rose between them, to be savored in intense silence.

"I could almost believe in myself, listening to you." He raised her hand to his mouth and left a lingering kiss in her palm. For a moment she felt the confusion of his thoughts, things he wanted to say but could not. Then he straightened. "Do you sense any animals that are not frightened?"

"The predators, once I can get past the aggression in their images. They seem interested in what is going on but not much more than that. Nothing concrete."

"As though they are waiting to see who would be ruler before they allow allegiance?" He nodded in agreement to his own statement. "It is the way of warriors everywhere."

"At some point, a warrior must come home. Why else would they bother to fight?"

"Because they must?" There was great sadness in his voice and his thoughts.

"Mykhael?" She stepped closer, daring to

press the issue. "What is it you aren't telling me?"

"I must leave." He said it baldly, dropping her hand but not yet turning away.

Already. Even before they met with Gabriel. She would be brave. She must be brave.

"I see. Of course." She drew a breath, controlling her voice, her thoughts, her damned tears. "Will you need anything from the house before you go?"

He tilted his head, staring at her as though she had suddenly lost all sense. Then understanding bloomed in his mind. A laugh, strained but genuine, filled the clearing with a moment of lightness.

"Kendra, Kendra. What will I do with you?" He grasped her arms gently above the elbows, pulling her into his body, swinging her from side to side. "Not forever. Just for now. Your zealous sheriff and his assistants are about to enter this part of the woods. I need to intercept them before they cause a problem. Did you think I would just walk away from you with nothing more than that?"

She shrugged, feeling suddenly foolish. His chest seemed very convenient to nuzzle, and her hands liked to rest against the lean strength of his hips. Whatever he said, their time together would be short. She soaked up the feeling of his body pressed against her, memorizing him one more time.

"In addition, I fear Gabriel will not come close while we are together."

"You aren't planning to face him on your own?" She stiffened, started to pull away from the comfort. His arms closed, holding her in place.

"We will face him together. It will take both of us to control what he has become. However, if he senses you alone, he will be more likely to appear with your cousin." He framed her face in his hands, smiling into the frown she could feel on her face. "Move toward the clearing where you first met him. I will be there with Danvers. Be very careful."

She nodded, not allowing her fear to show. His smile, his tender kiss, told her she was not in as much control as she had hoped. This time, she didn't care.

⁊〇⁊

The woods were not the same as when she had wandered them as a child. Nor even the same as the day before. In addition to the tense waiting of the predators, Kendra sensed a new watchfulness. There was a feeling of old power, both good and evil.

She remembered now where she'd felt the evil before. In Phoenix, at the theater. That night she had been drawn back as though by a compulsion. After the attack, as she lay under the heavy backdrop, she had sensed the approach of something so heinous, so foreign to everything she had ever known before, she had refused to acknowledge its presence. Nor had she remembered the next day.

Her dreams had been a shadow of the memories. It was only now, as she grew in strength and confidence in herself, that she began to remember all of that night. If this were the case, then the events were not random, but a culmination of months, perhaps years, of planning on the part of the immortals who wanted to attain more power on Earth.

She looked around, identifying her general location by the trees and granite outcroppings she had seen when she had first met Gabriel. There were no deer to guide her now, but she recognized the path easily.

In fact, there were no deer within a reachable distance of her location. She sensed a few timid minds, grouping together in a meadow far away. The feral, shifting, calculating minds of the predators increased in numbers, and proximity.

Mykhael was nearby, with Danvers and some of the men from town. A blank area appeared in her mind when she cast delicately for other images, the same blankness she remembered surrounding her when she spoke with Clarissa before.

There was no way around it. Sighing, she stepped into the clearing. The setting sun gave a russet cast to the stone and deepened the shadows that traced along the mountain face.

It would be a moonless night. Kendra remembered Gabriel was stronger in the dark and wondered how she would see to get around.

Then again, there was always light enough for those who knew where to look for it. Stars gave off light, faint but steady.

And there was the inner vision she had never quite trusted.

She felt again the pressure of the watching

predators. Stronger than ever, they seemed to try to dominate her, seeking now for acknowledgment, when she wanted only to track Mykhael, to encourage him to be here before his brother arrived.

So many minds demanded attention, until she commanded: STOP! Silence reigned in her head, only the shifting dark ooze of Gabriel's approach troubling at her like metal dragged across dry concrete. Coming closer, ever closer.

As the darkness at the far end of the clearing began to take shape, she felt a brief, warm stroking along her overwrought nerves. Mykhael approached from behind, Sheriff Danvers and a few of the men not far behind him. Calm came to her slowly, easing into the tension, releasing the knots formed by so many minds demanding so much of her all at once.

"You sure she's here, Mike? Damnation, I thought I put new batteries in this thing." Danvers could be heard cursing in what he probably thought was an undertone. It seemed like a roar, but she did not flinch openly.

"I'm over here." She spoke quietly

enough to spare her own ears. "Maybe the batteries are defective."

"First time for everything. You okay?"

She nodded then realized he couldn't see as well as she could and answered him verbally as he stopped at her shoulder, a solid, sane presence. Mykhael came up on her other side, reaching out to touch her physically while their minds aligned. Their fingers meshed, and they turned to face the gathering darkness at the other end of the clearing.

# CHAPTER 18

W ell, I'll be a son of a buck." Danver's harsh whisper echoed in the dark woods, cutting through the tension.

Not so dark as it had been. Light grew at the far end of the clearing. Not a true, clear light. More like a muddy graying of the oppressive darkness.

Forms took shape, figures of a man and woman of indescribable beauty. The few men who had dared come this close muttered devout profanities as the two became increasingly distinct.

This was Clarissa as she had seen herself but as Kendra had never seen her. Gone was the disheveled appearance, the lack of grooming. This woman stepped forward, perfect from head to toe, dusted in tiny sparkles. Clothed only in hair that had suddenly become much longer.

Gabriel took on the aspect of a statue, honoring deities from long ago. He seemed to embody a person larger, stronger, sleeker, wiser than anyone watching could ever remember having seen before. Covered only with shadows, he avoided indecency by the perfection of his male beauty.

For the first time in a week, Kendra remembered she was not the beautiful cousin. She chastised herself. Some of this feeling was projected by Gabriel, as a weapon. Logically, she knew that to be true. She would not let it affect her.

"Hello, little brother." Gabriel's voice was deep, smooth, unctuous. "It is good to meet with you again after—how many years?"

"Enough years," Mykhael answered easily, his fingers stroking Kendra's hand to increase the support he gave her mentally.

"And here you are, once more trying to protect one of your precious humans. Ah, but I forgot. You are human yourself. Part of you is, anyway."

An innocuous exchange, Kendra thought, listening to them continue to spar verbally. The undercurrents told her something else. There was so much anger here, so much bitter meanness. Beyond his nasty questions, Gabriel probed for some weakness, some fear or insecurity he could use. Again and again, he attacked Mykhael mentally. Again and again, Mykhael repelled him, while continuing to smile easily, as though this were truly a meeting between long separated relatives.

Scowling, Gabriel tried to reach into Kendra's mind, to establish control over her. To reach beyond her surface control and suck her into the same dark chasm that held Clarissa. Buoyed up by Mykhael's hand on hers, by his mental strength, she resisted, much as she would walk against an autumn breeze.

Cold enveloped her. Bitter, angry cold, with tendrils of frost seeking out her every fear. Winds gusted across the clearing, tearing at her hair, her clothes. Sucking the warmth out of the evening and howling in triumph when, one by one, the men behind them backed away into the shelter of the trees.

Danvers stood his ground to her right, shotgun held ready across his body, hat pushed low across his forehead. Kendra could see beads of perspiration across his upper lip and forehead, in spite of the frigid wind.

Echoes of his fear resounded in her head, in the tense effort it took for him to remain at her side. The sheriff was more frightened than he had ever been before. But he would not back down.

For a moment Gabriel allowed anger to control him. The wind screamed in fury, ripping at them until tears formed in the corners of their eyes. When it stopped suddenly, they nearly fell over from the lack of pressure.

"How foolish you all are. How futile your puny efforts to resist. You listen to my brother, surely the least among us, and risk eternal damnation."

"Whoa there, pretty boy." Danvers spoke through stiffly held lips, his gun clenched in white knuckled fingers. Still, he spoke with firm knowledge of the truth. "Whoever or whatever you are, you are not God. I doubt you've ever had much to do with him."

Kendra marveled at the courage of the large man. She could almost smell his fear, yet he argued calmly and logically, his upbringing and beliefs giving him strength to resist.

Gabriel's smile mocked as he moved forward, Clarissa close at his side. Kendra could feel the direction of his mental thrusts move away from her to center on Danvers. No matter how good the man was, how sincere his beliefs, he would not be able to withstand Gabriel's probing unaided. Nor could Mykhael support him in time to help.

With Clarissa and, she hoped, Hawkins to control, plus the display he was putting on now, Gabriel had to be taxing his strength, though she didn't know the limit of his power. If she could interfere with what he was doing, perhaps she could force him to divert some of his power.

"Clarissa," she said in a quiet voice, concentrating on her cousin as she spoke.

As she had hoped, the sound of her name caught her cousin's attention. Secure in her beauty, Clarissa turned slightly, offering a gracious smile.

"Kendra. How nice of you to join us." Her outstretched hand and wide smile only welcomed, but there was a dark double meaning to her words.

"No, Rissa, I'm not here to join you. I'm here to take you home."

The ethereally lovely features crumpled

into a brief frown before Clarissa tossed back her mane of hair and laughed, her nudity displayed without shame. There was a tone of dark power and lightning in the laugh. It was not, had never been, the laugh of her cousin.

Kendra stepped forward, reaching for her cousin, thinking only to pull her away. At the same time, she automatically reached out a mental touch. Mykhael's hand tightened on hers, and he drew her back to his side.

"Do not move closer to him. Gabriel is limited to how far he can exert power. If you move closer, it will make his job easier."

"But, I can't let her stay with him. He's...she's already..." She could not find the words to describe what she had briefly felt in her cousin's mind. A shiver that had nothing to do with the continuing frigid wind rippled through her body.

"You cannot help by losing yourself in him. You cannot risk yourself, Kendra."

His anguish, his worry on her behalf, was apparent in his face, in the convulsive grip on her hand. She could sense exhaustion from his encounter with Gabriel, but no fear, no loss of confidence. Not yet.

"What can I do?" she asked more quietly.

"Try to reach her. Try to see her the way you know she is, not the way Gabriel wants you to see."

She remembered how she had almost reached Clarissa before. She also remembered the grinding pain in her head afterward. Bracing herself, she turned back.

"Rissa. We grew up together. You know I was never interested in money then. Why would I be now? This place is all I ever wanted." As she spoke, she tried to picture her cousin as she knew she looked, ragged and worn. "Now that Tucker is dead, there's little chance of selling to a Japanese consortium. They'd have you for lunch and never miss a lick. What's in this for you?"

Clarissa stopped her seductive swaying and stood very still. Her hair fell limp around her shoulders as she focused on Kendra's words.

"Come with me now. I can help you. You can have a nice, hot bath, wash your hair. You'll feel so much better."

More of the glamour fell away from Clarissa as the cold wind lessened. She seemed persuaded by Kendra's words. Was it enough? Moving her mouth as though she spoke with herself, Clarissa started to step toward Kendra. When Gabriel spoke, she stopped, frowning.

"Your cousin speaks from jealousy, as she always did, my sweet. You cannot believe someone who is less beautiful than you are."

"That wouldn't be very many people right now," Kendra pointed out. She could feel his intense effort to control her cousin. Clarissa didn't seem to hear her. "Why do you want to keep her around, anyway? It's not as though she's all that great to look at any more."

"She amuses me."

"Has life become that boring for you lately, brother?" Mykhael spoke contemptuously.

"At least I have experienced life, instead of being kept locked away like a disobedient pet. I could ask you the same question your little friend asks. Why do you keep her around?"

"If you need to ask that, you have learned less through the years than you think you have."

"I have learned more than I will ever need to know. You will be learning much, soon, about pain. It is so much more satisfying to apply lessons of pain to an immortal. We will be listening to your screams for centuries to come."

Kendra shuddered at the image Gabriel projected of Mykhael stretched on a rack, experiencing pain beyond comprehension, coming close to death but never being allowed to die. When she would have moved forward she was again stopped by Mykhael.

"Do not let him worry you. It is what he wants."

She could sense no fear, no apprehension, in Mykhael. Instead he smiled, reaching up to brush a strand of hair behind her ear. Ignoring the wrath of his half-brother, he concentrated on her.

"Kendra, do you remember your little grotto?"

She nodded, remembering not only the grotto, but being there with Mykhael. Experiencing with him the healing peace of the secluded spot. Wanting desperately to be there now, with him.

"Why don't you go there?" he suggested in a low, intimate tone, supporting the thought with a gentle mental push. "You could wait for me."

She studied him, his sincere, intense eyes,

his distractingly beautiful face. There was so much he wasn't telling her. Even now, he attempted to protect her, to hide the worst of the evil from her. As if she had not experienced evil before.

She reached up in turn, laying her hand on his cheek, feeling the tension he tried to hide from her.

"Not without you," she said, simply.

"How very touching," Gabriel sneered.

Lifting his arms, he stepped forward. Clarissa stayed behind, sagging like a marionette with only half its strings. The wind died down completely, leaving an oppressive silence. Kendra could feel something stirring around her. An ingathering of power, like the beginning of a powerful electric storm. There would be no healing rain following this storm.

"Kendra, please." Mykhael spoke quickly. "Go to your grotto. You can make no difference here."

"I helped already."

"Yes, you did. You distracted him because he didn't understand before. He does now, or will very soon."

"Understand what?"

"How I have gathered the power to defy him. Please, sweetheart. Go."

Her heart ached at the endearment, at the torment in his voice and intensity of his eyes. Even if she could leave Mykhael, she could not leave Clarissa. Not until she was absolutely sure there was no further hope. It wasn't as though she had no other help. She cast a look over her right shoulder, knowing Danvers would be there, solid as his beliefs.

Danvers was not behind her. A quick glance showed him still at the edge of the clearing but further to her right. He stood stiffly, his jaw rigid, as though fighting something every second. His hands trembled as he moved the stock of the shotgun, racking it, preparing it for use.

She felt again the touch of the predator's minds. Gabriel began to glow, his hair raising. Demoniacal laughter echoed in the clearing, mingling with the rushing wind of power heading for him. Almost, she could see the shapes of wolves, cougars, bears swirling around them. Almost, she could hear their hot, hungry calls.

"Too bad, little brother. You almost made it this time."

"No!"

Kendra turned at the taunt, and at Mykhael's screamed reply—in time to see him leap past her, toward Danvers. In time to see Danvers, still shaking, still resisting, raise his shotgun, pull the trigger. In time to see the pellets fly out of the gun, propelled by powder and hate, directly toward her.

In time to see Mykhael throw himself between her and Danvers. A few pellets got through, ripping along her cheek, her chin, glancing off her shoulder.

The rest lodged directly in Mykhael's chest, ripping into heart and lungs. Disintegrating tissue. Harming beyond repair. She felt his shock, his pain. His triumph at saving her. His last, desperate mental thrust at her.

She felt him cease to be.

# CHAPTER 19

The grotto was in front of her, then around her. Clutching the walking stick to her chest, Kendra curled on the ground and let the peace try to help her. She had no idea how she'd gotten there— remembered only that last thrust from Mykhael as the pellets tore through his body.

There was no peace for her. Nor were there tears.

There was only a blank numbness, and a hole wrenched in her soul where Mykhael had resided.

Mykhael, who considered himself the lowest of the low, who once feared death so much, yet had come to fear life even more. Mykhael, who laughed at the concept of sacrifice, had gladly given up his immortal life so that she could continue her worthless existence.

She remembered his last, desperate

thoughts. Regrets, that he had not said more, done more. Longing. Fear. Love?

And herself, in those moments—striving to bring Clarissa out of her bondage, to give Mykhael more strength for his battle with Gabriel. Wanting to tell him, to dare to mention the word that she had never dared even think in his presence.

Love.

*No greater love hath a man, than that he lay down his life for his fellow man.* Did the poets have it right, after all?

Mykhael had laid down his life, for her. Could she do any less if there were the slightest chance she could defeat Gabriel? From despair came hope, and a rather pragmatic logic. Who else indeed? She alone had the shield, the ability to avoid control from the strongest of the immortals.

First, she uncurled herself from the ground. The walking stick was enough of a brace to help her rise. A wave of uncertainty, of dread, beat at her momentarily, tried to force her back down. She laid a hand on the ageless trunk of a tree that had always fascinated her. Let the leaves caress her face, the branches gently comb through her hair. Other memories crowded in, beautiful, positive memories overshadowing the pain, helped her to balance.

One last, deep breath of the air in the grotto and she stepped toward the opening. Not stooping now. The vines parted for her, trailing along her arms, her chest, easing across her brow and closing up behind her. She was left with a memory of Mykhael's last, unspoken words. Her never-voiced answer.

"And I you, my darling," she murmured, hoping he would be allowed to hear. "And I, you."

*♥♥♥*

It was as though she had left the clearing only seconds before. Gabriel's laughter still echoed in the woods.

The acrid smell of recently discharged gunpowder hung on the air. Clarissa knelt at Gabriel's feet, her beauty waxing and waning with his attention. Her hair shook with her shuddering.

Danvers had dropped his shotgun and taken a step toward where Kendra had been standing. His face was ashen, his hands outstretched.

She stepped forward, ready to move into the dim, red-tinged light. A delicate brushing against her leg stopped her. Looking down, she saw the shadow of a fox, sitting patiently, its full tail neatly hiding dainty feet.

Hesitating momentarily, she tried to step around the alert little animal. It moved, placing itself again in front of her. Kendra remembered the fox she had once befriended. Just so had the little female sat and watched her, more enigmatic than any cat. When one more attempt to enter was cut off, she gave in, for now. "But not for long," she mouthed at the deceptively delicate animal. From here, she could at least watch the clearing, and Clarissa.

"What the hell did you do?" Danvers shook with rage, with reaction.

"I? I did nothing. I cannot touch your weapons. You did it, my good man. Quite well, as a matter of fact." Gabriel looked down at the mass of torn flesh on the ground in front of him. "There is a limit to what can be repaired, which you have exceeded nicely."

With a snarl of impotent rage, Danvers lunged at Gabriel. The sheriff was heavier, if not taller, and in good physical condition. Gabriel stepped aside lithely in one of the blinding moves Mykhael had used. As Danvers stumbled past, Gabriel struck his fist down. Danvers fell to the ground and did not move.

Kendra would not look at Danvers, lying with fearsome stillness. Nor would she look at the unidentifiable mass Gabriel indicated. That was not Mykhael. She concentrated instead on Mykhael as she remembered him. Standing with his head back, feeling, hearing, smelling the world around him. He might never live again, but in her heart he would never be dead.

Gabriel hesitated, looking around. A frown marred his perfect brow, and he stepped away from the small group in the clearing. His narrowed eyes peered into the woods surrounding the clearing, but he did not step far from the granite.

Kendra understood what the fox had tried to tell her. Gabriel could not leave this area. Not yet, at any rate. Some new wisdom told her that would not always be the case.

"You can come out now," Gabriel called in a conversational tone. "I know you've had a bit of a shock, so come on out now. I can help you." A subtext to his words was strong mental images of good things for her, if she would come out. Nothing concrete, but intimations of great pleasure.

"Don't worry about my brother. His time was long past. He never really enjoyed the idea of being immortal, after all. Come on out. I need to tend to your wounds."

He was guessing at that, she knew. A calm settled over her as she contemplated the immortal. Somehow, the glamour, the beauty was not as strong as it had been a few minutes before. As he continued to call to her, at times enticing, at times commanding, Kendra sensed a note of desperation in his voice. As if he had some task to perform and only a limited time to get the job done.

In a flash of understanding, she saw the whole picture. Gabriel had to complete his purge in a limited length of time. Mykhael was gone, but as long as she remained, Gabriel would not be able to assume control, nor could he hide his actions from his superiors.

She could continue to hide, her essence somehow shadowed by the woods, or perhaps by the fox that still sat at her feet, bright eyes studying first her, then Gabriel. More than normal sharp fox intelligence looked at her, but she had no time to consider any more fantasies. If she continued to hide, Gabriel would be able to retreat, to draw back, regain some of his power and return next month, perhaps to harm many more people. He stayed only because he hoped to finish everything now, at his time of greatest strength.

Gripping the walking stick more tightly, Kendra drew a deep breath, and straightened. The fox stepped back, fading into the under-brush. A brush of feral intelligence touched her mind, hot and keen. She braced herself against the contact then welcomed the offered strength. Perhaps not all the predators were on Gabriel's side.

"Must you make so much noise? This was once a peaceful corner of the world." She stepped into the clearing with all the artistic style she had studied through the years.

Gabriel whirled. His hands raised then lowered, and he peered at her more closely.

"I worried about you. After the unfortunate demise of my brother, you disappeared. I was afraid you let yourself be too affected."

"So kind of you." She stepped fully into the clearing. "Yet, somehow, I must doubt your words. Clarissa, come, it's late. We must be leaving."

"Why do you insist on trying to 'save' your cousin?" He spoke with a forced, amused tolerance that rang as false as his solicitude. "Do you not see that she is completely happy as she is? Your cousin was meant for this life." He turned, extended a hand to the woman at his feet. "Come, my love. Rise up, and show your cousin how happy you are."

Clarissa rose, her beauty increasing as she attained her feet. Once again, she stood as a gorgeous, quintessential female. She turned her attention to Gabriel, a slight, knowing smile on her full lips.

As though drawn to her invitation, Gabriel leaned over to brush his mouth over hers, his hands across her body. Clarissa writhed, edging closer, her body taking on a new glow, a ripeness as she reacted to the touch of the immortal's long-fingered hands. As if he had all the time in the world, Gabriel kissed and caressed her.

Kendra ignored the erotic display, leaning on her walking stick as if bored. In fact she was repulsed, but she could not let anything distract her now. As the couple drew apart, she heard a slight sound off to one side of the clearing. Probably just the wind. It was promising to be a stormy night.

Gabriel released Clarissa with one last, lingering caress across her cheek. "My lovely," he crooned, stepping back. "Go now, and greet your cousin."

She turned obediently, stepping with consummate grace to where Kendra waited, scratched, dirty, weary. Her path was not straight, as she was forced to step around the bodies on the ground.

Kendra realized Clarissa's route was more convoluted than it needed to be. The blank expression on her face did not seem to be able to calculate. On the course she now stepped, she would step directly over the shotgun. No time now for subtlety.

"Rissa," she said urgently, drawing on all the weapons at her disposal. "Forget him, forget all of this. Come back with me. I'll take you home to your mother. You can have a bubble bath and some hot cocoa."

Gabriel's laugh boomed into the forest.

"Truly amazing, what you humans think is of value. Bubble bath and hot cocoa? Don't you see, you plain little fool. Clarissa will stay with me and be gorgeous forever. How can she turn that down?"

Kendra ignored him, concentrating on Clarissa, remembering what had pleased her as a self-centered child. She saw a trace of understanding, of comprehension, of longing. She hoped.

Next to the shotgun, Clarissa hesitated. Not going on, but also not reaching down. A fine trembling took over her limbs.

"If you do not obey me, you will be ugly for the rest of your life. And I can ensure you live a long, long time."

As a threat for most people, it lacked something in force. For Clarissa it would be dire indeed. Kendra saw her hesitate then crouch. Stand up with the shotgun, huge and ugly in her delicate fingers. Rack the gun with an odd familiarity.

Kendra gulped then braced herself. At least she would die by the same weapon as

Mykhael. Then Clarissa raised her head, and her lovely blue eyes, clear for the moment, looked directly at Kendra. There was a message, deep under the pain and confusion.

"Do not fire, my sweet, as long as she behaves. Come closer, Kendra."

"I don't think so," she said as stolidly as she could manage while staring into the ever-increasing muzzle.

"Come now. No need for any further theatrics. I do not wish to waste someone as valuable as you, but I can have no distractions."

Letting her shoulders droop, Kendra stepped forward. Perhaps she wasn't the stuff of which heroes were made. She leaned heavily on the cane as she shuffled toward her cousin.

Clarissa didn't step aside, nor did she lower the gun. When Kendra's chest, lifting with each erratic breath, pressed against the muzzle, Clarissa turned. The shotgun now pointed more in Gabriel's direction than Kendra's.

Snarling, he sent a bolt of mental fury directly at them. Kendra felt only a glancing impression, but it was enough to send her staggering. Clarissa dropped the weapon and fell to her knees. Gabriel's rage filled the clearing.

"What is wrong with you foolish human females?" Spittle flung from his mouth as he ranted.

Ignoring him, Kendra bent down to her cousin. Slipped an arm around her shoulders, attempting to give her at least a modicum of support. Clarissa's defiance was beyond her belief.

"Come on, Rissa. Stand up. I'll help."

"Get away, Kendra. He's weaker. I'll hold him off." Clarissa spoke between sobs, her face ugly now in pain and fear.

"Not without you. I can't leave you here."

"Don't you see it yet?" she asked, with a flash of her old arrogance. "There's no hope for me now, I've gone too far. You, though, you've always been so good. You can get away."

"For what? There's nothing for me now, Rissa."

Clarissa looked up, saw the huddled, bloody mass on the ground, and cried piteously. Cradling her cousin, Kendra slipped the walking stick into her slender fingers.

"Come on, Rissa. We'll do it together. I'll even let you use Gran's stick."

"This was Gran's?" With the wonder of a child, Clarissa stroked the smoothly polished stick. Then she stood, leaning on the support as though it were of great value. "Yes," she whispered. "It does help. Stay behind me, Kendra."

Swaying gracefully in spite of her weakness, Clarissa picked her way back across the clearing. Gabriel watched suspiciously but did not step further from the rock.

"You were right, Gabriel. I would rather be beautiful than good. Look what being good gets you." She looked back at Kendra, a sneer twisting her beautiful mouth. "Plain, bruised, and alone. She even gave me her cane."

Clarissa brandished the lovely old stick in front of Gabriel who stepped aside impatiently. Seeming not to notice his scowl, Clarissa followed, staying between him and Kendra.

"It's a lovely old cane, Gabriel. It belonged to our grandmother."

"I don't care if it belonged to the Queen mother," he snarled, pushing her roughly to the side as he strode toward Kendra.

"You should have more respect for our grandmother," Clarissa hissed, lifting the cane and bringing it abruptly across his back.

Gabriel roared in pain and rage, whirling. Before he completed the turn, Clarissa had managed to strike him twice more. Then his hand shot out, grabbed her by the throat. Shook her, until a sickening 'crack' filled the clearing. He tossed the limp, no longer lovely, body into the air. She flew against a tree, wrapped around it, and slid, broken and bleeding, to the ground.

Sickened, Kendra staggered back. Darkness threatened to overtake her again.

A roar sounded in the trees behind Gabriel. Screaming in anguish, Hawkins rushed forward, his beefy hands holding a hatchet. Gabriel laughed diabolically and waited, balanced, prepared for the attack.

Kendra looked for some weapon, some way to control this man, keep him from killing again. The stick had fallen next to the shotgun. She had only her hands. And her will.

Before Hawkins could get within striking distance, Gabriel stepped sideways, looking for better footing.

Kendra reached out, grabbing for a handful of his long hair, and pulled. As she did, she heard a snarling at her feet.

The fox tore at Gabriel's legs, rending gouges in his ankles.

Gabriel kicked out, his aim ruined by Kendra's pressure on his scalp. He tried to strike at her, to draw in enough power to bring her down.

Then Hawkins was there, his hatchet raised, poised to strike.

"Matt, no!" Whatever Kendra thought of Hawkins, she could not allow him to commit the murder, to risk himself.

Gabriel needed to suffer in different ways, and she intended for him to.

"You will not want to come near me with that, Hawkins," Gabriel panted. "You know I can make you hurt for a long time, as I did Clarissa."

Hawkins hesitated. Saw Clarissa crumpled under the tree and dropped the hatchet, stumbling forward. Forgetting everything else in his grief.

"So much for your defender, my dear." Gabriel turned, ignoring the pain in his scalp, at his feet. "Now, it is your turn." He took hold of her arms, his grip chilling into her bones. And stopped, looking past her.

Kendra heard the rustling behind her, felt the heat. The fox jumped away, taking up a spot next to her feet. Growling, threatening.

The snarling increased, and she felt the power of many bodies behind her. Panting, angry bodies.

Gabriel released her, stepped back. Tried to regather his control.

"No," he snarled. "You were with me."

Kendra dared to look around. Within the dark mist surrounding them she heard the stroking of owl's wings, the calls of hawks and eagles. Wolves, bears, cougars stood to either side of her, watching Gabriel intensely, as though deciding where to strike first.

The predators had chosen.

"I believe they have chosen for themselves, Gabriel. I don't have your ability to handle them so I suggest you just go on back."

She could see the breakdown in his eyes, the stress, the over extension. Gabriel had lost control of his surroundings, of himself. In a sudden show of weakness, he stumbled back. The predators stepped forward, their bodies brushing against Kendra's as they moved past her.

With a scream that could have come from any of the animal's throats, Hawkins jumped on Gabriel from behind, hatchet forgotten, his mind only on revenge.

The rest was lost in a cloud of dust kicked up by the howling winds and screaming animals.

# CHAPTER 20

Dawn slowly eased into the clearing. First outlining the treetops then removing shadows from beneath and between rocks and trees. Eventually, the light fell upon flat ground, upon the motionless body of a large man in a sheriff's uniform and a slender woman who sat alone, her head resting upon upraised knees.

Alerted by a curious sunbeam, Kendra raised her head. In the gentle early morning light the clearing looked as it had since shortly after the dust settled the night before.

Danvers lay face down just beyond her reach, his back rising and falling in a deep, slow rhythm.

As though he were asleep, but not hurt. In a while, when she had just a little more energy, she would move over closer to him, wake him to the new day.

Mundane thoughts filled her head, which

otherwise felt frighteningly empty. The undercurrents of voices, of thoughts civilized and feral, were gone. There was only herself in her own head. She had never before totally understood the concept of lonely.

Her knee hurt, almost as much as it had when she returned to the forest. She welcomed the pain as an indication that she was, indeed, alive. Although at the moment she could not be sure exactly why she wanted to be alive.

That would also have to come later. With a deep groan, Danvers woke, rising to his elbows and looking around. When his bleary eyes settled on Kendra, he hesitated then pushed himself upright, sitting on the ground like he wasn't sure he could stand just yet.

"Omigod," Danvers groaned, tensing and relaxing his back to ease the cramps from sleeping on the ground. "Kendra? Where the hell are we?"

"In the forest." A long night's contemplation had helped her decide to keep any and all explanations as simple as possible.

"What happened?" he asked bluntly, his tired eyes still commanding.

"We were searching the woods last night

and got separated from the others, so we decided to wait until morning."

He looked like he didn't quite believe her but was obviously still too off-balance to challenge her statement. Then his gaze fell on the shotgun, tossed to one side, barrel split down the middle. A tense silence rose in the clearing before he turned back to her. Comprehension woke in his eyes along with his awareness.

"Something else happened. I—" He gulped, then wiped at his face with a large hand. "Dear God, I shot your friend Mike."

Before she could try some of the explanations she had developed while she waited for him to wake up, the world caught up with them. With loud voices and heavy feet, the rest of Danvers' search party burst into the clearing. Time had run out.

Some of the men who had known her as a child came to help her. The rest hovered around Danvers.

Questions flowed too fast to be answered, until hot coffee and fresh rolls were offered and consumed.

Kendra leaned against a tree, not quite able to stand on her own but not willing to accept help from anyone. Not now. She would have to *learn* to stand on her own two feet. Might as well start now.

Through the growing pain in her head, she heard Danvers firm, decisive voice, rising above the babble.

"I tell you, I shot him. Point blank, with that shotgun there."

The crowd separated, and one of the deputies leaned down to pick up the ruined shotgun. Another one lifted Kendra's stick, now in three ragged pieces.

"I'll take, that, thank you," she said, trying to not speak too harshly because he was handling it. How could he know?

"It's all busted up, Miss Weiss."

"I realize that, but it's a family heirloom. I can use it for a decoration."

Once she had the pieces of the stick in her hand, away from strangers, she could think more clearly. Apparently a small amount of Gran's influence still prevailed.

"As I tried to tell you before, Sheriff, you did not kill Mike. He wasn't even here."

"Yes he was. And he wasn't the only one."

"Why would you want to shoot that guy

anyway, Sheriff?" one of the onlookers asked in a reasonable tone of voice.

"That part's not really clear."

"Because it never happened," Kendra offered, a solution building in her tired mind. If she could just get him headed in the right direction.

"I know what happened here, Kendra. Hell, look at your face. Some of the pellets must've grazed you."

"Don't be ridiculous. That happened when you tripped."

She had their attention now. Drawing a breath, she marshaled all her strength. This had to be good. If only they would stop looking at her.

"We did get separated and were thinking about resting for a while. You heard a rustle in the underbrush and thought it was a bear. When you turned to look, you tripped on that root over there. The gun went off when you fell, and a couple of the pellets brushed my cheek." She felt the growing burn of the gouges but continued to ignore it. "You must have hit your head on that rock. You were sure sawing logs for the rest of the night."

"What about your stick?" He wasn't ready

to accept her explanation, but at least he was listening.

"I got worried about something in the rocks and threw the stick that way. It was just a fox, but the stick busted on the rock."

Weak. The story was almost as weak as her head, her legs. Danvers stared at her suspiciously, taking in her obvious exhaustion, her soiled face, the scratches and gouges along her cheek.

"Look, if you shot Mike point blank with a twelve-gauge, where's the body? Or at least the blood?" It took most of the rest of her strength to ask the question. Wherever Mykhael was, he was gone from her. No need to let Gabriel ruin any more lives. "Trust me. If you had shot Mike, don't you think I would have used the stick on you?"

That brought a grudging grunt. Danvers scrubbed at his face, took a refill on his coffee, and drained the cup. The group waited, intent on his decision.

"Then where is he?"

"He left yesterday. Family business."

"He coming back?"

She hesitated. There was no way she could lie outright. Danvers could sense evasion—when he was not newly concussed. And the truth was not an option.

"I don't know. I hope so."

☙☙☙

Kendra stepped along the minted path, her stride careful but without pain. The late afternoon sun stroked her unbound hair, seeking out the lace spots on her loose dress to caress her bare skin with gentle warmth.

Setting the tea tray on her outside table, she paused to look around. The peace of the woods had finally taken over her thoughts and dreams. She could sleep most of the night through, in the window seat. She would never dance again, but she could walk without pain, and she could tend the gardens. She no longer cared about dancing. There was much more to life now. Once a week, she went into town to read stories with children at the library. It soothed her almost as much as her work at home. The fertile gardens, the welcoming woods had finally healed her. As much as they could.

She pushed aside the bleakness. No time now for tears, or negative thoughts. Mykhael had given his life so she could live. She would not throw this chance away.

The fox watched from its accustomed spot near the edge of the clearing. Since that night, this fox, or another much like it, appeared at least once a day. Occasionally wolves trotted through the gardens late at night, and she had once seen the shadow of a cougar among the high rocks when she walked deep in the forest.

No predators were harmed in or near her forest. Danvers ensured her wishes were carried out, even if he didn't fully accept them. He realized they had shared something far beyond his knowledge to understand, and she held to the story she concocted that morning. The fact that Clarissa and Hawkins' bodies had been found in a wrecked auto at the bottom of a canyon had encouraged his willingness to believe her.

Day by day, she grew stronger. Every morning she woke with a trifle more desire to rise and meet the morning. If all the colors had not come back to her life yet, she still had much more than she had ever expected. Kendra reflected on her life now as she sat herself determinedly in front of a plate full of sandwiches. Hunger was not yet something she thought about, but she would continue to make this effort as well and then leave the rest for the forest creatures.

"Are you going to eat all of those yourself?"

The voice, soft and deep, filled the garden, coming from nowhere and everywhere at once. She stilled, hand hovering over the dish and forgot, for the moment, to breathe.

"Or would there be enough to share with a passing traveler?"

A stirring, and the shadows under one of the largest trees began to take shape. She rose, leaning on the back of the chair, suddenly weak.

For a moment she saw no one in the deepening gloom. Then the shape moved, deep within the shadow of a redwood at the edge of the woods, and the form of a man stepped forward.

The sun's last rays painted the high cheekbones and newly deep valleys of an ascetically carved face and limned his hair in a halo of gold. Green fire flashed from his narrowed eyes as he eased forward, a warrior spirit returning home, hoping for a welcome.

Kendra remembered at last to breathe. As she expelled oxygen in a soft cry, she stepped forward. Was this the delayed product of that night of shock?

The form at the edge of the garden was lean to the point of gauntness and carried itself hesitantly. Loose linen trousers hung from his hipbones, and an open wrap shirt shadowed his chest. Would she conjure him like this, or rely upon her memories? Moments stretched to fearsome tautness as she hesitated, afraid to lose this precious hallucination.

Then he moved, a small step forward, his hand raised in supplication.

"If you could at least spare a slice of your bread? It has been long since I tasted its like."

The gentle whimsy was her undoing. Letting go the support of the chair, she moved forward. Daring her dreams, daring her hopes. The closer she came, the more she wanted to believe he stood there, the solider he appeared.

"Dear heaven, if you are a dream, a figment, please don't leave right away. Give me just a little time."

Unable to stop herself, she edged closer,

reached out to touch at least the end of his hair. His arm. The nearly forgotten heat of his smooth skin and the tickling roughness of the hair across his bare chest.

His cheek was smooth against her palm. She touched the arch of his brow and clean, taut line of his jaw. The tempting curve of his tightly held mouth. Hot breath warmed her fingers as she stroked his lower lip in ever-hopeful wonder.

"How?" she managed to say, sobs catching at her breath

"You believed in me," he said simply.

Then his lean, strong arms closed around her, and there was no more need for words.

Their mouths met in a kiss of past regret and gentle promise. Long, blissful minutes eased past them as they savored old tastes and discovered new ones. Kendra's fingers explored bones and hollows and fretted. Mykhael's hands encompassed smaller curves and deeper dips and worried. Not a lot. Just enough, because no one else had ever thought to.

"Your vocabulary has expanded, little one," he whispered against her mouth when he paused for breath. And to drink in the sight of her. His fingers brushed away any evidence of tears, and his eyes regretted even those.

"How do you mean?" The question was vague, but her eyes were suddenly seeing colors where she had forgotten they existed. Surely there was no other green like his eyes. Wonderingly, she cupped his face between her palms.

"You didn't ask, 'why?'" An impish mischief danced in his eyes as he turned his head to place a kiss in her palm.

"All that matters is that you're here. For as long as you can stay."

"Yes, that would be the next item on the agenda," a nearly familiar voice intoned from behind her.

Kendra whirled, automatically reaching to Mykhael for support. His hand never left her, easing her back at the end of her turn to rest against his chest. They faced the stranger together.

He was not tall. But his lack of height was not apparent as he stepped forward. Mere inches could not affect the power and inner strength emanating from the elderly man.

At least, he seemed elderly. White haired,

spare boned, slightly uncertain in his stride. Almost as if he were no longer accustomed to using a body to get around.

Kendra pushed the odd idea aside then stopped. The strange man, the remembered night of deaths, the mysteries all disappeared under the sudden onslaught of thoughts, dreams, and whims. As if she had stepped from a quiet, darkened room into full sunlight, her mind was no longer empty.

Wondering, she looked up over her shoulder to find Mykhael watching her. His hand cupped her jaw, played through her hair while his other arm held her closer against him.

"It was you," she whispered, understanding now why the color had come back to her life.

"No, precious," he corrected gently. "It is us, always. Both of us. Together."

"The boy's right." That officious little man interrupted again, demanding her attention.

She gave it reluctantly. Whatever he wanted, maybe she could placate him and get rid of him.

"Not right away," he answered her thought.

Kendra drew back. A suspicion was taking root in her mind, one she really didn't want to deal with at the moment. This man seemed more and more familiar, the more he talked.

"Do I know you?"

"Yes."

Terrific. He was into puzzles and enigmas.

"Not exactly. Let us sit, before you are overcome by your questions."

They arranged themselves at the table, the man on the chair and Mykhael on the bench he drew up.

Kendra was held close enough to almost be on his lap. Not that she fought him. At the moment, Mykhael's attention seemed to be more on the food than the conversation.

"Try some, sir," he offered the older man while working his way efficiently through most of the plate of sandwiches.

"Perhaps some other time. You continue."

"Haven't they been feeding you?" Kendra asked, allowing the whimsy of the moment to take over.

"He has been on his feet only a short while," said the stranger in a slightly chiding voice. "And we couldn't seem to find anything he liked to eat. Since he spoke often of your cooking, we decided to give over the rest of his convalescence into your hands."

"Conva—" She hesitated, afraid to look at what the opened shirt shadowed. Understanding now his gauntness, the hesitation in his step. "But, I thought..." She wasn't quite sure what she thought.

"Even our *magic* takes some time to perform, my dear. Particularly as badly as his tissue was damaged. His recovery was not helped by the fact that he refused to stay in one place. Kept insisting on knowing what went on in the tribunals."

"You mean with—" Even now, she couldn't quite bring herself to say the name. Mykhael's arm tightened in support, and she felt stronger.

"Gabriel, I believed he called himself. These matters are kept private, but it was decided you have the right to know." The man harrumphed, poured himself a small amount of water. Swallowed that before he continued.

"He did not act alone. All that company has been or will be disciplined in one fashion or another. You need worry no longer about him."

"Did he ever give you a reason?"

"Power. His superiors wanted power and believed control of this spot could give it to them. They developed the scheme to wrest this place away from your family."

"Then the attack in Phoenix and what happened to Gran were all a part of some conspiracy." She gave in to her need to move closer to Mykhael. Strong hands lifted her, until she sat in his lap, within the safety of his arms.

The stranger seemed hesitant to answer, almost as though he were ashamed of what he had to admit. At last, he nodded.

"Unfortunately, yes. Despite what you were apparently told, this is not an insignificant spot. Those assigned to oversee it let themselves be overcome by the idea of total control. They have been dealt with."

She shuddered, not wanting to know how. It was enough to know this area would be safe for a while.

"Then, of course, we needed to hold a disciplinary hearing on this young man."

"What?" She sat bolt upright, kept on

Mykhael's lap only because his arms tightened. She was held firmly against a suddenly shaking chest.

"How dare you? Mykhael risked everything to save your forest."

"He also disobeyed direct commands, not all of which were at fault. We held a long session of the Tribunal last night. Debate was fierce, but eventually reason prevailed."

"What did your precious Tribunal decide?" Kendra had never heard herself spit out words before. As a pressure relief, it worked fairly well.

"I'm afraid I'm out of a job, dear heart." Mykhael seemed to be speaking through an obstruction in his throat, but she could understand his words and some of his thoughts.

"You fired him for saving my life?"

"We released him from his pledge, because he no longer could perform his duties."

"I'm afraid I'm no longer much good as an immortal enforcer of the sacred places of the universe."

This was all too confusing, and Kendra had a strong suspicion that Mykhael just barely controlled his laughter.

"Please, no more of your Atrahasis games."

"Mykhael is mortal." The old man's voice was clipped, dry. Was there a suspicion of a twinkle deep within his shadowed eyes?

"So, how long will he live?" Hope began to try to take root inside Kendra. She fought it down.

"Barring accidents, I would say at least another fifty or sixty years. There are, however, a few conditions."

"Name them."

"You must allow him to remain here most of the time, to help guard this area."

The crafty old man paused, allowed himself another sip of water.

"Since he is now mortal, he will be expected to continue the heritage in another fashion."

She frowned, not understanding the man. Especially since he seemed to have some strange male joke in mind.

"It seems, my heart," Mykhael said, leaning forward and tilting his head to look into her eyes, "that I am expected to reproduce myself."

"Make the attempt, at any rate," the man

said gruffly. "Providing, of course, he can find a suitable partner."

"Do you suppose that could be arranged?"

Was that hesitation in Mykhael's voice? Kendra stirred on his lap, turning until she could wrap her arms around his neck. Trusting to his strength, she leaned back in his hold.

There was a question, deep in his enchanted green eyes. She wondered that he did not seek the answer for himself and realized this had to be entirely her own decision. An imp she had thought lost prompted her to tilt her head and crease in her brow, as if thinking it all through.

"If he must remain in the area and attempt to continue the line, it would be rather crowded to bring someone else up here," she ventured in as serious a voice as she could manage.

Reading her answer in the new-found hope in her eyes, Mykhael allowed his own mischief to escape.

"Would you allow another to stay here perhaps for a brief period of time? Just during the attempts."

"I wouldn't allow her here long enough to

ask directions back down the mountain." There was no denying the strength in her reply.

"So he can stay here?" The voice behind them was an intrusion Kendra wanted to ignore. Especially since Mykhael was busy rediscovering the feel of her body under his hands.

However, she had a feeling the man wouldn't go away until she answered him.

"He can stay. As long as he doesn't have any more visitors from his old life."

"I can promise you that." The man must have been moving away, since his voice became quickly dimmer. "If you have need of us, we will answer your call."

Kendra filed that for future reference. Her full attention was on the owner of the lap she sat on.

"He was serious, wasn't he? You're going to grow old like me, get gray, and eventually die?"

"Yes." A world of longing escaped with the small word. "But not for a while."

"No, you have—what did he say—fifty or sixty years?"

"A princely sum. All to spend with you,

my heart." He surged to his feet, holding her high against his chest.

Sudden shyness overcame her.

"Mykhael, what are you doing?"

"You just reminded me, I'm on a time schedule now. If I'm expected to recreate myself in only fifty years, I had better not waste any more time."

Laughter rose again in the garden, sprinkling the flowers with bright color. At the edge, the fox nodded to itself and padded off. The humans would be busy for a while. A long while.

## THE END

# About the Author

Mona Karel became convinced at an early age that her life would not really begin until she was about thirty five. She has no idea what precipitated that thought, but she claims she was a strange child. Until reaching that age, she led a peripatetic existence for many years, criss-crossing the country, working with horses and dogs—and waiting tables to support her other jobs. At thirty five, when many people are well into raising their families, Karel settled down to "real" work as a buyer and expediter. She married a high school teacher, which led to over twenty years in Southern California.

Karel can't remember a time she wasn't reading, though she doesn't remember much fun with Dick and Jane. Her preferred stories involved dogs and horses, and once she had gone through every horse book in the high school library, she started in on Civil War stories. They rode horses, didn't they? At that time Romance was swashbucklers and Gothic, and many preferred the stronger heroines of Mary Stewart and Victoria Holt. Then Karel discovered Romance in the form of Silhouette, Candlelight, and RWA, and her life was complete. Karel and her husband have since retired to New Mexico, where the live in the wind at 6,500 feet with their Salukis. When not writing or going to dog shows, Karel works at a solar related firm.